The Snake

By the time Ruston's body returned, he'd been processed by the medical profession, positively identified through dental records, and discussed by two governments. Though I didn't really know the guy except to say hello at university meetings, my early research in Guatemala made the story intriguing, and the situation was too odd to overlook. Friday morning, the day after the local stories aired, the national media picked up on the weirdness of Ruston's death. Since there hadn't been any real news for days, they dropped on the story like a hawk on a mouse. Every broadcast had something to say about Ruston, the early Mayan civilization, and ritual sacrifice. What it came down to was this: Robert Ruston had been killed in an ancient Mayan manner—tied to a scaffold, shot full of arrows, his heart ripped out. No one knew much more than that. Not why. Not who. Not even exactly when, given the state of his body. All anyone knew for certain was that the murder had happened in the heart of the Petén region in Guatemala in a pre-Columbian Mayan city unoccupied for more than a thousand years. Commentators played up the bizarre nature of his death, the links with early cultural practices, and Ruston's reputation as a world-famous scholar of Mayan glyphs.

By Friday no new details surfaced, but the national excitement made me think. After all, it wasn't as if Ruston had died of a heart attack in his office. There were bound to be local enquiries, and I wanted in.

What They Are Saying About
The Snake

"A snake, a ritual sacrifice, and an ancient carved marker—what do they mean? J.A. Kellman's debut mystery, set in Guatemala and central Illinois, is well-written and atmospheric. The author's deep knowledge of Mayan culture makes her story sparkle with rich detail and authenticity."

—Sarah Wisseman
Author of the Lisa Donahue Archaeological Mysteries
and the Flora Garibaldi Art History Mysteries

"Gripping suspense! *The Snake* takes readers on a tense, twisting trek from the American Midwest into the Mesoamerican jungles to solve a shocking crime. J.A. Kellman is a terrific new voice in mysteries."

—Molly MacRae
Author of the Highland Bookshop Mysteries
and the Haunted Yarn Shop Mysteries

The Snake

J. A. Kellman

J. Kellman

A Wings ePress, Inc.
Mystery Novel

Wings ePress, Inc.

Edited by: Jeanne Smith
Copy Edited by: Joan C. Powell
Executive Editor: Jeanne Smith
Cover Artist: Trisha FitzGerald-Jung

Wings ePress Books
www.wingsepress.com

Copyright © 2019 by J. A. Kellman
ISBN 978-1-61309-611-6

Published In the United States Of America

Wings ePress Inc.
3000 N. Rock Road
Newton, KS 67114

Dedication

To the Maya women of Guatemala

One

Unnoticed by the humans, the only witness to the crime had been a snake, a large female fer-de-lance, who often sheltered under a limestone ledge in the thick jungle surrounding the center of the ancient city of Tikal. The shouting, straining, struggling men and the howling man on the rack had made her nervous, but they had gone after the man had stopped thrashing. It had been quiet for some time.

This new influx of men, for the second time that week, upset her, talking and stamping in the area near her usual ledge. As soon as they moved away from her hiding spot, the snake began to slither, heading north. It was time to find new territory.

Big Grove, September

It wasn't until the Thursday evening news that first week in September that I learned of Robert Ruston's demise—his disappearance, his return in a coffin to Big Grove from Guatemala, the unusual circumstances of his death.

I'm Ann Cunningham, retired professor, forensic archivist, and a lifetime snoop. I've always been interested in learning more than is good for me, even as a child. Once I deliberately plunged into a nettle patch just to see what it felt like. And, this is another thing about me that often makes snooping difficult: I'm a fixer—a caretaker of the hopeless, the lost, the broken. If it's damaged, I mend it. If it's hungry, I feed it. If it's sad…Well, you get the picture. Instant involvement. Immediate commitment. It was a good quality to have when I was teaching, but otherwise it can make things complicated.

~ * ~

By the time Ruston's body returned, he'd been processed by the medical profession, positively identified through dental records, and discussed by two governments. Though I didn't really know the guy except to say hello at university meetings, my early research in Guatemala made the story intriguing, and the situation was too odd to overlook. Friday morning, the day after the local stories aired, the national media picked up on the weirdness of Ruston's death. Since there hadn't been any real news for days, they dropped on the story like a hawk on a mouse. Every broadcast had something to say about Ruston, the early Mayan civilization, and ritual sacrifice.

What it came down to was this: Robert Ruston had been killed in an ancient Mayan manner—tied to a scaffold, shot full of arrows, his heart ripped out. No one knew much more than that. Not why. Not who. Not even exactly when, given the state of his body. All anyone knew for certain was that the murder had happened in the heart of the Petén region in Guatemala in a pre-Columbian Mayan city unoccupied for more than a thousand years. Commentators played up the bizarre nature of his death, the links with early cultural practices, and Ruston's reputation as a world-famous scholar of Mayan glyphs.

By Friday, no new details surfaced, but the national excitement made me think. After all, it wasn't as if Ruston had died of a heart attack in his office. There were bound to be local enquiries, and I wanted in.

Guatemala City, Guatemala, the previous June

I managed to piece together the beginning of Ruston's story from conversations with friends. My own experiences made it easy to fill in the details.

On the first Monday in June, the Aviateca flight was on time as it touched down in the old terminal of Guatemala's crowded La Aurora International Airport. I could imagine Robert Ruston, a tall, heavy man with unruly gray hair, wrestling his battered bag from the overhead bin and joining the slowly shuffling queue of deplaning passengers filling the plane's aisles, clutching their shopping bags bulging with gifts for family and friends.

Free of the plane and its chattering occupants, he'd head for the old arrival hall—an echoing, high- ceilinged open space—to pick up his second bag; then he'd wind his way into the oppressive unair-conditioned, hanger-like baggage claim area.

According to Enrique Otzoy, anthropologist, longtime mutual friend, and part-time host during Ruston's yearly summers in Guatemala, Robert scanned the second-floor visitor's observation balcony, spotted Otzoy, and pointed toward the doors that exited into the street on the far side of customs. Otzoy took off to get his Land Cruiser as Robert headed toward the slowly turning luggage carousels and the passport lines beyond.

Finished with the entry process, Ruston must have struggled with everyone else through the heavily guarded doors into the open air, then pushed through the chattering crowd into the sun and toward the churning taxi rank, and scanned the endless stream of vehicles for Otzoy's familiar Toyota.

By the time Otzoy pulled into the pickup area a few minutes later, however, Robert Ruston and his bags were gone.

Otzoy parked and plunged into the melee. Taxi drivers yelled and jostled, seized luggage from passengers' hands, and shoved it in their cabs in an attempt to garner business. Newly arrived travelers shouted over the din to bargain with drivers, make their destinations heard, and converse with friends. No one had seen a big *gringo* with gray hair, or knew what happened to him.

Otzoy had returned to the nearby parking lot. He'd even braved the balcony over the arrival hall a second time, in case he might spot Ruston from that angle. Nothing.

Otzoy told me later it was like the Period of Violence during the 70s and early 80s when the government's Special Forces carried out a war against the people. Citizens and foreigners were dragged without warning into black Jeep Cherokees with tinted windows in that time of terror, agony, and killing. Maybe there'd be a smear of blood on the pavement, but more likely the person just vanished. Months later, a badly tortured body might appear in the dump, in a ditch outside of town, in an unmarked grave, in a small morgue on the edge of the city. Or maybe they'd never turn up at all. Professors. Teachers. Doctors. Social and religious workers. People that helped the indigenous, the poor, the downtrodden, the needy. All gone. All disappeared. All certainly dead.

After his fruitless search of the airport, Otzoy, agitated and increasingly upset, returned to his condo in a high rise near the embassies and museums and started making calls. He contacted police, friends in the United States, friends in Guatemala, Ruston's hotel in Tikal, the US Embassy in Guatemala City. A few hours later, he called them all again. No one had heard from Ruston. By the time he had exhausted his contacts and retraced his enquiries, forty-eight hours had elapsed. There was nothing. It was as if Ruston had never existed.

Two

Tikal National Park, Guatemala, the previous August

Weeks later, deep in the rain forests of the central Petén, park ranger, Tikal guide Officer Miguel Ochoa with a profile of an ancient Maya lord, rounded the base of Temple IV one morning in mid-August. He didn't notice the body immediately. What he saw first was the cloud of flies. He moved closer to the source of the insects. *"Madre de Dios,"* he muttered crossing himself; then he radioed park headquarters.

The source of the insects, the corpse—tied to a wooden rack in the undergrowth behind Temple IV under a towering ceiba tree—had only been dead for a couple of days, especially if one considered the effects of heat, insects, and animals.

While he waited for the emergency personnel, Ochoa photographed what was left of the body. The situation became clearer as he worked his way around the scene. The man had been tied with leather thongs to a structure that held him spread from corner to corner like a rug on a loom. He had been shot with a dozen carefully crafted arrows. Three paper strips had been tied to each wrist and ankle. His chest had been cut open and his heart removed.

As an anthropologist as well as ranger, Ochoa was familiar with the white paper ties and the arrows. The man had been a Mayan ritual sacrifice; the incision in his chest to remove his heart clinched it. When the officers from the Santa Elena police arrived an hour after Ochoa's colleagues from the park office, the man on the rack became a police, as well as a park, matter. Once the body was tentatively identified a day later as Robert Ruston, he became a problem for the Guatemalan government and US State Department, too.

~ * ~

Officer Ochoa was late returning home on the day of his discovery. He had been consumed with his find, with no time to give tourists tours. The multilayered enquiry into the probable identity of the dead man, questions from officials of every sort, endless forms, and countless cups of coffee all blurred together. When he finally parked his battered Land Cruiser in front of his small house on a dark side street in Santa Elena, twenty-five miles south of Tikal, it was nearly midnight.

At the sound of the Toyota, Esperanza, Ochoa's wife of thirty-five years, rose from the faded easy chair in which she had been reading and headed into the darkened hall to unfasten the padlock and chain securing the doors that opened into the street. Just as Esperanza pushed them open, he reached the front step, his courier bag dangling from one hand.

"What took you so long?" Esperanza asked as she fastened the doors behind him. "What did you mean when you said there'd been trouble? And why couldn't you talk?" Without a break in her activity or her conversation, Esperanza, not one to put things off, headed for the kitchen with its warm brick hearth. "Are you hungry? There's soup. I'll make tortillas."

Ochoa hung his jacket on a hook, paused, and considered whether he actually wanted to eat after a day with what he thought of as *La Problema de* Ruston.

"Let me think," he said, trying to bring himself back to earth, to this time, to his house, to Esperanza. He sank into a chair at the kitchen table. "Maybe a bowl of soup would help. I haven't had anything but coffee today. I feel as if I'd been poisoned."

Esperanza stirred the fire, adding a piece of wood, moving the soup to the center of the grate to warm. She placed the *comal*, a ceramic griddle for baking tortillas, on the grate next to the soup to heat.

The patting of Esperanza's slender hands shaping tortillas and the warmth of the fire soothed Ochoa. Slowly he began to relax enough to order his thoughts, to put words to what he had seen. He started with his arrival in the park, the familiar world of sounds and smells that had greeted him as he stepped from his truck. When he reached the part about Temple IV, the flies, and the man on the rack, Esperanza gasped at the details—the paper ties, the arrows, the missing heart.

"*Dios mío!* No! How can that be? Who would do such a thing? Bandits don't go to such trouble. They'd just shoot him. Besides, they wouldn't have a clue about classic practices, would they?" She paused, pushing a strand of still-black hair off her forehead with her wrist.

"I wouldn't think so. It was a lot of work—keeping him alive after they kidnapped him, building a rack, making arrows, carting him to Tikal. What for? It doesn't seem reasonable for an ordinary political group to do it, either," Ochoa said. "In the first place, why would they kill Ruston, a *gringo*? In the second, why go to all this trouble?"

Esperanza placed a bowl of steaming soup and a basket of hot tortillas on the table. "Try not to think about it anymore. Just eat. Then, after that, sleep. Nothing's going to happen tonight. You can worry tomorrow."

Dutifully, Ochoa spooned up the soup full of greens, onions, and pieces of chicken. He discovered he was hungry after all, but sleeping later was going to be another matter.

That night in the tiny bedroom behind the kitchen, with Esperanza breathing softly beside him in their narrow bed, Ochoa stared into the darkness. *What was it that had taken place? Why had the man died at Tikal? And why in God's name had it been a gringo who had been killed in such an elaborate manner?* As the roosters began to crow and the darkness faded, Ochoa slipped into uneasy slumber.

~ * ~

Two days after his discovery, after a multitude of questions asked by officials regarding his unpleasant experience, Ochoa returned to patrolling the park and leading tour groups. He hadn't forgotten the death of Robert Ruston behind Temple IV, though, and neither had the other park rangers at Tikal. The events of that day became the topic of conversation every time they got together, if for no other reason than everyone was edgy about blundering into a similar tableau. Though the questions they asked were the same impossible ones that Ochoa had considered in his dark bedroom that first night, something interesting came from a discussion in their thatched-roof luncheon shelter as their tour groups ate nearby.

The oldest member of the guide group, Jaime, who threatened to retire at the end of every tourist season, said there had been talk in the office the summer before that the *gringo* Ruston had discovered a stele, a carved marker of unknown provenance. This information hadn't surprised Jaime. His uncle, a lifetime resident of nearby Flores and former guide, had always maintained such steles existed deep in the jungle behind Temple IV.

"This is the interesting part. The steles were said to mark the edges of an ancient community," Jaime said, his mouth full of taco. "According to the stories, they outlined a small village that was here long before Tikal became a large city."

As the men finished their lunches, or lit up cigarettes before beginning the afternoon tours, they added what they had heard about unusual artifacts and early communities. Some shared rumors that drifted like bird song through the sticky jungle air, stories of strange sightings, current experiences, shadowy figures spotted flitting behind the trees. None of the information was completely new, but Ruston's discovery of an actual stele and his recent death shone another light on the tales. Suddenly they might be real—not myths, not imaginings, not just old men's winter tales.

Lost in thought, Ochoa scuffed his worn hiking boot in the dust next to the shelter's raised cement slab floor. Ruston's demise had opened up new possibilities.

Familiar with Ochoa's proclivities, it came as no surprise to the other guides when he began tramping through the tangle behind Temple IV during his free time. He had taken the Ruston business personally, and he wanted answers.

Three

As Ochoa struggled with *La Problema de* Ruston, late summer came down like a brass hammer on Big Grove. The grasshoppers, too miserable to fly, crept along the blades of tall grasses in Prairiebrook Park on the town's southern edge. The little creek that ran through the cottonwoods at its boundary had dried to a shallow pond behind what had been a beaver dam. The neighborhood red tail hawk panted in the heat.

I was getting a late start that Friday morning after the return of Ruston's body to Big Grove, when Luis Velasco, Mayan anthropologist and one of my closest friends, called. He was agitated, and due to his stroke a couple of months earlier, impossible to understand. His anthropologist wife Zoila took the phone.

"We knew Bob was missing. In Guatemala that is never good. But this latest news! Heart excision! Arrow sacrifice! It is unbelievable! He was a scholar, for God's sake, not an ancient captive!"

"Maybe he ran into something sensitive in his research, but what? Ancient Mayan glyphic writing isn't a likely reason for murder," I said, "especially a killing that was so carefully staged."

"It doesn't make sense to me," Zoila said. "Maybe Luis will have some ideas. Why don't you come for dinner? If nothing else, he can let off steam. This entire business is going to make him crazy if he doesn't feel he is doing something, even if it is just talk."

I'd met Luis and Zoila when we were grad students in Guatemala, and we became friends. When all three of us ended up at the university in Big Grove, our relationship picked up where it had left off in the cobblestone streets of Antigua, with one additional twist: Luis had become a Mayan calendar priest as well as a well-known anthropologist. As the direct descendant of the last Lord of the *Cauacs*, one of the five ancient *K'iche* tribes, and from his years of apprenticeship with a holy man in the Highlands, his ability to divine the future was formidable. Maybe he'd have insights into Ruston's death.

~ * ~

After dinner that evening, we took our drinks onto the balcony. We were still talking about Ruston, or rather, Luis was. He was having a hell of a time getting the words out with his stroke-fractured speech, but that didn't stop him and we were willing to wait patiently for him to say everything he needed to say.

"I knew Bob Ruston ever since we got to Big Grove, I hate to say it now he's dead, but I always thought he was a stuffed shirt. Self-important. I used to wonder how he could lord it over Zoila and me when we are the real deal as far as being Maya goes. He studied Mayan culture. We *are* Maya. His research was solid, though. Maybe that made up for his personality. No matter. He didn't deserve this. What a terrible way to die."

We grew quiet, thinking about Ruston's death—alone in a steaming jungle, face to face with his killers, pierced with arrows, suspended like a hide to be scraped, eviscerated. No way could it have been worse. Besides, he would have known what was coming as soon as he saw the scaffold.

"What was he working on?" I asked, just to break the gloomy silence.

"I don't know," Luis said. "Bob found something at Tikal last year, but that's all I know. Maybe José Polop could tell you. They were colleagues for years. I'd talk with Polop myself, but I hate the phone, and I don't want to go out in this heat. Zoila can call if you're willing to see him. Polop is one of those people with contacts everywhere. He's bound to have more details. Besides, he might appreciate advice about taking care of Bob's papers, since they ran in the same academic circles."

By the time I left that evening, José Polop, Mayan art historian, had agreed to meet me the following morning at his condo in a new development on the western edge of Big Grove.

"You can't miss it," he said. "It's the only house with a replica of the stele of Eighteen Rabbit, Lord of Copan, on the front porch."

"Eighteen Rabbit? Full size?" I asked, envisioning the fifteen-foot original in front of a suburban dwelling.

"No, I only wish. It's only a couple of feet tall, but it's a good copy. He appears to be watching the street. He's fierce enough looking...he keeps people from hanging ads on my door or pestering me with religious tracts."

"Thanks for the tip. See you tomorrow."

~ * ~

The following morning, I used my time on the way to Polop's to think about my questions surrounding Ruston's demise. How did Ruston get from the airport's passenger pickup area in Guatemala City to Flores three hundred miles away and then journey thirty-nine miles to Tikal without anyone seeing him? Unless, of course, he traveled by car—he and his bags bundled into a vehicle with tinted windows, just like the old days. That would explain his disappearance and reappearance miles away, dead in the lowland jungle. But what happened between the day he disappeared in June and August and when he was found behind the pyramid? Was this a return to classic Mayan ceremonies that included auto sacrifice and elaborate rituals or what? Whatever else it was, it was creepy.

All the condos in the Walnut Woods development were an uneasy mixture of Georgian pillars, brick facades, International Style panels, and angled rooflines. Without the stele on the low porch, I would have gone right by Polop's. I pulled into the short cement drive in front of his garage. A walk edged with prickly pear and yucca led to the low porch. Eighteen Rabbit stood next to the step surveying the street: regal, inscrutable, alien.

Polop must have been watching for me to arrive. No sooner did I raise the knocker than he pulled the door open.

"Glad you found me. Come in," he said.

"Who could miss Eighteen Rabbit?" I said as we shook hands. "I appreciate you taking time to see me and so does Luis. He's upset. He'd known Ruston for years."

Polop, a tiny solid man with spikey black hair, led the way into the house.

"Let's sit in the living room; it's cooler," he said. "Would you like anything? Water? Ice tea?"

"No, thanks, I'm fine."

Polop, settling on a hassock, began. "I'm not sure I can tell you anything that Luis doesn't already know. Ruston and I weren't close, more just longtime colleagues with similar interests. We only saw one another every couple of months. We were busy. Last time we got together was late April—I grilled steaks on the deck—we caught up on news, discussed our work. He was excited about an inscription on an ancient preclassic stele he'd found in the jungle in Tikal last summer. It's an interesting story. He'd been tramping around in the brush to the east of Temple Four, looking for architectural artifacts, when he fell over the thing. Once he pulled away the overgrowth, he knew it was unusual because of its size and shape, so he took photographs and rubbings, brought the material back to Big Grove at the end of the season."

"What do you mean unusual?"

"According to Bob, he'd never seen anything like it. It was small, thick, boxy, more like a small boundary marker than the later Mayan political, or astronomical statements. During the school year he deciphered it, made out the name of a ruler, K'in A'jaw, Sun Lord. That's when he got excited. Bob had never heard of K'in A'jaw, and no wonder. The date seemed to be in the early days of Tikal itself, around six hundred BCE."

"Six hundred BCE? Did Tikal exist then? I thought it was just a collection of villages."

Polop shifted on the hassock. "Yes and no. Some of them were beginning to coalesce, but still it wasn't a large community. I didn't hear from Bob again until he was ready to leave for Guatemala. He was taking off the first week of June, wanted to let me know he'd be staying with a friend of ours, Enrique Otzoy, in Guatemala City for a couple of days, and he'd booked a room in the Tikal Inn inside the park for the rest of the summer. I didn't hear from him after that, but that wasn't uncommon. He'd be busy packing, making appointments with people in Guatemala, planning his work."

"Ruston disappeared no sooner than he got into the airport in Guatemala City according to the news," I said. "At least Otzoy didn't see him after he left passport control. Ruston seems to have vanished into thin air. And this part is really weird. The autopsy report indicated he had been alive all through the months of June and July. The pathologist said he'd only been dead for a couple of days when Ochoa found him. What do you think happened?"

"It *is* odd. Where the hell was Ruston for two months? He certainly wasn't camping in the jungle; and where did he get that outfit? And who shot him full of arrows?" Polop asked, shaking his head.

"Ruston found that stele the summer before; might that be it?" I asked. "But when you think of it, how strange is it for a Mayan epigrapher to find a stele in the Petén?" I answered my own question.

"The area is covered with ruins waiting to be discovered, even though the rain forest is so thick one can't see more than a few feet in front of one's face. Why wouldn't Ruston find something after all those years spent poking around? The entire business is creepy, very creepy."

I thought for a minute. "Might Ruston's research indicate what he was thinking, what he was investigating in Guatemala, what caused his kidnapping and murder? Maybe someone wanted to learn what he knew and got rid of him." That last bit sounded way too TV, even to me. "After all, what could he have learned about the ancient Maya that was toxic thousands of years later?"

Polop grunted. "All I know is he wanted to see if there were similar steles hidden away in the jungle around Tikal, or tucked away in museums or private collections. Someone should take a look at his notes. He doesn't, didn't, have much of a family. I've got the key to his house, but I'm not up to the task. I've got my own work to do."

Not one to fool around, that was all I needed to jump into the situation with both feet. I was curious about the stele and didn't have another job on my calendar for weeks. I told Polop I'd do it if Ruston's relatives were interested.

Four

Tikal National Park, Guatemala, Early September

Ochoa tugged off his Forest Service hat and wiped his forehead with his bandana. His hair was wet, and his uniform stuck wherever it touched his skin. Despite his liberal application of repellent, he'd attracted a surging cloud of insects that had followed him ever since he'd crossed the Great Plaza. He was glad to break for lunch. He'd spent the morning leading a small tour group of German academics through the central heart of Tikal. Now they were eating in a thatched shelter near the Central Plaza, discussing what they had seen. A couple of them looked wilty, but sitting in the shade and drinking Coke seemed to be having a positive effect on even the most miserable.

As Ochoa waved away flies and waited for his clients to finish their meal, a small airplane headed high over Tikal's central courtyard toward the northwest border of the Petén. Strange. A small red and white plane, maybe a Cessna, flying over Tikal; there weren't any airports that direction, just a few big ranches and patches of jungle that hadn't been burned for fields yet. If the plane kept going on its current heading it would end up in Miami. Ochoa grunted. Maybe it was someone going to one of the ranches…it was daylight after all, but most often in this part of the country planes out of place meant drugs. And drugs meant trouble.

Five

I pulled into Ruston's drive a mile and a half from my condo in Burr Oaks at 8:30 a.m. on a sweltering, cloudless Monday, two weeks after the request to tackle his papers arrived from Ruston's sister in Omaha.

His house, a two-story, white brick contemporary, had an outside staircase, a gravel courtyard surrounded by a wall, and the bleak look of a dwelling whose inhabitant was never coming back. Four months of inattention had taken their toll, or maybe maintenance hadn't been high on Ruston's to-do list. Weeds sprouted through the pebbles. The mailbox to the left of the stairs was pulling loose from the wall. The small patch of grass was dead.

I grabbed my supplies—a plastic tub filled with cotton gloves, labels, and everything else I might need—and struggled up the steep steps, scraping my elbows on the rough walls as I went. I let myself in with Polop's key, pushing open the faded yellow door with my hip. A couple of months of being uninhabited had done nothing for the dwelling's interior ambience, either. It was hot, dark, fusty—a mixture of mildew, years of cooking, stale clothes, and cigars. Great. Not only would it be hot while I worked, but also smelly.

A glass-walled dining room and kitchen cantilevered over the garage to the left of the door. A hallway to the right led to Ruston's study at the back of the house. Aside from the view of the neighbor's garden, the study was all business—a light box and stacks of drawings and photos on an oak library table, computer and printer on a nearby desk, and a chair that had allowed Ruston to wheel from one work station to another. I set my water bottle on the desk between a wooden box decorated with images of highland village life and a ceramic figure of a Mayan ritual ball player.

Since an unair-conditioned house in Big Grove at the end of summer is always stifling, and dealing with a light box would make the situation worse, I'd come prepared. I dug a small tabletop fan out of my bin and plugged it into a nearby wall socket. The breeze wasn't cool, but a little circulation was better than nothing. Aiming it directly at my body and clamping my magnifier to my forehead, I settled into Ruston's chair, eager to tackle the piles of materials next to the light box.

Luckily, a quick riffle through the papers showed they were of the newly discovered stele. There were three kinds of images—photos on large sheets of transparent film, ink drawings, and rubbings on thin sheets of paper. Each had particular qualities that made them of special value for my purposes. The photos documented an area from an unedited perspective, presenting a richly colored tapestry of unsorted information.

The drawings, done on lightweight paper, contained the clearest descriptions of the subject from Ruston's personal perspective. The rubbings were somewhere between the photos and drawings, providing a topographical view of the stele's surface features in dark, soft crayon, looking for all the world like Wisconsin's rolling hills and winding valleys. Stacked together on the light box or laid side by side, the images looked as distinct as the patterns of a Mayan woman's traditional blouse, a *huipil*.

I placed the first drawing on the box and pressed the switch. The image suddenly glowed like Tiffany glass in the darkened room. Every line, form, recess, and protrusion was delineated; amounts and relationships were clear. Next, I added the photo and a rubbing illustrating the same view, searching the surface of the photo with the help of my magnifier, looking for anything unusual on the stele's surface—a vague shape, a change of hue, anything. With its two-power enlargement, details that were nearly invisible to the naked eye became large enough to see. Maybe I'd get lucky.

Working in an airless house on a hot day was miserable, but leaning over the battered old light box with an incandescent bulb was like bending over a stove with the burners going.

In half an hour I could feel perspiration trickling down my back; even my short hair felt damp when I ran my fingers through it. I exchanged the drawing for the next one in the stack, one with greater contrast and a closer view, adding the accompanying rubbing and photos. K'in A'jaw, the ruler's name according to Ruston's accompanying notes, filled the top-right corner of the stele—a pursed-lipped howler monkey face with a bean-shaped form containing the cross-like *k'in* shape floating in front and above it. I put on another set of pictures.

I couldn't distinguish a thing beyond what seemed a human skull looking left. Everything else had been worn away, leaving shadows, softened bulges, rounded depressions. The stele had been broken across the bottom sometime in the past, making it even more difficult to decipher. I had to take Ruston's word for what it said. From my perspective, nothing stood out as unusual—late preclassic size, boxy shape, badly eroded surface—only the name and the date were out of whack; they were way too early, according to Ruston, and he'd never heard of K'in A'jaw. I sighed. Why would I spot anything new if he hadn't seen it first? I bit my lip in frustration and pushed my glasses up my nose. I needed something more if I was going to figure out what happened.

On breaks away from the searing light box, I organized and filed Ruston's papers for disbursal. I learned a little about Ruston himself at the same time, but it wasn't much when one considered his age and international reputation. His interests lay almost entirely in Mayan glyphs and Mesoamerican cultures, even down to his fondness for Cinco Gallos, a Mexican–Central American restaurant located in a repurposed donut shack out by the interstate, if their dog-earred menu on his desk meant anything. His world was Guatemala—its capitol city, with high rises and ghastly traffic, and the countryside, where the smell of wood smoke and roasting corn hung in the air and small plots of corn dotted mountainsides. Big Grove was just an add-on. There was nothing to suggest a reason for landing him tied and butchered in the jungle.

The Mayan ballgame player next to my water bottle gave me an idea, though. He understood sacrifice. His game included plenty of it. So how did a frowsy epigrapher wind up as part of a similar ceremony? "What do you think?" I asked the ballplayer.

I swear he answered. "It was a ritual to nourish the gods, to keep the world in balance, predictable, stable—rain falling, crops growing."

It must be the heat. Now I was talking to inanimate objects, and worse, they were answering back.

But what about Ruston? Was he a sacrifice in the traditional sense, or was his death a cover-up, meant to look like a sacrifice, to steer people away from the facts, away from what actually was going on? Surely a group hadn't gone back to the pre-Columbian ways.

The sacrificial blood stuff gives a lot of modern Maya the willies—piercing tongues and penises, cutting out hearts. Not what the people I knew considered spiritually significant, or something they wanted to think about in a world with Internet and airplanes. So, if Ruston's death was a sacrifice, a real sacrifice, who would have carried it out? Could there be a small group of Maya hiding in the the Petén? Could the rain forest still be sheltering a little band in its depths, people isolated from modern life? Or, and this seemed another stretch, had a group of modern Maya returned to old rituals? If Ruston's death was a ruse, however, who would go through the trouble and why? Flaking points, making arrows, creating an obsidian knife. Let's face it. Killing someone by stretching him on a scaffold took work, organization, and a deep sense of purpose. It also made a statement of staggering proportions, a violent warning to anyone who was paying attention. No one could overlook Ruston's demise, that was for sure, but why would he end up dead in such a gruesome way? Maybe as I dug through the images and notes, I'd think of something. I swear the ballplayer snorted.

While I mused, I examined the little painted box next to the ballplayer. Inside, a jade pectoral—a simplified vulture—peered at me from a nest of cotton. I was stunned. It was beautiful. It was ancient. It was priceless. I could see from the style and its condition that it was early Maya, or maybe even Olmec. There was still dirt in the incised lines of the vulture's face; a cloudy rainbow sheen tinged the surface from being buried for years. When had Ruston taken to stealing irreplaceable cultural artifacts? The Guatemalan government would go nuts if they knew he had it.

~ * ~

After dinner, curled in my recliner with a glass of Bowmore 18 and my cat Rosie, I reflected on what I knew so far. According to Polop, Ruston was certain the stele included not only the name of the heretofore unknown ruler, K'in A'jaw, Sun King, but a startlingly early date for Tikal as a small city. The glyphs themselves were unusual as well. They were either early forms or hybrids of some sort.

I paused; that was something to consider—hybrids, mixtures, fusions. What two or more writing systems could have influenced one another? Given the small population in the Petén, how could such contacts come about? People weren't living next door to one another after all, so diffusion didn't seem reasonable.

Maybe conquest was the answer, one population supplanting another along with their writing system, but there would be archaeological signs—burned and shattered ruins buried deep in the jungle litter—or perhaps an outside elite replaced the first group's leaders through peaceful means. But how would that happen and why? And what about the vulture pectoral?

Something else interested me: the attack on Ruston coincided with his translation of and research into the ancient stone. He didn't have a lot of friends, but no one could recall enemies who might want to be rid of him either. He was just a self-absorbed, obsessive middle-aged academic with dry scalp, if all the bottles of Selsun in his bathroom were an indication. Then the year after he found the stele and started his research, boom! He's murdered. That might suggest some sort of connection between the two; why would the events occur so close together? Of course, coincidence explains a lot of things, but it seemed a stretch with Ruston.

The dull headache I'd had behind my right eye since noon was becoming insistent. Since I wasn't going to solve the problem overnight, I headed for bed. At least I could try to shake the headache.

As the early autumn wind rattled the windows and drove thready clouds across the moonless sky, Rosie tramped and pawed before settling behind my knees. Maybe this Ruston business was making her restless, too. I certainly was wide awake. My brain was in overdrive.

As the sky began to lighten, I took a couple of Benadryl. I finally fell into a restless sleep, dreaming in fits and starts of the rain forest dotted with small villages of thatched houses and Mayan people in traditional garments going about their daily lives. Far beyond the villages and miles from the tidy homes, though, deep in the dark and tangled jungle, something roamed, something that didn't belong there, not then, not now.

~ * ~

The next morning, groggy from antihistamines, I scanned the vulture pectoral into my computer, sending copies to Polop and Luis and Zoila, but I got shifty when I emailed the Mesoamerican curator at Dumbarton Oaks, a research center and museum in Washington, DC. I didn't send him an image, just asked questions. I sure as hell didn't want to start a witch hunt, not with the priceless pectoral on my desk.

I hate sleepless nights. Not only had I not figured out anything with all my agonizing, I felt like dirt. I stopped at the South Seas Café for an iced cappuccino on the way to Ruston's. It was blessedly cold in its paper cup as I let myself into the airless house and settled into my spot in front of the light box. At least this would be the last day I'd need to bake my brains out.

To celebrate the approaching end of bending over the light box, I'd arranged with Bill Paulson, one of the two other people on my floor, and one of my closest friends, to meet for lunch at Cinco Gallos. Pat Barr, the other member of our usual threesome, couldn't join us; she was scheduled to volunteer at the local library. We'd all known one another since we moved in about the same time years ago and felt more like siblings than neighbors. They'd been in on the Ruston business from the start.

Bill, marathoner, former Navy SEAL, and retired police officer, co-owns a sport shop with his brother. He is our little group's trainer and tactician when we need one. Pat is a retired research librarian from Health Sciences. What she doesn't know about medical issues isn't worth knowing, and better yet, she is acquainted with everyone remotely part of the health-care field in the Midwest. The three of us in combination are formidable researchers, investigators, and snoops, or at least we like to think so.

I shut off the light box at noon and hurried down the stairs to the RAV4, eager for lunch and to hear what Bill had to say about my recent discoveries at Ruston's.

According to the address on the carryout menu, Cinco Gallos was in the old Dunkin' Donuts out near the interstate. It was easy to spot. Its bright colors and Spanish language sign made it stand out in the jungle of car washes, payday-loan joints, and gas stations at the end of the steeply curving off-ramp of I-74. I pulled into the busy gravel parking lot.

The restaurant's architecture vaguely hinted at what it had been, a boxlike fast-food establishment with a drive-through window, though efforts had been made to disguise it. A glass-roofed sunroom filled with plants and an adobe-walled patio with bright umbrellas advertising Mexican and Guatemalan beers had been added, and large planters of impatiens marked the entrance.

Any trace of the former donut shop disappeared once I got inside. A tall wooden cashier's desk sporting posters from western Mexico faced the front door; the dining space had been transformed from grab-and-go Formica counter to a real restaurant with murals of winding cobbled streets, hanging ferns, and *norteño* and salsa on the sound system. No wonder Ruston liked it. It was as close as one could get to Mesoamerica in Big Grove.

Bill sat in a booth just beyond the entry, sipping iced tea and reading a menu. I slid in across from him, savoring the icy air, the smell of grilling meat and onions, and the cool Naugahyde against my damp back. An iced tea magically appeared at my place as soon as I arrived, as well as a basket of hot homemade tortilla chips and an array of sauces in small dishes.

"I figured you'd want tea in this heat," Bill said. "The menu is stunning," he added as he pushed his copy toward me.

After we ordered, we sat back to watch the action. The place was surging—dark-haired men in jungle-print shirts ran between tables. Most looked like they pumped iron; a couple had gang-banger eyebrows shaved into lines, patches, and peaks. Over the music, we could hear the greasy laughter of men full of self-satisfaction sharing a joke in an office just beyond the entry.

"They're having a hell of a time in there," Bill said.

"I wish I were feeling as pleased with myself as they are," I said, scowling. "Nothing stands out from all those notes and images I've examined, except Ruston clearly hadn't become interested in K'in A'jaw until last summer. In fact, according to him, no one had even heard of the ruler till he tripped over the stele.

"What made his continuing research complicated was that it wasn't just K'in A'jaw he wanted to uncover, he wanted to piece together his world, to discover how closely linked the ancient people were to those who followed them later."

Bill nodded as he scooped salsa onto a chip. "You're probably right," he said with his mouth full. "That doesn't seem like much after all that work, but it's something. And it tells you where his research might have gone next and maybe what people didn't want him poking into in the future."

Our lunches arrived in a sizzling cloud of steam. The grilled steaks were perfect—as were the homemade tortillas and black beans with thyme—just what I needed after a morning spent bending over the searing light box. Bill smiled as he rolled a tortilla full of guacamole and fresh cheese and licked his fingers happily. Customers poured through the door in a steady stream while we ate—construction workers, truck drivers, people from nearby businesses, glassy-eyed travelers off the interstate.

Traffic into the parking lot hadn't slowed by the time we left an hour later. Two large semis were pulling into the lot next to the restaurant as we crossed the hot gravel to our cars. A group of students parked near the entrance and darted inside.

The guy who owns Cinco Gallos must be rolling in cash. Maybe that helped explain the new British racing green Jaguar F type coupe parked in the "Reserved for Owner" space near the rear entrance.

Bill whistled when he spotted it. "You know how much that costs? Sixty-three thousand dollars, give or take. We aren't talking only selling tacos to buy that thing. If we are, I'm changing jobs!" He gave me a half salute and headed for his battered old Land Cruiser parked near the dumpsters at the rear of the lot.

~ * ~

Back in Ruston's study, I examined the remaining pile of materials. So far there wasn't anything about the stele that meant anything to me beyond what he told Polop in the first place. I'd start packing his papers and books tomorrow. I'd be done by late afternoon if I kept moving. I was eager to wrap things up. The heat and stale air were getting me down.

By Friday morning, nothing new had appeared in Ruston's papers except a short description of a jade green vulture pectoral at the end of his field notes. He'd made a rough sketch of it, too; it was identical to the one I'd found on his desk. By noon I'd heard from Luis and Zoila about the vulture's possible meaning. They suggested it was an image of transition between sky, earth, and the moisture that flows between. Polop proposed a water connection as well, a link between earth and sky in which the vulture played a role in moisture and fertility.

The Dumbarton Oaks curator said the same thing—water, sky, rain, moisture, fertility, and jade itself carried similar watery connections. Just before we hung up he added, "Here's something interesting, around six hundred BCE there was a lord called Grandfather Vulture, K'utz Chman, in a large community near the west coast."

Huh. Curious.

The other information I'd gleaned during my time at Ruston's, aside from his use of Selsun, was that his interest in cigars was more than casual—if the large wooden humidor on an office shelf and the lingering odor of tobacco after several days with a window open were indicators. There was his fondness for Cinco Gallos, too. I guess that counted as a discovery, but still, taken together, there wasn't much information about Ruston as a person or his stele after a week spent digging through his papers. Nothing suggested what had happened to him. Nothing indicated the role of the stele in his demise or the jade pectoral's place in his enquiries, either.

Six

Big Grove, First Week in October

A week after my Ruston job, Big Grove was jolted out of its early fall routine of football, tailgating, and raking leaves. At six o'clock Saturday evening, on I-74, at the north edge of town, a battered white Cintas truck—The Uniform People, it said in blurry letters on its side—was blown off the road near the Sutter Avenue turnoff behind Cinco Gallos, according to the ten o'clock news. The driver tried to swerve back onto the road, but the front tire caught in a depression in the gravel below the sharp edge of the pavement. The truck skidded onto the narrow shoulder on its side, slid down the embankment, and came to rest upside down below the tight curve of the highway exit. An hour later, as emergency personnel began the process of documenting and cleaning up the site, the truck burst into flames due to a gas-tank leak.

Several things made the accident notable, the newswoman continued: the driver and his companion had disappeared, and they had been hauling a substantial quantity of drugs. According to her, a number of brick-sized plastic-wrapped packages had fallen from the truck and spread across the grass behind Cinco Gallos as the vehicle skidded down the incline. The police, always alert to the possibility of drugs, brought a dog to check the scene. The officers were right.

The dog was eager. The packages on the grass appeared to contain heroin, as did the bricks stacked floor to ceiling in the back of the truck. The dog, her work complete, was returned to the back of the squad car, just before the truck caught fire.

Emergency personnel from several jurisdictions kept bystanders away from the burning truck, but they couldn't do anything about the smoke. The north end of Big Grove was blanketed in a thick cloud by the time the flames were put out, a couple of hours later. During interviews the next morning, people who lived in the area joked they would be high for weeks.

~ * ~

In the investigations that followed, officers learned that two days before the accident, a mason on his way to work saw the boxy white van as it turned north out of El Paso toward Wichita. Other people, too, took note of its rapid northeastward progress, since speeding Cintas trucks aren't common in interstate traffic. A semi driver spotted the van heading east from Wichita toward Kansas City. A day later, an Illinois Highway Patrol officer saw the truck on the interstate between St. Louis and Effingham. Then it turned north.

Evening traffic was thick by the time the truck approached Big Grove. Several people interviewed after the accident had seen the truck exit I-57 and turn east on I-74, where crosswinds—always tricky on that stretch of road—caught it and rolled it down the off-ramp incline. The truck's flaming demise was well-documented, for by then several people were using their cells to take pictures.

~ * ~

Our Burr Oaks group gets together at least every couple of weeks in someone's apartment for what we call cocktail hour. Our evenings are BYO and everyone brings snacks to share. Bill, runner thin, can be depended on to have a bag of Cheetos or salsa and tortilla chips and a microbrew of some sort. Pat, short and chunky, leans toward vegetable sticks, homemade spreads, and a glass of pinot noir. I usually have a hunk of nice cheese, crackers, and

Bowmore neat. We gather around a kitchen table, spread out the hors d'oeuvres, and dig in.

"Where the hell was all that stuff going?" Bill mused at our cocktail hour the Friday after the news broke. "Chicago? Detroit? Indianapolis? I mean, millions of dollars of heroin and fentanyl, too. Who could buy that quantity? Where else could that be sold but a big city?"

We were in Bill's kitchen this time. Plenty of Cheetos, potato chips, and onion dip. Pat brought her new baked ricotta and herb spread with crostini. I'd gone all out and purchased smoked salmon, a change from my usual cheese and crackers.

"Was the truck exiting, do you think?" I asked as I bit into a layer of salmon on thin, buttered brown bread. "Or did it just blow off I-74 at that point?"

"It's hard to know," Bill said, dunking his potato chip into the dip. "Maybe they were pulling off for the night. There are a lot of cheap motels in that part of Big Grove."

Pat sipped her wine. "But where was the driver?" she asked. "There wasn't a sign of him."

"Long gone after that accident," Bill said. "He wasn't going to stay around for the finale."

"Do you think someone set fire to the truck or did it catch on its own?" Pat asked, not expecting an answer.

We kicked the questions around for a while, then drifted into other considerations: Pat's enthusiasm regarding new seating in the library, Bill's plans for running the marathon in the spring, my growing interest in taking a real holiday. An hour later, as we packed the leftovers, Bill promised to see what he could find out from his police buddies at the gym about the truck and drugs. Maybe they knew something.

As it turned out, none of them knew anything that wasn't in the paper or on TV. In fact, nothing more came to light about the crash until months later, but in the meantime things continued to go wrong in Big Grove.

Seven

Big Grove, Second Week in October

Father Diego Muldonado sighed as he locked the back door of St. Patrick's social hall. It had been a long day. It was eight o'clock and nearly pitch black. Parishioners called good night as they moved to their cars, keen to reach the warmth of their homes after the parish board meeting. Father Diego waved.

At least they had finalized the parish holiday arrangements—a Day of the Dead Fiesta (they'd have to hurry their preparations, since they had waited to the last minute), a communal dinner on Thanksgiving, and a tamale supper and gift exchange on Christmas Eve after midnight Mass. There also had been decorations that needed to be discussed, since the women were eager to make the large open space of the hall as festive as possible. They would do most of the work—the decorating, the cooking—but they were excited despite their family obligations and the fact that making tamales would mean several of them cooking all day in the steamy parish kitchen.

Father Diego had one more thing to do before he could go home to his old brick rectory on the corner. He palmed his car keys, clicked open the door of his Corolla, and eased under the wheel. He headed out of the parking lot and turned north toward the interstate and

Cinco Gallos. If he were lucky, the meeting with Eduardo Guzmán, owner of the restaurant, would be brief.

Father Diego's parish covered the entire length of Bloomingdale Road between Sutter and the I-57 exit and paralleled I-74. It wasn't much to look at. On the east, at the interstate's intersection with Sutter, a McDonald's, bright with lights and colored plastic play equipment, faced a payday-loan office in a former fast-food restaurant. To the west, Bloomingdale was lined with tired, inexpensive motels surrounded by gravel parking lots dotted with semis, the trucks of workmen, and the cars of people saving money. Interspersed among the motels, small businesses waited for customers—a seafood shack smelling of hot fat and fish advertised hush puppies and fried okra on a white plastic foldout sign near its door; a faded, yellow concrete-block liquor store announced its weekly specials in hand-lettered signs behind its window grates; a bait shop listed minnows and night crawlers on its sign out front.

Businesses that serviced trucks—semis and large truck repair, a retread tire business, a welding shop, a truck wash—backed up to the interstate. Tiny houses built after World War II, the homes of parishioners, dotted the neighborhood, struggling to avoid the encroaching trucks.

St. Patrick's Catholic Church, a red, wooden building that resembled a ranch house with a tiny square steeple topped by a small white cross, sat in the center of a large grassy soccer field. It looked more like a rural, southern Protestant chapel than a Catholic church—no statues, no stations of the cross, no stained glass. The parish hall was located in front of and to the right of the church: the rectory, a tidy brick two-story, was situated next door to the hall on the corner.

When Father Diego left the restaurant three hours later, Cinco Gallos had been closed for an hour, and the parking lot was empty except for his car, Eduardo's Jaguar, and the battered vehicles of two women mopping floors and readying the restaurant for the next day.

The wind had increased while he was inside, causing the traffic lights to sway, hurling sandwich wrappers, sales flyers, and trash can lids into the air, blowing dirt from the interstate across the restaurant's parking lot toward the tiny neighborhood beyond. Despite the late hour and the dirt, Father Diego was smiling. He headed home, full of wine, with a substantial contribution to the church in his pocket.

The sound of I-74 seemed unusually loud that night, the whining noise that endless traffic makes as it moves along an interstate in any American city. Maybe it was the wind, but it sounded like *La Llorano*, the weeping woman, calling her dead children, or the wail of a creature in distress.

Eight

In the far southwest section of Big Grove, Eighteen Rabbit watched blankly as José Polop's garage door rose with a rattle just after midnight. *I feel like a rat about Quesito,* José Polop thought as he threw his carry-on bag into the front seat of his car and slid under the wheel. *I'd like to take him with me, but I've got to disappear. I'd stick out like a sore thumb walking through O'Hare with a cat carrier at this hour.* "Yeah, I saw a little Indian guy with a cat. He was buying a ticket for Guatemala." *I've left plenty of food. The Lunds will check when I don't pick up my paper tomorrow morning. They'll take care of him.* He backed out of his garage and headed for the interstate.

It was 12:30 when he turned north on I-57. The wind tugged at his car as he drove up the ramp. Unlike some early mornings, the road was empty. If all went well, it would be two and a half hours to Chicago, then a half hour more to O'Hare. He'd done this trip so many times on his way to research in Guatemala or visit family that he could drive it in his sleep. He'd buy a ticket for the five o'clock morning flight to Miami and then one from Miami to Guatemala. Once he got to Guatemala, he'd disappear. Visit a friend in Xela, or Quetzaltenango as they call it now thanks to the Spaniards, or maybe

Chichicastenango. This whole Ruston business was so Guatemalan: there was nothing like torture to keep the wheels of time and existence turning. Whatever had gone on with Ruston probably wasn't going to follow him to the Highlands, and the black Jeep Cherokee that had been driving past his house the last couple of days may have been someone visiting in the neighborhood. Probably he was paranoid, but he couldn't take a chance. No one outside of friends and family knew where his former schoolmates lived. He'd be okay with them while he figured things out.

When he got to O'Hare, his luck held. There was still parking in the long-term lot. Polop pulled into one of the remaining spots, grabbed his carry-on, locked his car, and hurried toward the shuttle for Terminal Three. His tickets were going to cost an arm and a leg, but he didn't care. When he got to Guatemala it would all be worth it.

The immense echoing ticket area was nearly deserted except for two or three scattered groups waiting for ticket agents' desks to open. A rumpled family of four slept curled against one another on a couch in front of the huge front windows, their bags at their feet.

Buying the tickets was easy. The sleepy-eyed clerk who emerged from the back hardly looked at him. Polop hurried through the remaining travel processes—TSA, passport screening, then headed toward his terminal, stopping for a coffee on the way. A half hour before the flight was called, he went to the men's room nearest his gate to avoid using the airplane toilet later.

The blue tiled space was deserted except for two janitors who followed him in, pushing carts loaded with trash bins, plastic sacks, and cleaning supplies. The largest of the men set up a pair of yellow plastic signs in the entrance saying that the toilets were closed for servicing and warning of wet floors. An arrow pointed to the still open section on the other side of the entrance. The second man parked his cart in the middle of the room, removed a mop and a container of cleaning solution from his cart, filled his bucket at a service tap near the door, and began swabbing the floor under the sinks.

Uninterested in the janitors but eager for privacy, Polop chose a stall at the end of the row away from the activity, pushed open the stainless-steel door, and stepped inside, fumbling with his bag, his jacket, the sliding latch. Suddenly the space behind him exploded. The door flew open and Polop was slammed forward into the stall. "What the hell? Get out!" he yelled as he struggled to keep his balance and turn to face the intruder. It was useless. He was penned in the limited space in front of the toilet, restrained by his jacket, the clumsy carryon, the arm around his throat. Rubber gloved fingers pressed hard on the pressure point below his right ear. It felt as if someone had jabbed an electric probe in his neck. He dropped his bag, staggered, fell back into the arms of the largest janitor who hauled him out of the stall.

"Don't say anything. Don't make a sound. If you do, I *will* hurt you," the man said in Spanish as he and his partner lifted Polop over the edge of the nearest cart's trash barrel. "If you shout, move, anything, you're dead."

Something hard, maybe a gun from its size and shape, pressed against the top of Polop's skull. The second janitor scooped up Polop's bag, threw it in on top of him, then covered him with the bulging, leaking trash sacks they'd gathered from the gates in Terminal Three. As the men moved into the echoing concourse pushing their carts of supplies, the smell of coffee, popcorn, and greasy french fries filled Polop's lungs like poisonous gas: brown landfill-like leach trickled over his head and shoulders from the bags above.

When Airport Security made enquiries later, passengers waiting outside a nearby gate remembered nothing unusual, just two janitors doing their nightly rounds, shoving carts with supplies in front of them as they headed for the main terminal. The airport employee monitoring passengers at the terminal exit recalled seeing two janitors push a single cart out a sliding door into the passenger pickup area, perhaps to empty the waste cans along the drive. The employee didn't see the black Cherokee parked at the far end of the exit curb turn on its lights. When he looked later, the car was gone: the cart stood deserted on the sidewalk, bulging trash bags piled nearby.

Nine

"Second Mayan Scholar Disappears," the local headlines read, further disturbing Big Grove and the university. Even national news picked it up, especially since it was similar to the Ruston story earlier in the year—same university, same area of scholarly interest, and the two men had been colleagues. American Airlines verified Polop had bought a one-way ticket at their counter but failed to board his flight. TSA acknowledged he'd entered their system.

According to Polop's neighbor, Peter Lund, in a TV news interview, Polop had been uneasy a few days before he disappeared. Ruston's murder and the Jeep Cherokee driving past his house had triggered memories of Guatemala at its worst. From the state of Polop's condo and his appearance later in Chicago, however, he hadn't been burgled or kidnapped. And he'd left plenty of food for his cat. Maybe, Lund suggested, the airport was the first step in a sudden trip to visit relatives, but where did he go after that? And why hadn't he said anything about Quesito to the Lunds before he left?

~ * ~

I left my coffee in the kitchen as I headed into my bedroom to dress. Polop's disappearance was a shock. I knew Luis and Zoila would call as soon as they read the paper. The world of Mayan scholars was shrinking. Two former colleagues gone: one dead, one missing. I wasn't wrong; the phone rang just as I pulled on my sweater. Zoila was upset. "Can you come over? Polop's disappearance has hit Luis hard. First Ruston. Now José. Just like the seventies and eighties."

The drive to the retirement community was rainy and cold. The wind had picked up; it buffeted the RAV4, making it lurch from side to side. Dried corn leaves and scraggly weeds tumbled onto the brown lawns and trimmed evergreens on the far side of the road. I got to the Velascos' apartment fifteen minutes after I talked with Zoila.

"This is terrible. Luis and José have been good friends ever since university in Guatemala City," she said as she took my coat.

Luis was in the living room looking grim. He hadn't touched his coffee or sweet bread, but my appearance seemed to rouse him. He pulled himself up straighter in his recliner and adjusted the red and purple blanket over his legs.

"It started when Ruston was sacrificed in Tikal. Now Polop disappears in O'Hare. It doesn't make sense," he began without saying hello.

"I've had sheet lightning running on my skin ever since Ruston died," he said, mentioning the effects of his divination abilities as a calendar priest. "It's been clear something is amiss, but starting last night, the warning of trouble has become even more pronounced. I'll cast the seeds. Maybe the ancestors will tell us something."

Luis began to plan for the ritual. "You need to be here, too." He looked at me over his reading glasses. "You were just talking with José about Ruston and his stele a few days ago and Ruston's discovery seems to be the beginning. Let's plan for four o'clock. That gives us time to pull everything together."

"I'll get the offerings," I said. "Flowers, candles, anything else?"

"How about a couple of cigars? Cheap is fine. Even cigarettes would work in a pinch. With Ruston's interests, it makes sense to have tobacco on the altar." Luis Valasco, calendar priest, daykeeper, mother-father, Mayan holy man, diviner, smiled grimly.

By the time I returned with the offerings later that day, Zoila had swept the balcony, apartment, and stone altar, lit copal incense in the broken potshards that lined the balcony's railings and set pots of thyme from her herb collection among the shards.

The autumn wind still blew down from the north, winding the incense into thin blue strands beyond the balcony, sending it back through the partially open door as I settled in my chair across from Luis. The curtains twisted in the gusting wind.

Zoila positioned the little table with the striped cloth over Luis's knees and placed his divining sack in the center. Then, she arranged the offerings on the altar.

Luis emptied the red seeds and clear quartz crystals into the middle of the table, then sat, eyes closed, hands resting in his lap, listening to the wind, the voices only he could hear, his lips moving in silent prayers. He swept the seeds and crystals counterclockwise with his right hand, spreading them out, then swept again, chanting softly, requesting the lords of the *Cauacs* to heed his voice, asking the ancestors to listen, inviting them to come closer, requesting guidance and help. Luis paused in his prayers to place ten large crystals in a row along the front of the table. He arranged piles of seeds and crystals behind them. He waited, scrutinized the tiny heaps, gathered them up and threw them down again—throwing and reading four times, resting in between throws, eyes closed, oblivious to everything but the seeds, the crystals, and the patterns they made.

Zoila and I sat quietly, focused on Luis's circling hand, his chanting, the smoke wafting in from the balcony. The copper disk of the autumn sun slid beyond the haze of trees on the horizon; the orange light of sunset spread and thinned. The room darkened.

Finally, Luis spoke. "It's clear. We must go to Tikal. That is where the story began thousands of years ago, when the early people began to build their cities. Those stories reach into the world today, touching us all. Maybe Ruston and Polop were caught in a related struggle, something between indigenous rebels, or the cartels moving out of the Highlands. Perhaps we can find a trace of the two men, as well as information about the rising interest in Tikal's narrative."

"I don't like it. You'll be a sitting duck in that wheelchair if someone is after Mayan scholars," I said. *Besides,* I thought, *what the hell kind of demands are being made on Zoila? Had the ancestors thought of that? And why and how do I, a retired* gringa *professor, fit into their schemes?*

"And Luis, the walker. How can we manage?" Zoila asked. "You tire easily. And I don't—"

Luis waved his hand dismissively. "The situation demands it. Besides, how else are we going to find out what is really happening? And we haven't visited the relatives for months. The trip itself isn't a big deal. All I'd have to do is sit. So, what's new there?"

It became clear there was no sense arguing with Luis, or the ancestors either. By the end of the evening, we were deep into plans for a trip to Guatemala. The decision wasn't as precipitous as it seemed. I'd been talking about a vacation for weeks, and Zoila and Luis hadn't been back to Guatemala since Luis's stroke. They were eager to see relatives and friends again.

Despite my misgivings, I could spend a week in Tikal with them, reacquaint myself with the site and visit museums in Guatemala City after they left for the Highlands. Mrs. Bertramson, who'd lived upstairs for years, could look after Rosie as usual.

We couldn't pretend we hadn't noticed that the experts in an entire area of study seemed to be disappearing from the university. Tikal would be a good place to look for answers, since that was where Ruston died and Polop's research was focused on precontact Mayan art imagery—just what one would find in the ancient site.

That night, as I hurried to the RAV4, the air held the first hints of winter. I smelled snow on each gust of wind as it wrapped my coat around my legs and drove dried leaves across open spaces between buildings. The trees fretted and complained, uneasy against the dark sky.

Ten

Ciudad Juarez, Mexico, Late October

It was midmorning and the heat had begun to rise when José Polop and his four escorts landed in Ciudad Juarez. His airport exit was the reverse of his entrance into Midway from O'Hare. They hauled him through the lounge, his feet barely touching the floor, then frog marched him to curbside parking. A black Jeep with tinted windows waited near a flowerbed of prickly pear. *Was there no other vehicle for this sort of work?* Polop wondered as he struggled to remain upright. The two guards—janitors, thugs, whatever they were—dragged Polop with them into the back seat. The small-boned jumpy guy in charge who'd been in the Jeep at O'Hare, got in next to the driver. The last kidnapper, as before, was somewhere behind him in an extra seat. Polop could smell his cheap aftershave.

It was like a Gabriel García Marquez short story—surreal images, fragmented conversations, cloudy dreams—held together with the hum of the auto engine, the hiss and thump of tires over rough spots in the road. At night, they pulled into isolated *ranchitas*, tiny rural houses with tin-roofed porches, ever-present pots of *nixtamal*—corn and lime in water—simmering over small fires, and scruffy dogs, patchy, and nervous, that barked when they arrived, then hurried behind the house as they opened the Jeep's doors. The dream included tortillas and frijole, beer if they were lucky, silent people in worn clothes, stars thick as smoke wheeling overhead, night winds rattling rusty roofs.

He slept in sheds behind the houses, tipsy with beer, exhaustion, and fear, shackled to an iron ring for tying animals to the shed's wall or trussed like a calf in a roping contest when there wasn't a ring. Three days later, by the time the car stopped for the night, Polop had gleaned a few scraps of information from the muttered conversations among the men. They were headed south. He was supposed to arrive safe and sound, then do something, look at something. His escorts smoked, worked puzzles, listened to music. The guy in charge fiddled with his cell when there was reception. Polop slept, tried to think, slept again.

That night, like the first, Polop was chained to the back wall of the tiny storage building attached to the house. He squirmed to make himself comfortable on a rough woven mat under a filthy burlap bag. The cold desert wind blew dirt against the door. Rodents skittered among the feedbags. Polop shivered. *What the hell is next?* he wondered.

~ * ~

The drive to the Lacandon National Park in Mexico, just over the border from Guatemala—at least he'd found out where he was going for certain last night—was murder. The roads were lousy and Jesús, the leader, was on edge. He kept poking at his cell, craning his neck to see the road ahead, consulting a hand-drawn map spread on his knees. The thugs on either side watched the roadside like Rottweilers at a fence, their hands close to guns in holsters they'd strapped on that morning, holsters like those seen in pictures of SWAT teams. Who knows what the guy behind him was doing? Probably the same thing.

When they finally stopped that fourth night, God knows where, it was dark. They pulled through the open gate of a small compound surrounded by an adobe wall on the edge of what had appeared in the fading light to be a tiny *aldea* or village scattered in the nearby jungle. Their destination, a small cement-block building at the back of the compound, was dim inside, except for a smoking kerosene lantern on a crude table in the center of the room. Polop counted a half dozen men seated on rough chairs in the flickering light. His throat tightened. They looked like ancient Maya, *Yukatek* Maya if their language meant anything—ponytails over their foreheads, earplugs, jade-inlayed teeth, which flashed in the feeble light— except they were dressed in commando outfits that included sidearms, bandoliers, and thick belts sagging with radios. A dozen assault rifles leaned against the walls. Two men dressed in street clothes sat well back from the table. They were Mexican from their appearance as well as their Spanish. No one smiled. His escorts didn't either.

That night they let him in on their plans. There was a cave with murals, north of Santa Elena, Guatemala, the Mayan leader, a guy named Kan, said—fantastic images of a pre-Columbian Mayan lord of an unknown early city-kingdom holding court, a woman offering a pot of chocolate, warriors standing guard, a Vulture Lord ancestor hovering over the scene in a cloud of incense. They needed a Mayan art expert. Wanted Polop to explain the figures, to give them a date, to verify the murals as a document of their ownership of the Petén and surrounding lands. They wanted an anthropologist to read a document, too. See how those fit in. *Great.* There were endless ways he could fail.

The rack and arrows hovered at the end of it all like a gate to hell no matter what he did.

Eleven

Tikal National Park, Guatemala, Early November

At the end of the rainy season in Guatemala, people in Flores and Santa Elena began to plan for the Christmas holiday, but Ochoa had something other than the holidays on his mind. Ever since Ruston's death, hoping to find something that would explain the professor's murder, he'd continued to comb the area behind Temple IV, a dense expanse of understory that had seen little activity for the last twenty years. That afternoon he'd pushed further than usual into the region of unidentified stones and ancient building materials. It was hard going and Ochoa was sweating. If it hadn't been for his heavy boots, he would have turned his ankles a half dozen times.

Suddenly, he tripped over something hidden under the vegetation and fell on his hands and knees in the thick tangle of foliage. He muttered as he pulled himself up, brushing off his pants as he stood. Whatever he had fallen over was substantial. He crouched down in the undergrowth to investigate, pulling back the plants. He'd caught his toe on a stone—the size of a German shepherd—half buried in the jungle duff. Using the small trowel he carried on his belt for just such occasions, Ochoa carefully removed the earth from around its base; then he rocked back on his heels.

"Madre de Dios! Es el mismo! Es el mismo que tiene Ruston," Ochoa said as he carefully dusted its surface with his handkerchief. The ancient carving was the twin of Ruston's. The date was in the upper left, the lord's name in the upper right, but at the bottom where the earlier stele had been broken, a seated lord stared up into the face of a vulture leaning out of a cloud of incense rising from a brazier near his feet. A pectoral in the form of a vulture hung from the lord's necklace of large jade beads.

What are the chances? Ochoa asked himself as he pulled out his camera and set to work documenting his find. *Two stele, the same lord?*

"There's a lot to do before I go home—record the new stele back at the office, lead a tour of visiting academics, reread the reports on the possible relationship between Tak'alik Ab'aj on the coast and Tikal around six hundred BCE." Ochoa muttered as he covered the stele with vines. After all, Grandfather Vulture was the lord of Tak'alik Ab'aj at that time. Maybe the vulture imagery was connected with him in some way.

First I have to tell Ríos about the stele. Everything else can wait. He barely heard the howler monkeys calling in the distant jungle as he flipped on his radio.

~ * ~

Captain Ríos, director of Tikal National Park, a short, heavy man in a brown park service uniform that befit his role as director, even if it did strain over his stomach, responded immediately. Never restrained, he began talking before Ochoa finished his second sentence. *"Jesús!* We've got to get someone out there as quickly as possible. Rope the site off. Post a guard. Tomorrow morning at the latest, before someone steals the thing. Start digging. Did you cover it?"

When Rios stopped to breathe, Ochoa assured him that the site was invisible. The wheels of Tikal National Park had begun to turn.

~ * ~

By the time Ochoa pulled up in front of his house six hours later, not only had he finished his other tasks, he'd also learned enough to begin formulating questions about the stele and its seated lord, K'in A'jaw and to begin to worry. Ruston hadn't lived long after finding the first stele. Ochoa didn't like his chances with the second one. He'd keep his concerns from Esperanza as long as possible, but it wouldn't take her long to put two and two together.

Even before he unlocked the front door, the odor of wood smoke and baking tortillas reminded him he was hungry, distracting Ochoa from his pre-Columbian considerations. There was something simmering, too, maybe frijoles with meat. Once he was inside, he locked the door and padlocked the chain for the night, hung his jacket in the dark hall, and headed for the kitchen, just as Esperanza poked her head out of its doorway, her face flushed, wisps of black hair pulling out of her thick braid.

"I thought I heard something. I'm glad you're home. What is going on now? Is someone else dead? And you said something about another stele."

"I'll tell you the whole story while we eat. It's amazing," Ochoa said, following her back into the warm, fire-lit kitchen. "Something smells good. I'm starving."

Over bowls of steaming frijoles and a basket of fresh tortillas at the tiny table near the hearth, Ochoa described what he had learned in the library that afternoon—the vulture pectoral that gave K'utz Chman his name, the city he'd ruled, and the fact that the city had existed for two thousand years.

"Tak'alik Ab'aj was on a ridge in the jungle near the Pacific—they had trouble with erosion in the city center, so water control was an issue just like it was in Tikal," Ochoa said, spooning a piece of beef out of his frijoles. "Ancient people always had trouble with water—too much, too little, wrong place, whatever. The lord, in this case K'utz Chman, was responsible for dealing with water."

"But why the name Grandfather Vulture?" Esperanza asked, refilling Ochoa's coffee mug.

"Because the vulture was associated with moisture and agriculture, its image shows up in a lot of places—Tak'alik Ab'aj and elsewhere. It reflects the lord's water-related duties. Makes sense if you think about it. Vulture equals water, lord equals vulture, crops, prosperity."

He paused a moment to watch Esperanza fuss with the fire and pat more tortillas before he continued. "On the stele I found today, K'in A'jaw of Tikal is wearing a vulture pectoral and looking into the eyes of a vulture rising from the smoke of a brazier. Maybe his spirit animal, maybe something else. So, right there we have the vulture as a holy being or maybe an ancestor in an interaction with K'in A'jaw himself.

"I've begun to wonder if Grandfather Vulture and K'in A'jaw were related in some way, if the figure in the smoke and the vulture pectoral indicate their relationship, that we'll find a connection between the two." Ochoa scooped frijoles out of his bowl with a tortilla. He knew it was bad manners, but he didn't care. "We have to dig."

Esperanza looked concerned as she stirred sugar into her coffee. "I don't like it. You know what happened to Ruston after he found the first stele. A year later he was dead. Are the same people going to come after you?"

"I don't know, but I figure there are a couple of things in my favor—I'm not a *gringo* for one thing, and for another, I'm not taking information or anything else out of the country. Everything stays here where it belongs, where it's protected from looters, dealers, and wealthy collectors, and I'm not researching the stele, either. All I did was trip over the thing."

Esperanza didn't look convinced. "Still, be careful. Who knows what motivated the people who grabbed Ruston?"

Ochoa tried to steer the conversation to family matters and the Christmas season to get her mind off ugly possibilities. "What are the family holiday plans?"

"Mother's volunteered to have everyone at her house," Esperanza began, knowing full well that he would have preferred to remain at home with her eating chicken instead of tamales with the entire family, but there you have it. Her mother hadn't held a celebration since Esperanza's father died three years ago.

Ochoa grunted to show he was listening.

"This will be good for her," Esperanza said, perking up. "All the women in the kitchen making tamales just like the old days."

Ochoa nodded in agreement, half listening, absorbed in the problems of traversing several hundred miles of jungle between Tikal and the southwestern Pacific coast community a thousand years or more ago and the mounting evidence of an ancient link between the two.

"She's going to roast a turkey in the patio oven for you and Uncle Roberto, and I'll make tortillas to mop up the sauce." Esperanza was getting excited, despite Marta and Pedro, their two grown children, being elsewhere—Pedro at Stanford and Marta in Spain with her husband. "It'll almost be like it was before the kids left home."

Ochoa nodded again, pleased that Esperanza was more cheerful, but his mind was elsewhere. Water. Vultures. Jade. Two lords. Two cities. Ruston hanging on a rack buzzing with flies. There was more to the situation than these several facts, some level he was missing, something that might mean the difference between life and death. Ochoa only half heard Esperanza's remark about the turkey.

Twelve

"Half the trip completed and everything is fine," Zoila said that Monday evening before Thanksgiving as the dense Guatemala City traffic smoked and roared fifteen floors below Enrique Otzoy's apartment. She took a handful of cashews from the bowl on the table at her elbow. "We still have our luggage, nothing bad happened, and Luis is holding up. What more can we ask?"

"And tomorrow will be a short day," I said, sipping my wine. "It's only an hour flight to Flores."

"So, what's new on the missing scholar's front?" Otzoy asked Luis as he handed him another beer.

Luis shook his head. "Nothing."

We sat in silence then, sipping our drinks, contemplating what the complete absence of information might mean.

~ * ~

The flight to Flores early the following morning was rough. The Avianca thirty-seven-passenger, twin-engine Embraer ERJ 145 dropped and shuddered in the turbulent air. Bottles and cans rolled down the aisle, clattering against the seat legs and bulkheads at either end. The seat belt sign glowed the entire time. By the time we reached Flores, several people were queasy, if the gagging sounds around the cabin were any indication.

The pilot must have been sick of flying because he dumped the airplane at the end of the runway like he never wanted to see it again. The impact brought down a rain of coats and bags from the poorly secured overheads, and cries of fear from the passengers. They grumbled as the plane turned toward the terminal and nosed into an empty bay. Once the pilot cut the engines and the door was open, though, they didn't care about the quality of the ride...they just wanted to get the hell out.

Exiting the plane proved to be the hardest part of the trip—Luis, the steep airplane stairs, the collapsed chair, the walker, the carry-ons—the three of us struggling on the metal stairs to stay upright and to get Luis safely in his chair at the bottom. I was sweating by the time we headed toward the terminal. Luis and Zoila went ahead, weaving through the baggage carts and airport workers who were servicing the plane for its return to Guatemala City. I trailed behind, intent on retrieving our remaining luggage.

~ * ~

Guatemala's terminals are interfaces between worlds, I thought, resting my arms on the handle of the luggage cart as I waited for our bags. *They're where my familiar self is replaced by someone else. Maybe part of my sense of stepping through a looking glass is that I don't look like most Guatemalans, and I'm aware of not fitting in. I'm taller, for one thing, lighter—a white giraffe in a herd of gazelles.* I smile at the image.

The flashing red lights and blatting horn of the lurching conveyer pulled me out of my musing. Backpacks, cardboard boxes tied with twine, baby carriers, shopping bags with handles roped together, battered suitcases emerged from the far opening, circled around the central island, exited through the door on the other side, to return a few minutes later accompanied by additional cargo. I grabbed our luggage as it juddered past, heaved it on my trolley, and headed for passport control. Luis and Zoila waited for me near the beginning of the line.

Despite the crowd, we were through the process in no time.

"Looks like the shuttle has arrived," Zoila called as she shoved their bags onto a luggage cart and began to push Luis toward the door. She nodded her head toward the green Ford van parked at the curb, sending out a cloud of exhaust.

Tikal National Park, Guatemala

The Tikal Inn, a ten-minute walk from Tikal's Central Plaza, is a collection of low brown thatched bungalows around a swimming pool and tropical garden and two multistory buildings, the largest with a dining room and bar. We'd opted for rooms in the main building, easier for Luis.

We met later for dinner in the glassed-in dining room, an airy space with flowers on every table and a view of the jungle. Next to the hostess's desk, a scarlet macaw, shifting from foot to foot on his perch in the center of a wirework cage, watched over the area with beady eyes...periodically remarking on his job as a hotel mascot. While we waited for our dinner of beef grilled over a wood fire with plenty of salt, we discussed our plans.

"I want to see that stele for myself," Luis said, putting down his beer. "Get a sense of where it's located in relationship to the rest of the site. Get a better idea of the stele as a boundary marker, the direction of a line of demarcation, the scale of a possible enclosure. And I want to know what has been written about the ancient peoples, the early preclassic history of Tikal. See if I can develop an idea of who might have erected it, and why Ruston is dead because he found it."

Zoila nodded as she sipped her wine. "I keep thinking that water lies at the heart of the whole Ruston thing. Let's face it...the vulture imagery is about water and elite power, too. Water's always been a big deal. The lord would have to provide rain through rituals and maybe oversee the engineering of hydro projects. Look around. People in the Petén still have to depend on rain, retention, storage, bringing water in. Somehow Ruston touched that ancient nerve and then—"

"Poor guy," I said. "He probably stepped into what amounts to a two-thousand-year-old wasp nest. I wonder if I followed through on his scholarly plans, if I could uncover anything about the stele or the pectoral. The pectoral has to mean something, or why else did he bother to mention it in his notes, or steal it for that matter? Where the hell did he get it? Why is it important?" I sloshed my wine in my excitement. "Surely there is information that will shed light on it." I pulled my drawing from my purse and spread it in the center of the table as if it might help me think. "It isn't just an ornament. It has to be more than that, and it's bound to tell us something about Ruston's inquiries."

As dinner arrived, a dark shape fluttered toward us from an elaborate cage in the corner of the room. The inn's resident toucan was eager to introduce himself. He settled in the center of the table, moving his blue feet carefully among the dishes, peering hungrily at our food, fluffing his yellow bib. I handed him a piece of papaya. He took it in his graceful red-tipped beak, tossed it down, clacked his bill for more.

On the porch later, watching the evening mist rise in the jungle undergrowth in inky shadows, the soaring canopy fading into darkness as stars powdered the sky, I started to relax. Luis sagged in his chair. Even Zoila, who usually had energy to spare, looked worn out. We went to bed early. Maneuvering Luis's chair around Tikal tomorrow wasn't going to be easy.

Thirteen

Tikal National Park, the Following Day

The roar of howler monkeys jolted me awake the next morning. They sounded as if they were about to attack the hotel. I slid out of bed and crossed to the window. No dark forms headed toward the buildings through the mist, only ferocious howling indicated the monkeys' presence. They were probably just telling one another their plans for the day. They didn't care about the hotel—or humans, either. We were nothing.

The strangely inorganic cries of other jungle creatures—sounding like steel strings struck with tiny mallets or tinkling glass chimes—and the drone of insects followed me into the dining room.

Before we sat down the toucan hurried over, taking over the middle of our table. When our fruit plate arrived, he clattered his bill in enthusiasm, eyeing the slices of pineapple, papaya, mango, and bright magenta pitaya. He poked the tiny red bananas with his thick beak as if to ascertain their ripeness, and then he arranged himself, tail and wings tucked as if he were in his nest hole, waiting to be served. I handed him a large piece of ripe papaya as a reward for his good manners. His bill felt like plastic as he gently lifted it from my fingers and tossed the entire slice down his throat in a single swift motion. He made a couple of passes at the breadbasket, too, so I ripped off pieces of sweet bread to round out his breakfast.

~ * ~

When Captain Ríos gave Miguel Ochoa the letter from the internationally known anthropologist, Luis Velasco, requesting a private guide and describing his interest in seeing the unusual stele discovered last summer, neither was aware of Luis's special travel requirements. All Luis indicated was his current interest in early Mayan cultural interactions, his wife's research in hydrology, and their companion's particular focus on vulture imagery and its social implications.

He hadn't said anything about his wheelchair, so when the small party of academics rounded the end of the front desk, Ochoa was stunned. He'd known the group was comprised of retired scholars, but the frail man in the wheelchair with a red and purple blanket over his knees and two older women carrying bulging backpacks as they pushed his chair destroyed Ochoa's careful plans.

How the hell are we going to get from the hotel to Tikal? Ochoa thought. How was Velasco going to stand up to the heat, the rough ride over grass, the hours of sun and humidity? And how were the women going to hold up hauling backpacks and pushing Velasco? Or, if he were the one shoving the chair, how was he going to give a tour, answer questions, think, while wrestling the thing over rough ground? He was in shape, but dealing with Luis and his equipment would be miserable. He'd had a wheelchair visitor in the past—a young man with upper arms like hams and a huge companion who could propel him over the worst terrain. That situation worked. But this was different. The professor was in no state to help with the process, or endure the jolting over an archaeological site for hours on end. The women were in no shape to play mule, either. He needed to find an alternative to the chair. Fast.

"My name's Ochoa, Miguel Ochoa," Ochoa said as he rose from his chair. "I'm your guide in Tikal. I've read your request and have a general idea of why you're here, but we need to consider transportation before we begin our tour." Brushing his silver streaked hair from his forehead, Ochoa plunged on. "I have concerns about the wheelchair. The terrain is rough. Even though it's covered with grass, it isn't lawn. One of the guides has a pony and a special saddle. He's gentle. Kids play with him all the time, and the saddle was made for people with disabilities. If you're okay with riding, Professor, I'll ask if we can borrow him during your visit."

Luis nodded. "I should have said something before we came; I didn't think. But I've been worrying about mobility since we left home. A pony can't be worse than my chair. I'm afraid none of us is going to live till the end of the week if we have to struggle with it in the heat."

Ochoa activated his radio. "Jaime. Miguel…Fine. You? I need to borrow Poncho for a couple of days. Professor Velasco is in a wheelchair. He isn't going to be able to use it on site. We're at the hotel. Could you have someone bring Poncho with his adaptive saddle? Good. How long will that take? Half hour? Fine. Believe me, we aren't going anywhere." Ochoa clipped his radio back on his belt. "Jamie got that saddle and pony when his daughter wanted to ride. She was born with cerebral palsy, and Poncho and the saddle made a world of difference for her. Poncho has come in handy with other people over the years, too."

While we waited for the pony, Luis shared our story with Miguel—Ruston's life in Big Grove, the pile of images of the stele, Polop's disappearance, Luis's mounting sense that something was enormously wrong. He didn't mention the vulture pectoral.

"We're all interested in related things—the library, the museum, the stele, the place where Ruston died. We'd known Ruston for years. His death was a shock. Seeing the place where he died might help us lay it to rest," Zoila said.

"We can go to Temple Four first, visit the spot where I found Ruston. After that we can explore the most recent discovery in the

park—a second stele behind Temple Four near where Ruston found
the first one. Then we'll stop for lunch. You can spend the afternoon
in the museum and library, if that suits you. It would give you time to
do some research and see some of Tikal's other treasures. Make
sense?" Ochoa looked at us each in turn.

"A second stele! I can't believe you found another one so soon,"
Luis said. "I can't wait to see how it compares with the first."

Ochoa grunted. "It's in one piece, too. That's the most amazing
part. At the bottom, where the other stele is broken, there's a vulture
hovering in a cloud of incense over a seated lord—presumably K'in
A'jaw, the lord mentioned on the first stele."

"A vulture with a lord!" I said. "Amazing!"

Half an hour later, Jaime's nephew appeared at the edge of the
porch with a tiny pony. "This is Poncho," the boy said, patting the
pony's neck. The pony snorted. A bay with dark mane and tail and
huge brown eyes, Poncho had a saddle which looked like a chair with
arms and a seatbelt, and the air of an animal that knew his business.

"We better get started," Ochoa said after we all patted the pony's
neck, "before it's too hot." As the nephew held the lead, we lifted
Luis onto Poncho's back. It was surprisingly easy once we got his leg
over the saddle. "Is that okay?" Ochoa asked, tightening the seatbelt,
strapping the walker behind the saddle. Nodding, Luis settled in.
Giving the pony a final pat, the boy, fifty quetzals richer, headed to
the museum with the rattling, bucking chair.

Ochoa took the pony's lead and, with Poncho walking sedately
behind, started west toward the main plaza and Temple I and II.
Temple IV lay beyond, through the dark passage between the gray
bulk of Temple II and the 230-foot wall of the Terrace with the North
Acropolis behind it. Zoila and I trailed.

I'd forgotten the size of the structures and the vastness of Tikal.
Its central area is staggering—sprawling, incomprehensible, alien, the
scale of buildings daunting. The temple stairs were meant for
giants—the steps reach one's knees, their precipitous angle make

climbing difficult. What would it have been like to be a Mayan priest, or worse, a captive struggling from step to step in the jungle sun?

Tikal is ancient. By 600 BCE it had begun to rise from the jungle; by 200 CE it had grown to a city of twenty thousand; between 250 CE and 800 CE, it may have had as many as eighty-thousand inhabitants. It was a trading hub, a ritual and administrative center, a place of palaces and temples, and beyond the edge of the city, thatched houses and farm fields. It had been beautiful, too, bright with fresh plaster and paint on every surface, temple facades rich with multicolored reliefs of gods and animals. Pierced roof combs, many-hued tributes to gods or rulers, crowned the temples and towered over the plazas and ballcourts. Roads and causeways covered with lime plaster led into the jungle toward distant temples and far off communities. It had been intended to overwhelm when it was built. It still did, even as the jungle took it over and most of its buildings crumbled, disappearing under the encroaching vegetation.

"We'll pass Temple Three on the Tozzer Causeway," Ochoa said over his shoulder, pulling me out of my musings. "Next will be the Bat Palace, then Temple Four. Everything we want to explore is behind, or beyond Temple IV in the undergrowth."

Poncho snorted, swished his tail at bothersome flies.

"This isn't bad," Luis said, patting Poncho on the neck. "I always wanted to be a *charro* when I was a kid. My friends thought I was nuts. A Mayan *charro*."

Poncho snorted again.

"I'd love a picture of this," Zoila said. "Luis, Poncho, Miguel, the two of us sweating behind. Research at its most stimulating."

The Tozzer Causeway became Maudslay Causeway in front of Temple IV and headed northeast. We turned south, skirting the bulk of Temple IV to reach the tangle of plants and trees beyond.

"Temple Four is probably the largest aboriginal structure in the New World," Ochoa said. "Like the rest of Tikal, its two-hundred-twelve-foot height was meant to overpower, to make clear the importance of Yi'kin Chan K'awiil, the twenty-seventh king of Tikal who commissioned it."

"No doubt as to the status of this guy," Luis said as we rounded the pyramid's southeast corner.

"None," Ochoa said. "It's taller than any other structure, except maybe the Temple of the Sun in Teotihuacan. No way could anything else measure up."

The undergrowth behind the temple still showed the effects of the murder investigation. Even the postholes that marked the corners of the rack were there, though nothing of the structure remained. Ochoa described his discovery from his first bewildered encounter with the cloud of flies, the growing investigation that spread from Tikal personnel to the embassy, to the governmental agencies that followed; and the unaccounted-for time in Ruston's life between the airport and his death months later.

"Nothing more has come to light since then. Nothing. It's as if he'd been kidnapped by aliens," Ochoa said. We peered at the postholes in silence. What was there to say?

Ochoa led us further into the brush behind Temple IV, using his machete to widen the narrow trail for Poncho. "Next the steles," he said over his shoulder.

After an hour of shoving through tangled brush and vines and tripping over the broken stumps of small trees, a hundred yards ahead, barely visible in the dense undergrowth, two blue plastic tarps covered the steles and their surrounding areas. We had been stumbling over rubble ever since we left Temple IV, and I was eager to reach our goal. I was running with sweat, and my bug repellent was giving out. Insects formed a thick ball around my head, waiting for the last bit of spray to wash off with perspiration. To add to my misery, I'd fallen over a stump, and my shin was bleeding. I'd also begun to imagine a fer-de-lance under every stone.

When we finally pushed into the little clearing around the first stele, Ochoa pulled back the plastic covering. It was more astonishing than I'd imagined and smaller, too, the tiny blocky form surprising in the world of soaring temples, sprawling platforms, and imposing monuments. The second stele, a hundred yards on and similarly covered with plastic, was even more amazing. Even though the markers were earlier than anything else in Tikal, their imagery was recognizably Mayan. It was K'in A'jaw, according to Ruston's research: his soft, rounded form, familiar garments, and carefully detailed hands and feet made that clear.

The stele showed K'in A'jaw peering intently into a cloud of billowing incense rising from a low bowl at his feet. He appeared to be listening to a vulture, an ancestor perhaps, that loomed over him out of the smoke. Its large, round eyes peered at the mesmerized lord; its long-pointed beak reached its chest. The bird itself was simple, unmarked except for deep incisions marking the edges of its folded wings. I pulled my drawing of the pectoral out of my bag and carefully held it next to the carving on the stele.

"They're similar," I said, as the long face of the bird stared at K'in A'jaw across the surface of the stone. "What did the vulture mean besides water and transformation?"

"Bountiful crops, moisture, all the necessary outcomes for a lord who was supposed to provide agrarian success," Ochoa said, wiping his face with his handkerchief. "Water was always an issue in Tikal. It's sitting on a ridge of limestone. Water sinks right in. At the beginning, it had one or two small natural springs. There aren't any rivers or lakes, but the springs were enough for a small group of people. As the city grew, plastered plazas and buildings covered the recharge area, and the springs began to fail. Then the people collected runoff, built reservoirs, and later constructed an enormous dam.

"Water is still a problem in the Petén."

"Sky, rain, vulture, lord, crops," Luis said. "They're all tied together."

"But why a vulture?" I asked.

"Mayan farmers practiced slash and burn agriculture—they still burn fields to clear them," Luis said, patting Poncho's neck absentmindedly. "After the fire, vultures circle the fields to collect dead animals. It looks like they're guarding the crops and transforming the animals' deaths into agricultural offerings; and they were associated with the sun since they soar into the light and disappear.

"Think of how powerful they are: they transform death into sacrifice, oversee crops, consort with the sun; not only that, they're messengers. My grandfather used to say that if someone dreamed of vultures, the rainy season was coming. Since the lord was in charge of agriculture and rain, everything fits together—the bird, successful agriculture, the lord. It makes sense he would use a vulture as a personal symbol." Ochoa tucked the plastic around the steles.

"The return trip won't be as hard as it was getting here. We made a good trail coming in. Do you think you can hold together till lunch, then make it to the museum and library?"

"I can't wait to stop moving," Luis said. "I'm bug bit and hot and the saddle's starting to chafe."

Zoila and I nodded. I hoped Ochoa was right about the way back being easier. Getting to the stele had been a small-scale horror show. Ochoa turned Poncho in the direction we'd come. The little horse picked up his pace. I wasn't the only one eager to get the hell out of the jungle.

A trace of wood smoke from the southeast followed us through the undergrowth. None of us paid attention.

~ * ~

Just as the library closed at five o'clock, the boy led Poncho to the front porch. Using the top step as a mounting block, Zoila and I got Luis into the saddle without much trouble. We were getting the hang of lifting, and Luis had figured out what he could do to help.

"I'm beginning to enjoy Poncho," Luis said on the way back to the hotel "When we get back to Big Grove, I may take up riding.

We'll have to get an adaptive saddle, of course, and a horse. What do you think?"

Zoila snorted. "We can discuss mounts and gear later. Right now, I want a shower, clean clothes, and a glass of wine. How about meeting at six-thirty in the bar?"

"Good plan," I said as I headed for the stairs. I couldn't wait for a shower. I felt like I was wearing a rubber sheet.

Later, a plate of tapas in the center of the table, drinks in hand, we agreed the hike had been a tramp through hell, or Xibalba, as Luis calls it.

"It could have been worse, though. Think of Ochoa," I said. "He was the one widening the path. It had to be a nightmare swinging that machete all the way in."

By the time Luis had a second beer and Zoila and I were on our second glass of wine, we were ready to discuss what we had found in the library.

Zoila went first. "I spent the afternoon reading articles about Tikal and Takalik Abaj, the pre-Columbian city near the Pacific coast. It is interesting how much alike they were. They began about the same time, and both lasted over a thousand years; they were located on ridges in tropical forests with high rainfall, but water was an issue for various reasons; and each had steadily growing populations.

"Takalik Abaj had a lot going for it—rivers on either side of the ridge, lush tropical forest filled with resources, including the city's main export cacao—and it was on the commercial routes between Mexico and the Guatemalan Highlands."

Zoila thoughtfully tapped the side of her wine glass for a moment. "Their main problem was erosion. The city sits on granite. Water couldn't sink in. When it rained, it eroded the temples, ballcourts, plazas, everything. So, they built a drainage system— stone canals to move the water away from building and subterranean channels to carry water to residential areas. They even built a sauna.

"Tikal had its own problems. It was perched on a ridge as well, but it was surrounded by lowland, swampy jungle with no consistently available surface water. They had plenty of rain, but the limestone soaked it up like a sponge. As Ochoa told us, there'd been a couple of springs on the site in the early days, but once the city grew, the springs practically dried up." She nibbled a tapa. "The city was desperate for water—for drinking, households, crops, everything. The only available water was runoff from the plazas and other plastered surfaces, so they built catchment basins, reservoirs, channels, filtering systems, even a coffer dam." Zoila paused again, taking a sip of wine before continuing.

"Hydraulic engineering made life possible in the Petén for a city as big as Tikal with its growing population. It made it feasible for it to develop into a major trade center on the east-west trade route that went all the way to Teotihuacan in Mexico."

"What you found makes me wonder," I said, putting down my glass. "Even though the cities were in distant parts of Guatemala, they existed at the same time, and their problems were is some ways similar—growing populations, water issues, the need to develop hydraulic systems."

"Well?" Luis asked, biting into a tiny bean-laden tortilla.

Not one to believe in mere coincidence, I continued with my list of considerations. "I mean, could there have been contact between them as early as seven hundred BCE? They both grew to be influential cities at their height, both had hydraulic issues, both used vulture imagery, and the clincher is the vulture pectoral on Ruston's desk is similar to K'in A'jaw's pectoral, and a Vulture Lord appears in the incense smoke on those new stele, too. There has to be a connection."

Luis was quiet for a minute. "I've wondered about the possibility of a link myself. There is something else that suggests connections between them. About the time of the Grandfather Vulture in Takalik Abaj, there seems to have been a shift from Olmec to Mayan style in that city—in sculpture, ceramics, imagery—as if Mayan influence had begun to affect artists. It's as if when the Vulture King came to power, things began to change. It wasn't the result of an alien population taking over. There's no sign of that. It was subtler...Olmec and Mayan characteristics began to appear side by side at the same time, as if the two different groups of people were working in close proximity to one another."

"So, this is what I think we've got," I said, "Tell me if I'm wrong. Vultures in both places, concerns about water, and Takalik Abaj, a crossroads in a trade network that ran all the way from Mexico, through the Highlands, then to the Petén. So, let's say a Mayan group goes from Tikal to Takalik Abaj for some reason—trade arrangements, political matters, curiosity.

"A prince, let's say K'in A'jaw, the guy on the steles, goes along as an envoy. That would be natural, a young lord taking part in Tikal's business, learning the ropes of negotiation, of lordship, that would explain the image on the stele. He meets the K'utz Chman, Grandfather Vulture. They exchange gifts. K'in A'jaw is feted, toured through Takalik Abaj territory, and impressed by what he sees—the developing municipal water channels, the sauna, the astronomically oriented temples, the Olmec sculpture, and most of all, the lord's oldest daughter. He stays for months." I looked at Luis. He nodded in encouragement, and motioned for me to continue with his good hand.

"He and the lord talk about trade, exchanges of craftsmen and ambassadors, and finally, after a night of feasting, a wedding. Relatives and dignitaries from Tikal are summoned. A couple months later they appear. It's a long trip on foot—mile after mile of mountains, arroyos, jungles, highland plateaus—and they had to carry supplies, bundles of gifts, their own finery. They'd stop to put on their best clothes before they reached the city. They're tired, but they want to impress. After all, they've come to meet K'utz Chman, to visit his kingdom, to see his daughter, and, if all goes well, to arrange the marriage."

The waiter brought another plate of tapas.

"Weeks later, after complex negotiations and countless fiestas, K'in A'jaw starts home with his new wife. Everyone is laden with presents from K'utz Chman—cacao, feathers, brocade garments, jade and shell jewelry—and a jade vulture pendant, a token of the new alliance, hangs from K'in A'jaw's neck."

My story was complicated, but it was as reasonable as anything else. What else would include all the variables? Besides, I love to make things up.

Zoila nodded. "It makes sense. It even might explain the similar channels in both communities."

"And the ancestor on the stele," said Luis. "And the pendant."

But it sure as hell didn't explain Ruston. How did he become discoverer and then victim? There was Polop, too. We were overlooking something.

After dinner that night, lying under the slowly revolving fan and awash in the metallic drone of insects and the roar of howlers, it was hard to sleep. I missed Rosie, missed my own bed, missed the prairie wind rocking the world.

Fourteen

Flores, Guatemala, Late November, the Following Day

The next morning, before the mist had completely cleared, Luis and Zoila headed to the museum and its priceless artifacts and archives with Poncho and Ochoa. I climbed into the hotel van with a young English couple on their way to explore the caves near Santa Elena. I was going to Flores to meet Ochoa's wife, Esperanza, in her gallery. Not only was I looking forward to getting to know her, I was eager to see her weaving collection, and I was hoping to poke around in Flores for signs of Ruston. Maybe with my fresh perspective, I'd notice something the police had missed.

Flores, the capitol of the Petén, is the island heart of the lowlands. It, like the Petén, is its own world, a tiny island floating at the end of a causeway, a mirage in the middle of Lake Itza drifting in the morning light. The Petén is island-like, too—disconnected from the rest of the world by a vast jungle. There are some vehicles on the single highway coming in from the Highlands, of course, and planes land in Santa Elena and a handful of smaller airports, but there is not much else.

I'd wondered why anyone didn't notice a *gringo* like Ruston in such an isolated setting. Where was he for those months between his disappearance and death, if not nearby? Others had to be with him, too. Someone took care of him during that time, and he sure as hell didn't sacrifice himself. So, where was he, and why had he been snatched? What did he have that someone wanted? And how about Polop? Surely his disappearance was related to Ruston's. The two men had to have something else in common besides academia.

The van let us out at the roadway that connected the mainland to Flores. With its close-packed, red-roofed buildings and waterfront shacks, small boats, and countless sagging docks, Flores seemed suspended in the middle of the lake—untethered, surreal. The young couple headed south to the caves. I turned onto the narrow land bridge into town.

The warm breeze from the southwest, smelling of water and wood smoke, ruffled my hair and tugged at my pants as I walked along the uneven surface. The land stopped a few inches on either side of the road, leaving it adrift on the lake. The view from the causeway was magical. In the distance, a slight chop rocked the handful of boats, low black shapes against water silvered by the morning light. Near the jetties protruding from the island, cormorants fished from pilings or rocks, or dried their wings, turning slowly with stately steps, huge black birds dancing in the sun.

At the end of the causeway, I hurried across the narrow strip of beach surrounding the island and darted across the ring road, through the cars, vans, and shiny rental motorbikes that circled the island, belching smoke.

Beyond the road, Flores' streets are few—narrow cobblestone lanes that contain the island like a net. Five minutes from the causeway, I reached the plaza with its church and tiny park. Families in their Sunday best strolled around the square, greeting one another with polite nods; children chased up and down the church steps, and clots of tourists sipped coffee in the tiny cafés. The restaurants and shops selling boat tours, souvenirs, and guided trips to Tikal were busy.

According to the map Ochoa had given me, Esperanza's gallery lay just beyond the plaza on La Avenida Libertad in a neighborhood of businesses devoted to Mayan arts and crafts. Her shop was easy to find once I hit La Avenida: *Hilos de Tempo, Arte del Maya* was painted in large gold and black letters on the front window, making it hard to miss despite the milling tourists window-shopping the length of the street.

Four *huipiles*—San Martín Sacatepéquez, Patzún, San Juan Comalapa, Sololá—pinned to gray felt display boards, brightened the window with multiple colors and complex patterns. Inside, a woman folded garments, placing them on the shelves behind her. A younger woman swept near the back of the store.

A bell tinkled as I pushed open the door. "Esperanza?" I asked. The woman sorting garments looked up with a smile...her long black braid, laced with red cotton ribbon, was coiled around her head like a crown.

"Ann? Welcome! Miguel has told me about you, as well as Señor Ruston," Esperanza said, stepping from behind the counter. "He said you were interested in weaving, too. If you would like, I thought we could look at some *huipiles* and then have coffee on the square. After that we could ask around about poor Señor Ruston if you are still interested. Juana can watch the store while we're gone."

"Sounds perfect to me," I said. "If the *huipiles* you have in the window are an indication, your collection is amazing."

~ * ~

Four hours later, after examining countless *huipiles*, drinking coffee, and making visits to the hotels and bars that catered to tourists, we decided to tackle the docks. "Maybe someone there can tell us something," Esperanza said.

"I've been wondering," I said as we started toward the water, "What does NM stand for? I saw it painted on several walls on the way to your gallery. It was even on the steps of the cathedral. I've spotted a couple of stepped pyramid outlines, too. They're all done in red paint. What's that all about?"

I nearly tripped over a broken cobblestone, but Esperanza gracefully hopped over it onto a strip of sidewalk. "I don't know. I imagine it has something to do with the young men I see lounging in the plaza with ponytails in front of their eyes and earplugs. I've asked Miguel, but he doesn't know. He's seen the graffiti and the kids as well. As far as he's heard, the boys don't do anything. Just look like pre-Columbian toughs."

The waterfront, a jumble of coiled ropes, beached canoes, boat motors in need of repair, nets, and traps, smelled of fish, fuel, mud, and weeds. Half a dozen men were hard at work overhauling engines or scraping boats. A man, younger than the rest, seated on a white plastic five-gallon bucket, mended a net. The nearby boathouse had been tagged with the familiar initials and a tiny outline of a pyramid.

Out on the lake, ferries from smaller communities plied their daily routes, and boats loaded with tourists hoping for fresh coconuts, zoo visits, or picnics headed for lakeshore landings on one of the tiny islands that dotted the lake. Small fishing canoes with single occupants and boats with two or three men and large nets searched the water for fish.

"*Buenos días*," Esperanza began. The men looked up briefly. A couple of the younger ones had earplugs and ponytails over their eyes; the others were ordinary boatmen, their short black hair spikey with sweat. Esperanza introduced us. Conversation wasn't their strong suit and unknown women—one a *gringa* at that—made them nervous. The conversation lurched along: Did they know anything about Ruston? Had they met a man named Polop? They knew nothing.

No surprise. This was getting us nowhere. It was like dragging a dead horse. Would they let Esperanza know if they heard something about the two men, she asked as we turned to leave. They nodded.

"Back to the gallery?" I asked Esperanza. The guy who had spent the entire time sewing on a dip net looked up for a moment, his ponytail nearly covering his eyes. Since I had his attention, I plunged in. Why not? Nothing ventured, nothing gained.

"I'm curious. What does NM mean?" I asked him. "Is it a social group? A team? I've seen the initials and the pyramid drawing in several places." I tried to look harmless, just an old, retired *gringa* professor asking stupid questions.

"Maya Nuevo," he said, returning to his net. No hope of further eye contact there, either. His hair screened his face, but I'd glimpsed a jade inlay in a front tooth, another ancient touch.

"Maya Nuevo? Who are they? What do they do? Is it a club?" I asked.

"*Yo no sé,*" he replied, continuing to mend.

That didn't help. There is no good way to respond to flat denial without sounding aggressive.

"Maybe it's the new soccer team in Santa Elena," Esperanza said, breaking into the awkward silence that followed. "They just started playing this year,"

I knew that wasn't the case, but the guy wasn't going to say anything else, at least not in front of me. How could he not know the name of a local soccer team, or who or why someone else might be tagging all over Flores? He probably lived here his entire life, and his hairstyle and decorations suggested he wasn't out of the fashion loop either: he at least followed young men's local styles.

On the way back to Esperanza's shop, we talked about weaving, a more satisfying topic than tagging, Ruston, or the missing Polop, given how little we knew. "I've always thought of weaving as threads of time," Esperanza said. "I imagine weaving has held our world together since the very beginning. Ixchel the moon goddess weaves; the universe is measured by lengths of thread; ancient Maya portrayed fabric patterns in their art because they were significant."

Juana was behind the counter when we opened the door to the gallery. "Lots of shoppers today. I sold four *huipiles* to a woman from California, a belt from Santa María de Jesús to an American couple, and two shawls to a man from England," she said, returning piles of garments to the shelves behind her.

"Coffee?" Esperanza asked. "My poor feet. What a day."

We settled at the table at the rear of the gallery as Juana pushed through the curtains into the tiny storage area. She appeared a few minutes later with two mugs and a plate of cookies, placing them in front of us.

"Snacks should help," I said, adding sugar to my steaming coffee. "I feel like I've aged ten years." I bit into a cookie. "All that walking and nothing to show for it."

Then, motivated by the closeness created by our day together, I told Esperanza the whole story—Luis, the lightning, Ruston, the jade vulture, Polop. I even threw in K'in A'jaw and our developing reconstruction of his life. Why not? She was part of the story now, too. There is nothing like misery to form bonds.

~ * ~

An hour later, after promising to keep in touch, I was on the van headed for the hotel. How the hell had I gotten into this Ruston/Polop business anyway? There were the concerns of Luis and Zoila, of course. Their worries were the immediate reasons, and then my archiving business had gotten me involved with Ruston, but what had motivated me to keep going? Nosiness? A maddening desire to know the answers? Probably a mixture of both. Inquisitiveness isn't always a good thing; I'd learned that earlier. Poking around is not always useful. Not at all.

The van swerved around a pothole, another, larger hole loomed ahead with a branch sticking out to mark its location. The only other passengers, a retired couple from Cincinnati we picked up as we passed the airport, gasped and grabbed one another's hands as the van veered across the road then back into our lane. I smiled at them reassuringly. We swerved again.

Before we reached the inn, something small and dark darted across the road, disappearing into the jungle without parting the undergrowth. The couple from Cincinnati didn't see it.

Tikal National Park, Guatemala

That night at dinner we shared information, or rather Zoila and Luis did, since all I could report was a guy with an inlayed tooth and a bad attitude and the presence of tags and pyramids in red spray paint on buildings in Flores.

Zoila was looking pleased. The water thing, the connection between communities, must have panned out. It turned out that wasn't all.

"The type of hydro construction on Tikal began to change around five-ten BCE. They built channels and reservoirs for the runoff from buildings and plazas. Then the population began to grow as available water increased." Zoila paused and sipped her water. "Maybe a link was formed with Takalik Abaj as well, maybe with the princess we imagined, maybe someone else. Then something happened a few years later to upset everything. For one thing, there was one of those periodic Petén droughts, perhaps made worse by increased forest clearance to enlarge the cornfields. It became drier in Tikal, not catastrophic, but life was more difficult."

"Anything else?" Luis asked.

"The article I found said there was social unrest, too. I don't know what that means." Zoila shook her head. "Maybe people became edgy. Maybe the streets felt unsafe. Maybe neighbors began to eye one another as if they had angered the gods. Maybe rumors of evil spirits and spies were whispered in the market."

I waited impatiently as Zoila sliced her steak, took a bite, chewed, and swallowed.

Finally, she continued. "The royals made every effort to bring back the rains. The prince with the rest of the royal family let blood in elaborate rituals, prayed, burned copal, let more blood; they oversaw the sacrifice of captured warriors, but nothing seemed to work."

Zoila paused to consider, began again. "I'm guessing at this part, but maybe the traditional elite of Tikal, the scribes, the military officers, the advisors who had always had been uncomfortable with a princess from the coast and wary of her children, who would certainly usurp the places of their own families, began to agitate."

"You always have to watch the scribes." Luis smiled at his own joke.

"Not only was the princess from another world," she said, momentarily slowed by Luis's joke, "she was distinctive in a lot of ways. Everyone could see that. Usually a foreign princess came from a city in the Petén, someplace in the world of dense jungle, jaguars, ritual warfare, and bright macaws. Such a woman's language would be similar to theirs; her clothes would look like the garments of the women of Tikal, too, but not this one.

"Maybe the rumor started that her family was the source of trouble with Tikal's water supply, the failure of the rains. Maybe Chaac, the lord of rain and storms, felt Tikal deserved to suffer because of an alien princess and her upstart children in their midst. Who or what else was there to blame?" Zoila asked.

"Advisors from Takalik Abaj had helped build the original channels at Tikal," she added, "but maybe it had been a trick, for now the city needed more water than before, had more people than it could care for."

"I can imagine it," I said. "More people, less water, tension, spreading unease."

"There was something else that worried them, too: trade, the fear of losing Tikal's place in the commercial network that tied them to the huge city of Teotihuacan further north if their power waned.

Trade was more important than anything to the lives of the elite, even more critical to Tikal than the princess and her children."

Zoila stopped. "It sounds plausible, doesn't it? It is always the stranger's fault," she added as she scooped up frijoles. The toucan, seated as usual in the middle of our table, nodded his head as if in agreement.

"I don't have as much as Zoila, but it's interesting," Luis said after sipping his beer. "I read everything I could dig up on Ruston's stele, but now there is a second one, maybe something more will come to light. The thing that strikes me, though is the apparent connection with the ruler of Takalik Abaj. An ancestor, maybe K'utz Chman himself or someone similar, is leaning out of the cloud of smoke rising from the sacrificial bowl on the second stele, bending over K'in A'jaw while the prince looks up, entranced."

The toucan, moving slowly, carefully snagged a piece of lettuce from Luis's plate.

"If we draw a line between the two steles, we get the suggestion of an enclosure in the surrounding rubble, as if the stele were markers of a precinct that existed before Tikal began to expand, before the jungle was cut down." Luis traced a curved shape with the handle of his fork on the tablecloth to illustrate his point. "Maybe the prince and princess settled there, at least for a while. They would be safe. The terrain was rough in that part of the jungle. It would have been nothing but swamps, limestone ridges, impenetrable vegetation, poisonous snakes, jaguars, and who knows what else? It would be nearly impossible for Tikal to attack. Don't forget, Tikal was still small then, too."

Our waiter appeared. I ordered another glass of wine. "Sounds reasonable. At least as sensible as anything else. After being in Flores, seeing that tagging and those retro Mayan guys, I've been thinking about Ruston, how he fits into the Tikal picture, how we got from an unknown stele, to cultural rebirth, to human sacrifice."

The waiter returned with my wine along with a plate of fruit. "What if the Nuevo, eager to reestablish their ancient dominance, kidnapped him?" I asked, helping myself to slice of pineapple. "He was world famous, after all. They might have heard about him and that he had information about the ancient Maya. On top of it, he'd found that stele and the vulture pectoral. Maybe they didn't know about the pectoral, but we can't be certain. It's reasonable to think they wanted to learn what he knew about their early ancestors, then get rid of him. He was a *gringo*; maybe he shouldn't have any important Mayan knowledge at all."

The idea of the vulture pectoral hidden in my spice cabinet gave me the creeps. *What if the Nuevo or some other group interested in control of the Petén found out? I could end up like Ruston.* I shoved the thought from my mind and plunged on.

"So, first, kidnap the guy at the airport. Take him to a tiny *aldea* on the far shore of the lake. Find out what he knows; maybe have him translate any material in their possession. Then a few weeks later, ferry him to the shore of Tikal, load him on a donkey, take him to a spot behind Temple Four, and kill him. The sacrifice of an important man would be a perfect statement of their power and presence, as well as a gift to the ancestors. And he'd be off their hands."

Luis and Zoila nodded in agreement.

"Makes sense," Luis said. "It's a plausible explanation of Ruston's disappearance. It didn't have to be weird or mysterious at all. Just the same old Mesoamerican power, sacrifice, terror thing."

Just as we gathered ourselves to leave the dining room, the toucan politely removed a final piece of banana from the edge of Zoila's plate and tossed it down.

That night the wind came up, flapping the curtains and rattling the thatch on the cabanas around the pool. The howlers redoubled their efforts. Perhaps they were agitated by the wind. Maybe they needed to make themselves heard over the blowing trees.

~ * ~

On our final day in Tikal, after our farewell tour of the site, we sat on the porch with our drinks as we had the first evening, watching the jungle darken and the mist rise between the trees across the small lawn, listening to the high-pitched songs of insects and the hoots of other jungle dwellers. I stirred in my chair, still musing about what I had seen on Flores. Who were those young men? What did they know about their ancestors and the thousands of years of Mayan history? What did they have to do, if anything, with the people who lived here in the distant past?

"I've been thinking about the Nuevo, their hair, piercings, teeth, and something we talked about yesterday. Might there still be descendants of the prince and his followers living in the Petén, maybe mixed in with everyone else, but still remembering some of the old stories?" I asked Luis.

He thought for a moment. "Maybe." He pulled himself up a little straighter in his chair with his good arm. "That period saw a lot of cultural change: from Olmec to Maya on the coast, trade across all of Mesoamerica, populations intermarrying, language changes in Tikal, populations coalescing into cities with heterogeneous population, and entire groups of people shifting from one place to another. The disappearance of a small group early in Tikal's history would hardly be unusual. Their reappearance years later, perhaps elsewhere in the Petén, wouldn't be strange either. That's the way it worked."

I nodded, visualizing the little group that left Tikal.

"It could have looked like this," I said, plunging into a story. "Once the prince and his family decided returning to the coast didn't make sense—they had kids to worry about—they began to build a community deep in the jungle: a small palace, plaza, and temple, houses for their retinue. They cleared land for crops as soon as possible and marked boundaries with little stele to separate their world from the untamed wilderness."

"The group would include everyone necessary to begin a new community, too, everyone a village would need to start from scratch," Zoila interjected.

"Yes, Tikal didn't cover much territory then, and its population wasn't very big, so the group didn't have to go far in that rough environment to get away from the growing city and its soldiers. No way was anyone going to march through snake-infested swamps to attack them. They might as well have been on another planet, as far as Tikal was concerned." It sounded plausible, at least to me.

"Their group could have been safe from the Spaniards years later, too," Zoila said, taking up my tale. "The Spaniards probably weren't any more eager to push through the swampy terrain than the folks in Tikal had been.

"Maybe they're still here. Maybe those kids in Flores are part of that group. Maybe Ruston blundered into them. The Nuevo may be an offshoot of the original population. Or maybe they're just wannabes."

We went to bed early that night. The next day was going to be busy—fly to Guatemala City where Luis's and Zoila's relatives would pick them up and take them home to Xela; I'd go into the city, spend a couple of days visiting museums, and then head to Antigua to see friends. Two weeks later, we would meet in the airport to begin our journey home.

The drive and flight the next morning were easy: the road had been graded, the plane was on time, takeoff and landing were smooth, and the plane was nearly empty.

We spotted Luis's two brothers and their wives waiting in the arrival hall as soon as we got our luggage. After greetings and a flurry of activity, the men took the bags, the walker, the handles of Luis's wheelchair, and swept Zoila and Luis away toward the exit, everyone talking at once.

I made a beeline for the taxi rank—first the hotel, then the Ixchel Museum. Maybe their exhibits of ancient regalia and clothing would be the keys to the meaning of the steles. After all, what else was there to see in those steles' images besides ancient garments and stylistic conventions?

Guatemala City, Guatemala

The Museo Ixchel del Traje Indígena on the campus of Francisco Marroquin University explores the Mayan traditions of dress throughout Guatemala; its collections of textiles and jewelry are known throughout the world. I'd spent hours poking through their collection when I was in grad school and could locate various materials in my sleep. I headed toward the rear of the lower level and the section on early dress that included a display of pre-Columbian coastal cultures' garments.

Clearly the small exhibit had been redone into a diorama since I'd last visited. It portrayed the central market plaza in Takalik Abaj, according to the description on the nearby wall. The mannequins were dressed like characters in what must have been a daily scene in the busy Olmec-Mayan city that dominated coastal trade for more than a thousand years. The freshly painted background mural made the scene come alive—men trading bright feathers of jungle birds, elaborate pottery from far north, and pieces of jade for salt, and cacao. A young lord, looking a lot like the guy on the five-gallon bucket in Flores, was seated cross-legged in front of temple, watching the scene, wearing a jade vulture pectoral much like Ruston's on his necklace. That retro guy. A jade vulture. I took a photo then headed for the director's office.

Isabella Gutiérrez, director of the Ixchel, her black hair in an untidy bun, was seated on the floor of her office sorting through a pile of files when I knocked on the half-open door. She clearly hadn't heard me coming because she let out a tiny squeak before floundering to her feet.

"I'm sorry I startled you," I began. "I won't take much of your time. I'm Ann Cunningham, retired professor of art and culture from Big Grove in the States. I visited your museum years ago. I can't believe all the changes. Your new diorama of the market in Takalik Abaj is wonderful. What a great setting for those garments!

"The mural is spectacular as well. Could you tell me something about it? Who painted it? Is the artist from around here?"

"Come in," she said, pushing the door wide. "Have a seat. I'm glad for a break. I've been sorting these files since I got in this morning; I'm trying to get organized, make more room for the paper that accumulates despite computers. Paperless society, ha! I'm Isabella Gutiérrez, but I imagine you figured that out." She offered her hand and we shook briefly before we both sat.

"The artist owns a studio in Antigua. She does most of the museum work in Guatemala and much of Central America. Her name's Ruth Wiseman. Her parents immigrated here during the Second World War. I have her card somewhere," she said, digging in a box on the top of her desk. "Here's her address and phone number, if you'd like to know more. Tell her I told you to give her a call."

"I'm going to Antigua in a day or two: I'll get in touch with her then, but maybe you could tell me a bit about the coastal mural itself. Did you have input, or did Ruth choose the content?"

"A little of both. We discussed what I was thinking. She did a couple of preliminary sketches. I took a look, made some suggestions. She did a final drawing. I approved it."

"I'm interested in preclassic garments and the work of an epigrapher named Ruston," I said. "How about details like the lord's pectoral? Did you suggest it or did she just include it? And how about the lord himself? Do you know who the model was?"

"I know before she started work she looked through our collection of jades and coastal garments. We don't have a vulture, by the way. She did some research at the National Museum of Archaeology and Ethnography, too. I don't think they have a vulture there, either, but you might check, or you could just ask Ruth. As far as the lord is concerned, she said he was a friend, a guy she's known a long time who was willing to pose."

Conversation drifted off to other topics: the Ixchel's recent acquisitions, Ruston's demise, and the recent disappearance of yet another scholar, Polop. It was after four o'clock when I left, too late to go anywhere but back to the hotel. The Archaeology Museum could wait till tomorrow.

~ * ~

I got to the Archaeology Museum as soon as it opened the next morning. At that hour, I had the place to myself, which made my life easier. I could take photos without having to dodge tourists and school kids on a field trip. Everything that looked like a vulture—carved in limestone, painted on ceramics, hinted at in jade, painted in murals—I documented in excruciating detail, with my camera as well as in my notes. I didn't have much luck finding a jade vulture pendant until just after noon.

In a dark corner of an exhibition hall, in a poorly lighted glass case full of early classic polychrome ceramics, a cylinder-shaped vessel caught my eye. Around the center portion, under a border of glyphs, a lord leaned forward to accept a bowl of chocolate from a high-ranking woman with a jade necklace.

The only thing strange about the otherwise ordinary court scene—with a seated lord, petitioners bearing gifts, and a servant standing behind the lord with a fan—was the lord wasn't human: he was a vulture. What the hell? Hundreds of years after the date on Ruston's stele, a Vulture Lord crops up again, and this one is wearing a vulture pectoral, too.

I nearly dropped my camera in my excitement. Once I calmed down and recorded every scrap of information I could find on the label and in the guidebook, I took photos from multiple angles. I could chase this thing down when I had more time.

If I'd missed anything here, it wasn't because I hadn't been looking, I thought, as I headed for the exit.

~ * ~

I didn't spot the car following my taxi in the dense city traffic on the way to my hotel later that afternoon. I didn't see it pass my cab and turn down a dusty side street of workshops, garages, and small businesses a block beyond my hotel, either, but it must have been there. How else could anyone explain what happened next?

Two men dressed in jeans and black T-shirts, wearing sunglasses blank as welder's goggles, rounded the corner of my hotel, just as I started toward the front entrance.

"*Uno momento, señora*," the tallest man said as he crossed the short distance between us.

I turned, startled. Something wasn't right. I grabbed my purse strap with one hand and balled my other into a fist. Men don't stop women in the streets in Guatemala. Young men don't accost older women, especially. And why were they dressed like killers in a cheap thriller? And why their urgency? If it was a joke, it wasn't funny.

I turned to face them just in time to be hit square on the cheekbone by the shorter man and to be engulfed in the choking grasp of the taller one as he grabbed my neck and tried to wrench my bag from my shoulder. My purse, one of those steel-reinforced, impossible-to-read-credit-cards-through, don't-screw-with-me travel bags, wasn't going anywhere. Its heavy strap crossed my body from shoulder to hip. The steel-reinforced band sawed on my shoulder like a cheese slicer. They'd have to kill me to get it off; it was a bad thought to have as I was being assaulted.

"Where is it, bitch?" the tall man snarled, tearing my blouse open with a single jerk.

"*Fuego! Fuego!* Fire, fire!" I yelled as I kicked the short guy in the shins as hard as I could—according to my periodic training with Bill, calling "help" makes people nervous and they run; yelling "fire" draws them in. I felt a bone crack in my hand with a tiny jolt as I slammed my fist into the tall man's nose. I didn't care. His nose wasn't in good shape, either. I screamed and punched and kicked for all I was worth as my defense lessons—bless Bill's Navy SEAL's aggressive little heart—swung into gear. Those afternoons Pat and I spent with him behind Burr Oaks were paying off.

I rammed my knee into what I hoped was a crotch just as the doorman–hotel guard jumped into the fray. There wasn't much else he could do but join in, since the three of us were rolling on the cement like brawling dogs, and he couldn't use his gun without running the risk of shooting me.

Once the fight included the guard, though, the men, seeing their plan had gone awry and they were losing ground, broke away and ran like hell. The guard, stopping long enough to make certain I was okay, ran after them, unsnapping his holster, pulling his gun, and firing in one smooth practiced motion, but by then the thugs had rounded the corner.

The rest of the action was a blur. The guard hauled me into the hotel and seated me in the nearest chair. He called the police. The manager called an ambulance. A hostess from the restaurant brought ice wrapped in a towel for my hand and a sweater to cover my ruined blouse. Finally I fainted, carried away by the receding wave of adrenaline.

Fifteen

Tikal National Park, Guatemala

Ríos had been discussing the month's duty roster with Ochoa in the rangers' headquarters early the following morning when the phone rang. "What? What? She what? No!"

He put his hand over the phone as he turned to Ochoa seated across from him. "It's the American Embassy. A pair of thugs attacked Ann Cunningham when she got out of her cab in front of her hotel late yesterday afternoon. She was coming back from the Archaeology Museum."

"No! Now what?" Ochoa asked. "Ann assaulted in broad daylight in front of her hotel. Is she okay? What the hell is going on? What can we do?"

"She's banged up, but fine except for a broken bone in her hand. They kept her in the hospital for observation, but she'll probably be released this afternoon. The embassy can't reach the Velascos—the phone reception is terrible in that part of the Highlands. They've contacted two of her friends in the States, but it is going to be a couple of days before they get here." Ríos listened to the person on the other end of the phone for another minute before ending the call.

He turned back to Ochoa. "Embassy folks want us to stay with her till the friends arrive, since Ann knows you. We need to keep an eye on her safety, too, since they're shorthanded. No one knows what happened, maybe just a random mugging, maybe something else, given what has been happening to people who have anything to do with Ruston and his stele. *Jesús!*"

Ochoa thought for a moment. "Listen. I have an idea. Why don't Esperanza and I go? Esperanza can stay with Ann. I can keep my eye on them both and poke around till her friends show up."

Ochoa was already making a list of things to take. One thing for certain, since this was an official assignment, he'd wear his uniform and take his weapon. He wasn't going to be much of an official presence if he didn't look like one. He'd need extra magazines, Mace, his bulletproof vest. This sure as hell wasn't going to be like delivering a lecture on the fine points of early Tikal architecture. Who knew what kind of weirdness was going on?

~ * ~

By the time Bill and Pat showed up two days later, Ochoa hadn't learned much more. He'd checked the police reports—nothing. After all this was, by police standards, a nonevent, especially in Guatemala. Besides the hotel doorman, there was only one other witness, the elderly woman who sold *atole* on the corner at a small temporary stand—one crate with her supplies and a stool for her customers.

"Two men jumped out of a car at the corner as soon as that woman left the taxi, the *atole* woman said," Ochoa told Bill later as they drank beer in the hotel bar. "They ran at Ann. One grabbed her purse. The other hit her in the face and ripped her blouse. She screamed. She wouldn't let go of her purse. They dragged her down the walk by the strap, but she fought like a jaguar, according to the woman. When the hotel guard came out, the men ran. One was bent over limping; the other was holding his hand over his bleeding nose. The *atole* woman enjoyed the hell out of the spectacle.

"I figure it was the two men, plus a driver. A well-planned attack. And they didn't get what they wanted. Who knows what they thought was in Ann's bag, unless they wanted her research notes and camera. And what did they think was around her neck so they needed to rip her blouse open? I don't have anything to go on. Zilch. At least Ann and Esperanza enjoyed their visit. Oh, Ann told me she recognized the model for a lord in a mural she saw in the Ixchel. That's something."

Sixteen

Big Grove, December

It was the first day of December, another cold night in a string of steel-cold midwestern evenings, the kind that made people close the curtains and put on their warmest sweater and slippers. It was made more miserable in the Bloomingdale Road neighborhood with dirt from the nearby parking lots blowing across the road in eddies and peppering exposed skin like buckshot. A white panel truck with Texas plates pulled off I-74 and stopped in front of the self-storage business that marked the edge of Saint Patrick's immediate neighborhood. The driver punched in the business's entry code and turned the truck toward the units at the opposite corner of the facility, stopping in front of the last space.

The driver of the truck, a large man in a black cowboy hat and fleece-lined jacket, opened its door, leaving the engine running. He muttered as he slid from his warm cab into the cold. His helper, bundled in Carhartt coveralls against the weather, had been faster getting out. He already had unlocked the chunky padlock and shoved the garage door up when the driver reached him. The driver aimed his flashlight into the dim interior. Good. Just what he hoped to see—nothing. So far everything was going to plan. The driver returned to the truck, turned it around, and backed as far as he could into the opening. This time he cut the engine.

It took three quarters of an hour to unload the truck and stack the contents in the storage space. After they stepped out of the building, the driver swept the beam of his flashlight across the darkened storage area a final time. The plastic-wrapped packages filling the back half of the unit glistened like wet bricks in the shaft of light. At a nod from the driver, the smaller man pulled the door down and snapped the lock back in place.

Delivery complete, the men hurried back to the truck. The driver fired up the engine and turned across the gravel mews toward the entrance of the storage facility; he stopped the truck at the checkout station so he could reach the keypad.

The truck headed for the on-ramp and disappeared into the steady flow of red taillights, two tiny spots of light, red blood cells in the capillary of I-74 heading west.

The rest of the truck's trip was the reverse of its journey to Big Grove, except for the conclusion—Effingham, St. Louis, Kansas City, Wichita. Disappear.

~ * ~

As the men in the truck headed west on I-74, Father Diego parked his car in his garage and let himself in the side door of the rectory, glad to be home and out of the wind. Off the road. Rid of his most recent passenger. The back entry, lined with hooks filled with outerwear for all seasons, smelled of damp wool and wet foot wear. He slipped out of his topcoat and changed his shoes for carpet slippers. What he wanted next was time to sit in his library, have a glass of port, take time to consider his situation.

The library was at the back of the house, overlooking the church and playing field. Beyond lay the industrial buildings on the far side of Bloomingdale Road, the interstate perched on a low berm. When the wind blew from the north, the traffic sounded as if it were under the library window, but when the windows were closed, one could usually ignore the hum. Tonight was a north wind night, a night of high tire whine and rumbling Jake brakes belching and growling, as truckers slowed to turn onto an off-ramp. The sound was impossible to ignore.

The priest poured himself a drink at the small bar built into the bookshelves. As the wind rattled a loose shutter on one of the library windows, he settled into a leather chair next to the reading lamp, glass in hand, and closed his eyes. The parish Thanksgiving the previous week had been a success. The activity hall had been packed with diners, the food had been wonderful, and the decorations had added a festive air.

December, with all its holiday preparations, had begun. It made his head ache to think of it. More meetings and planning. More cooking and dinners. More decorations and entertainment. At least this year they could do whatever they wanted in their newly refurbished kitchen. One more job for Eduardo and the money for repairs and extras would be secure, and he would be free of the nerve-wracking business of being at Eduardo's beck and call.

He sipped his port, trying to remember how had he gotten into this mess. As far as he could recall, it had begun last year on All Souls Day when Eduardo Guzmán, owner of Cinco Gallos, came to church for the first time and left a healthy contribution in the offering plate. Why all that money for the repose of the dead in a parish Eduardo had never visited? There were other sizable contributions to the church, too, but that was reasonable, considering Eduardo had no other parish. Eduardo didn't reappear again till Christmas Eve. He showed up at Lent—Ash Wednesday when he received ashes like everyone else and Good Friday—then Easter. Before the annual Easter brunch in the community hall, Eduardo invited Father Diego to join him after church the following Sunday for dinner at Cinco Gallos. Maybe he should have begun to wonder then, but he didn't. The meal was wonderful: a feast of fruit, grilled beef, fresh tortillas, carefully cooked beans, flan. The waiters were attentive, seeing to his every need, pouring wine before his glass was empty. That was the tip of the hook, the beginning.

He was flattered by Eduardo's attention, delighted with the rich meals and money, happy to have the gifts that were delivered to the rectory on special occasions by one of Eduardo's assistants, pleased by Eduardo's interest in him and the church. He basked in the attention; he deserved it after all; he worked hard. He told himself the presents weren't out of line, just an occasional box of expensive cigars, a bottle of good port, and dinners at Cinco Gallos. Nothing seemed like a bribe; it just meant Eduardo enjoyed his company.

Then, it was payback time. Requests came from Eduardo to drive silent men in dark glasses—men who weren't from the neighborhood—to airports, to unfamiliar locations in Chicago, Indianapolis, or Saint Louis, or to pick someone up and deliver him to Big Grove. Once he even had to drop off a suitcase in a Pilsen seafood restaurant in Chicago that Eduardo claimed one of his innumerable cousins had forgotten. That's when Father Diego realized something was amiss, and the only explanation was something illegal was going on, probably drugs, and he was in it up to his eyes. He groaned.

Father Diego was heading for the stairway and his bedroom over the library when the phone rang. He was still tired from the holiday and from the drive to Chicago earlier in the day to pick up Eduardo's brother at Midway, Chicago's old Southside airport. He was eager to shower and get into bed. This couldn't be good.

"St. Patrick's Rectory. Father Diego speaking."

Eduardo began without preamble. "My brother is going to need a ride back to Midway on the fourth, Thursday morning. Pick him up at eight o'clock at the restaurant," he said. He hung up before Father Diego could reply.

"I can't stand this," Father Diego said to himself while replacing the phone on its base. "I feel like I'm walking along the edge of a cliff. This is the last time I'm going to play taxi. I won't accept any more money for the church either, even if we can use it. We'll manage. We did before. And I don't need cigars or expensive port. After all, what could happen if I say no?" He tried to push his discomfort away.

Though he was tired, sleep was slow in coming. Maybe the banging shutter and the whine of traffic were louder than usual. Or maybe it was the shadowy figures of Eduardo and his silent thugs that seemed to watch with dead eyes from the corners of his bedroom.

~ * ~

The following Thursday, Father Diego eased the garage door closed behind his car after his trip to Chicago and then headed for the rectory. He had plenty of time to change into his cassock and have tea before the five o'clock service. He could even relax, since he had told Eduardo that morning he wouldn't act as a driver anymore. This was his last trip. Eduardo tried to convince him to carry on, to consider the benefits to the church, to think about his own future. Then Eduardo got angry, furious, calling him a dick and worse; Eduardo pointed out that no one quit a job with him without repercussions. The way he had said it made Father Diego's skin crawl.

Maybe saying Mass would help my unease, Father Diego thought an hour later as he walked to church through the windy dark.

He didn't see the quick, dark form next to the east wall of the church as he turned to slip inside the sacristy. He didn't hear the two breathy metallic wheezes of a gun with a suppressor, didn't consider further the coming evening Mass, or the wind, or his supper of *pozole*. With his thoughts flickering like loose connections in an old lamp, he sank to the floor, the exit wound in the back of his head oozing. His shattered heart convulsed and stopped; his eyes twitched, his hands moved restlessly, and he stilled.

Seventeen

Tikal National Park, Guatemala, December

Ochoa was on his third cup of coffee. The warmth of the kitchen felt good. Mornings could be cool even in the Petén, or maybe he was just getting old. Over the sounds of Esperanza washing dishes in the corner sink and the crackling fire, the growing sound of an airplane heading their way interrupted the quiet morning routine.

"What the hell?" Ochoa was suddenly all business. He ran onto the small patio behind the house to catch a glimpse. Esperanza followed him, wiping her hands on her apron. Single engine. Heading north, descending. It definitely was easing down somewhere on the far edge of the park, or just outside. Not good. Not good at all. It looked like drugs were coming to the Petén in a big way, and the park seemed to be included in the picture.

"What is it?" Esperanza asked. "Smugglers?"

"Yes, and maybe a cartel moving in. I've heard talk at the office that there've been changes in the Highlands, where the smugglers used to land their cargo. That route is too well-known now, for one thing, and struggles for dominance between South American suppliers and the big Mexican cartels have intensified as the demand in the States has increased," Ochoa said. "Maybe someone figured if they set up in the Petén they would be less obvious. It's full of national parks, several archaeological sites, big ranches, tourists, planes in and out bringing people in along with supplies for ranches and everyone else. There is plenty of jungle cover, a small population, more places to build bigger landing strips ..."

Later that day while his tour group was busy in the museum, Ochoa returned to headquarters. He wanted to tell Ríos about the plane. Get his take on the situation.

Captain Ríos was bent over a topographical map of Tikal he'd spread on his desk. He was muttering to himself when Ochoa appeared at his office door. Without looking up, Ríos started talking before Ochoa could say *"Buenos días."*

"I heard it, too, if you are here about the plane this morning. We're in trouble. This is the sixth sighting in a month, all heading toward the north end of the park. I've talked to the park service's main office in Guatemala City," Ríos continued, waving Ochoa toward a visitor's chair. "There's a rumor it's the Sinaloas bringing cocaine, heroin, Fentanyl. They'd attracted too much attention in the Highlands and worn out their welcome, so it seems they decided to shift where they wouldn't be as obvious, where they could process, pack, and store drugs, as well as ship them to Nuevo Lorado in Mexico for distribution. Using the Petén would allow them to use their previous cross border routes—Ciudad Juarez as jumping off spot for the States, El Paso across the Rio Grande River—as warehouse and transportation hubs where drugs could be packed for individual distributors and to load American trucks. Shipments could be routed straight to Chicago, St. Louis, Indianapolis, Detroit, Des Moines, or wherever, without having to transfer the shipment again."

"Anything about Los Zetas?" Ochoa asked.

"So far, nothing firm, but the story goes Los Zetas might be pushing into Sierra del Lacandon Park just over the border in Mexico. There've been hints—fights in bars between locals and Mexicans from up north, indigenous people shoved off their lands so strangers can construct who knows what—airfields from the sound of it. We'll know if they start to muscle into Tikal, too. There'll be carnage if Los Zetas and the Sinaloas bump heads here. We've got to stop them before that happens. The park would turn into a battleground; we'd have to close." Ríos groaned. "We've got to get to the north end, see what's going on."

Eighteen

Eduardo Guzmán sat in his office in the yet unopened restaurant, nursing a cup of coffee and tapping his pen on the desk top. He could hear the cook in the back, chopping vegetables, and he could smell frijoles simmering. Otherwise, the place was empty, if he didn't count his two bodyguards drinking coffee in a booth near the front door. All of a sudden, he had a lot on his plate. There was the usual transfer of goods from El Paso to Big Grove to Chicago, of course, and running the restaurant, but now there was the shift of smuggling operations from the Highlands to the Petén with its new buildings, runways, personnel.

If that weren't enough, at breakfast his wife, María, brought up his older brother's youngest daughter's *quinceañera*, the traditional Mexican celebration of a young woman's fifteenth birthday, coming up in April. She wanted to go. María was eager to see the relatives, and she wanted to let them know how well they were doing. The *fiesta* was going to be held on his brother's ranch in the Yucatán—a weeklong family reunion with entertainment, dances, fancy dinners, and plenty of time to catch up with one another's lives and to enjoy the warm weather after what had been a winter of frigid temperatures and blowing snow in Big Grove.

Not that Eduardo was eager to watch his brother strut and brag about his wealth or talk with his idiot relatives, either, but he was wavering. The *quinceañera* was a big deal, and he could show the rest of them he hadn't just been making tortillas and frijoles since he moved to the States. María could prance around and flash that big diamond he had bought her. It might be worth it, even though his brother was a prick and his sister-in-law, that skinny bitch, had a voice like a Skil saw.

They could even spend a few days on the beach in Cancun on the way home if they planned things right. He hated to leave his business with shipments coming in, but it would be a perfect opportunity to check on the new transfer facilities and landing center in the Petén, since they weren't far from his brother's ranch. At least the trip to the Yucatán could include business as well as a vacation, so he wouldn't completely be wasted. He'd tell María when he got home and have her start making arrangements.

The problem was he had to find a new courier ASAP. Business was picking up, for one thing, and moving people and money without calling attention to what was happening in the Yucatán was an increasing issue. It would be impossible to find someone with such good cover as the priest, but what could he do? Why the hell had Father Diego suddenly developed *cajones* after all the money he'd poured down the priest's throat and into St. Patrick's? What a dick, taking advantage of hospitality like that. This whole courier thing had turned into a total pain in the ass. Eduardo shook his head.

Nineteen

Big Grove, December 10

A snow squall was blowing in from the northwest when we arrived home. The plane waddled, dipping and pitching, before its wheels finally hit the ground. The weather was a shock after the tropics, but otherwise the trip was easy. We made our connections and we had plenty to talk about in the airports.

Luis and Zoila were full of news from relatives—kids growing up, a young cousin's wedding in the spring, Luis's nephew's new accounting business in Guatemala City. All I had to share were the details of my mugging and my visit to Ruth Wiseman in her studio in Antigua, but that hadn't yielded much.

I blamed my halting conversation with Ruth on the fact that I felt like hell, and I looked like I'd been in a bar fight. Who wants to chat with someone with the appearance of a police incident photo and who groans when she moves? I had managed to find out that the model for the young lord in the mural was the younger brother of a friend of hers from Flores. She had given me the boy's name: K'in Kan. Everyone called him Kan. The vulture jade was nothing, merely an adaption of something she had seen in a museum. At least Ruth had promised to get in touch if she remembered something else.

Flores. It was a start. I wouldn't be surprised if the guy was related to the man I had seen mending fishing equipment.

Big Grove was not the peaceful college town we'd left. The local paper was full of speculative articles about the killing of Father Diego: updates on the investigation appeared on local nightly news and in the Chicago media. His murder seemed to excite particular interest, not only because he was a priest, but also because his death looked like a professional hit. He hadn't been robbed. His pricey phone and wallet were still in his pocket. It wasn't some macho, clumsy kid trying to steal, who pulled the trigger. It was someone who wanted him dead and knew how to kill. But who would murder a priest—who, by all accounts, was important in the community and popular with his parishioners—and why?

Some reporters suggested his death might be linked to something in the Hispanic community itself. Then there was the drug crash behind Cinco Gallos; maybe that played a role. In many inventive minds, his killing fit right in with everything else: anti-immigrant hostility, drugs, gang wars.

Even though it wasn't much, I emailed Ochoa with the latest developments and the name of the man in the mural, just to keep him in the loop. Maybe he could find something about the kid at his end. It would be something.

A couple of nights after we got home, I sat in my recliner with Rosie, trying to put together what I knew of Ruston and Polop. Was destruction seeping out of Xibalba, the Mayan underworld, as Luis suggested, or was it something more mundane? And if it were something run of the mill, what would cause a priest to be assassinated? It sure as hell didn't have anything to do with squabbles over plans for church Christmas festivities.

There were other signs of unease in Big Grove as well. Just before exam week, a young woman was found nodding in a women's bathroom stall in the student union; she still had a needle in her arm.

A few days later, two high school kids from the southeast side of Big Grove overdosed, ending up in the emergency room. Drug arrests and stops were up, too. According to the authorities, no one knew where the sudden flood of high-grade heroin was coming from or how to stem the tide.

Twenty

Tikal National Park, Guatemala, December 18

When Ochoa walked into Captain Ríos's office early one morning just before the holidays, Ríos was already working on a list of things to be done before the park closed for two days at Christmas. "We need to send a small expedition to the northern boundary of the park before the break," he said, removing the tip of the ballpoint pen from his mouth that he had been gnawing. "There is too much plane traffic heading that direction. We can't ignore it any longer. Add that increase to Ruston's murder and other events—Ann and her purse, for example—it's clear something is up. I want you in charge. You know the park inside and out. Take Jaime with you and maybe the two newest guys; it'll let them see what that part of the park looks like.

"Just don't go snooping in Mexico," Ríos added. "That would start something nasty. I want you to just document what you find and leave, but don't let anyone see you while you are at it."

~ * ~

It was just after dawn six days before Christmas when Ochoa pointed the Forest Service Land Cruiser, which was packed with tents and enough food and water to last a month, along a dirt track toward the northern edge of the park.

"What's with all the supplies?" Jaime asked. "I thought we only planned two days away. We're not going to hang around in the jungle for Christmas, are we?"

Just then the SUV lurched. Ochoa grunted as he jerked it back onto the smoothest part of the track. "No, we aren't, but Ríos wants us to be prepared for anything. You know how he is. This is supposed to be an in and out. We see what we can see, photograph anything of interest without anyone—if there is anyone—spotting us, and then we head back."

As they drove past central Tikal and headed deeper into the jungle toward the ancient city of Uaxactun, the road turned ugly. The unusually frequent rains during the rainy season had done nothing to improve its surface. Ochoa clasped the jerking steering wheel, his knuckles white, muttering under his breath as he addressed the ruts. The others braced themselves, silent, except for the occasion gasp as the SUV jolted over rocks. By the time they reached the park boundary, Ochoa was eager to get out of the Land Cruiser. His shoulders and wrists hurt from the effort of holding the Toyota on the road, and his spine felt as if it had been driven through the top of his head.

"It's like riding a bronco," Ochoa said. "The road makes steering a nightmare. I need some water," he added as he slid from under the wheel, unscrewing the top of his canteen at the same time. "Then let's see what the hell is happening. I don't see anything here, but Mexico may be another matter."

Jaime grunted in assent and returned his own water bottle to his belt; then he walked to the back of the SUV and unloaded the spotting scope from behind the seats. The new guys, looking queasy from the jerking drive, still leaned against the Toyota sipping from their canteens.

Ochoa stepped to the edge of the undergrowth, scanning the distant open space with his binoculars. Things had changed since he'd been there six months ago with a group of archaeologists looking for possible dig sites. Where once there had been no sign of humans, an airfield had sprung up just over the border, complete with control tower, hangers, and airplanes of all sizes—medium sized transports to Piper Cubs. That wasn't all. Three large pole buildings with logos on their sides lay beyond the hangers: "Maya Jungle Gold" stated the logo in red and gold letters around an image of Temple I: "World-wide exporters of fine, wild-grown organic cacao beans," was written below in large red and black letters. Trucks arrived and left in a steady steam to and from the loading docks of the largest building. Workers in blue jumpsuits with the Maya Jungle Gold company logo on the pockets unloaded burlap sacks stamped with the same logo, pushing them inside on flat-bottomed trollies, or moved sacks between buildings.

Ochoa let out a low whistle. "Take a look at this, Jaime," he said lowering his binoculars. "It's an entire community."

Jaime raised his binoculars. "*Jesús y María*! An airport, too, and guard towers!"

Jaime had set up the scope in a small clear spot in the vegetation with a sight line through the trees to the bustling scene. Ochoa switched to the scope for a better view. Beyond the runways and tower, he could see a low building with *Oficina* written over the door in red letters. He also noted what appeared to be a bunkhouse, wash house, and mess hall with a thatched outdoor eating area just beyond.

"This used to be scrubland. Now it's an industrial development," Ochoa said. "Look at all those trucks and planes! How many cacao beans can one company sell: enough to fund all this construction in a space of a few months? Three runways? A tower? Living quarters? Guard shacks? If this is about selling chocolate, I'll retire right now. There can't be enough cacao in the whole of Guatemala to keep this place operating, but it's perfect for drugs. Ríos is going to hate the hell out of what we tell him, but what can we do? It's in Mexico."

"The authorities are probably in on it anyway," Jaime added.

Ochoa pulled his camera from its bag behind his seat, twisted on a lens, lined up his first image. "Let's document and head home. We can't peek in their windows. Talk about trouble, that would be it." Ochoa paused. "But at night, if we're careful…"

"Two perspectives are better than one," Jaime said, carefully easing his bulk through the undergrowth as he attached his long-distance lens. "Let me know if you want to poke around once the sun goes down, or better yet, come back later on our own. I don't want to drag the kids into something ugly," he said, glancing at the two young rangers busy with their binoculars on the far side of Land Cruiser.

~ * ~

Deep in the duff in the understory near the SUV, the snake stirred uneasily. Humans were poking around her new resting spot. She would have to move again.

~ * ~

When Ochoa and Jaime arrived at Captain Ríos's office two days after Christmas, he was already at his desk. He was humming under his breath but stopped when he saw them.

"Sit," he said, waving his hand at the two battered wooden visitors chairs in front of his desk, but he wasn't smiling. "How were your holidays?"

"Excellent," Ochoa said. "My mother-in-law went all out. Even got a turkey."

"Tamales and chicken at our place," Jaime said, "and all the kids were home. That made it special. How about you?"

"Fine," Ríos said. "Fine. Or it was fine until I got a call from the border patrol. They'd spotted a couple of guys in camo driving a Forest Service truck right up to the Mexican frontier late the day after Christmas. The patrol figured they better see what was going on, so they waited. Once it got dark, the two guys snuck into Mexico, past the empty guard shack at the far end of the compound, headed to the back of the pole buildings behind the hangers, and went up to the window of the one nearest the border. The guys took photographs, did the same at the remaining two structures." Ríos paused, made a steeple with his fingers in front of his face.

Ochoa groaned to himself. *They'd taken a chance, but who'd think a patrol would be out so close to Christmas? What the devil were they doing at that location anyway? Watching the action as well?*

"I have the feeling it must be you two, from the sound of the operation. You know, two men with binoculars, cameras, side arms, Forest Service truck."

Neither Ochoa nor Jaime said anything.

"I thought so! You could have started an international incident! I can see the report now! Tikal Park Rangers invade Mexico on Christmas!" Ríos was nearly shouting. His face was red. "Well?"

He paused, waited. Still neither Ochoa nor Jaime said anything. Losing patience, he demanded an answer. "What the hell did you see?"

"Drugs," Jaime said. "Drugs and guns."

"They're packaging heroin in one building, cocaine in another, warehousing in a third," Ochoa said. "And it looks like they're mixing something in with part of the heroin in that first building, too.

"They don't seem to be doing anything else, just repackaging in smaller amounts, like they're preparing it for distribution."

Ríos chair creaked as he sat back. "What the hell can we do?" he asked no one in particular.

Twenty-one

Big Grove, January

The holidays following Father Diego's murder had been muted, but once the New Year began, life in Big Grove settled back into a more familiar routine and a cold-weather pattern. People dreamed of blazing fireplaces, good books, and chili and soup. Rosie and I spent our evenings curled in the recliner reading in a warm pool of lamplight, and Pat, Bill, and I went back to our biweekly cocktail evenings.

At the end of month, I began a new commission…organizing the papers of the village of Riverview for transfer to the local historical society. A town west of Big Grove with a population of 350, Riverview had been founded in 1850 with a handful of rough houses, general store, a church, and one saloon. After the railroad came through and corn from the elevator could be shipped, it had grown to a good-sized community with a business district, bank, and a second church. Then grew it to its current size as shipping of corn and beans moved from rail to truck.

In the end, the job turned out to be more interesting than I first imagined. The city council had saved everything from the earliest days—meeting minutes, agendas, receipts, correspondence, every copy of the *Riverview News,* announcements for social gatherings, school plays, church suppers, photographs—all stuffed in no particular order in cardboard boxes in the tiny storage room behind the city offices, which were located over Bud's Place, one of the two bars in town. I parked the RAV4 in the icy gravel behind the Victorian building that held Bud's and the offices. A peeling, white wooden door led directly into the dark and quiet of the midmorning tavern, where Bud, a stout man in his sixties with a halo of white wispy hair, was reading the paper behind the old mahogany bar.

"Hi, Bud," I said, resting my plastic tub of archiving materials on a nearby stool. "I don't know if you remember me. I'm Ann Cunningham. We met at the last city council meeting. I was there to answer questions about preserving city papers."

Bud peered at me over his glasses. "I remember. Glad you're here," he said as he led the way to the narrow stairs at the back of the room. "We should've organized things years ago. Papers are a real mess now." He looked at my jeans and turtleneck. "Looks like you're dressed for it."

I struggled up the stairs in the back of the bar with my box of supplies and down the narrow hall that led to the storage room at the back of the building. There wasn't much to see once I got inside, just shelves of boxes, bundles of papers tied with twine, a single light bulb in the center of the ceiling, and the sense that time had stopped in the tiny space. It was musty, too. I had just managed to open the window across from the door when Bud appeared with a chair.

"Thought you could use this," he said, placing it in the only clear space. "Let me know if you need anything else. I'm always downstairs. Just give a shout." He cocked his head to one side as if listening. "I better go. Just heard someone come in. I'll check on you later. See how you are doing." He gave a wave as he turned to leave. I could hear him retreating down the creaking narrow stairs.

The first box I opened was a mixture of old mouse nests, brittle paper, and dirt. The nests smelled, the papers fractured like glass, and dust rose in clouds into the pale sunlight that filtered through the single window's cloudy surface.

~ * ~

I was about half way through the job a week later when I found something that sounded strangely familiar. The story unfolded over several years in crumbling copies of the *Riverview News*. In 1870, the banker's son brought home his new wife. He'd left home ten years earlier to go to college in the east, take the Grand Tour, see the world. A faded picture of the stolid German banker's son and his delicate bride—an indigenous woman from another world, if the braids wrapped in ribbon and coiled around her head and Mayan dress meant anything—showed the pair staring, unsmiling at the camera. According to the accompanying interview, the young man came back with dreams of a business empire of grain sales and shipping, a rich and productive farm, and a big house on the hill north of town. His bride, he said, was from the Yucatán, daughter of a community leader named Kan. They'd met on one of his trips.

Later papers announced the birth of children: first a boy, later a girl; the creation of the grain business on a spur of railroad next to the river that ran east and west through town and the construction of the palatial dwelling on the hill. The business prospered according to the paper, but of the family there was nothing more after the daughter was born. It was as if they disappeared. The banker's son died twenty years later, alone in his grand house. His obituary didn't mention his wife or children.

Bud didn't know much about the story either, just that the woman and her children left years before the man died. "People figured she went back where she came from. Not much room for strangers in Riverview then," Bud said.

It reminded me of K'in A'jaw and his princess—the foreign wife, her rejection by the husband's community, the flight—but at least K'in A'jaw accompanied his wife and children into the jungle, not like the banker's son who let his family leave without him. *I wonder where their descendants are now*, I thought as I headed to the icy parking lot, remembering the sepia image of the tiny woman, the stolid businessman, his growing list of properties.

Big Grove, February

Polop was sent home from Guatemala by the US Embassy at the beginning of February, twenty-five pounds lighter, jumpy as a cat, and nursing a flesh wound in his thigh. We'd nearly given up on seeing him again. He was staying with Zoila and Luis until he could tolerate being alone. They invited me for dinner, so I could see him and hear his story.

"Managed to escape on the way to the toilet one night," Polop said after supper. "There was an outhouse on the edge of the compound. I'd been with them so long they were getting lax: they let me go alone. That's when I ran. Lucky for me it was dark and the compound backed into a grove of trees. I'd been in Santa Elena long enough to have a sense where things were—main street, causeway, road to the airport. Besides, there isn't much else there. I headed north staying on back streets. I thought I'd get to the airport or the road to Tikal that way. There aren't streetlights to speak of, so it was easy to hide most of the time. I was crouching behind a tumbled-down section of wall, trying to catch my breath, when I got shot. They must have seen me in the shadows. I ran anyway. There's nothing like fear to keep me moving. I didn't have money, my leg was dragging, and I must have looked terrible, but once I got to the airport, the guards were willing to listen. They knew about my kidnapping from a police watch list."

"Sounds like Indiana Jones," Luis said.

Polop snorted. "Ha. Some adventure. Looking back, I still can't believe what happened. Those men with their front-facing ponytails give me the willies. I hate the jungle. And all I could think of was Ruston. I imagined I was next. Otherwise, why were they hanging on to me? They probably were waiting for a propitious moment, the right day in the calendars, Venus rising or something.

"I just remember pieces of the ordeal—the jolting car, the rickety ferry across the Usumacinta, the hike north to a limestone ledge deep in the jungle, the narrow cave, which was wet and full of bugs." Polop paused for a moment, then plowed on.

"They felt they had to look like the ancestors for this holy journey and didn't wear their usual combat gear. *Jesús y María!* They dressed as classical period warriors—breechclouts in those awful weeds full of insects and snakes, then crawling on all fours in a cave piled with bat dug. They're...they're *possessed.*"

"Nasty," Zoila said. She shuddered slightly.

"By the time we reached the central chamber, the men were electrified, beside themselves. They'd reached the holy of holies, and now they believed they'd learn the secrets of the universe.

"They were right to be excited. The mural *is* amazing, even in lantern light. The colors are still good, though some paint has flaked off. In the center of the mural, a young lord dressed in a plain white loincloth, green quetzal-feather headdress, and jade necklace is seated cross-legged on a throne. A young woman, maybe his wife, offers him a pot of chocolate. Two guards with spears in court regalia—jaguar capes and sandals, quetzal headdresses—stand behind him. Another figure, badly eroded, but maybe another lord, approaches the throne from behind the woman. His clothes didn't look familiar: long, white sheer robe, more like the Lacandones today, simple bead necklace, maybe jade, it's hard to tell; plain sandals and hair done in a bun. He looks older, too; he's got a paunch. And he's carrying a necklace with a vulture pectoral, maybe as a gift for the young lord."

"You're joking!" I exclaimed, leaning forward eagerly, not wanting to miss a word.

Polop shook his head. "The mural looks early, late preclassic maybe. Kan, the leader, wanted to know if the jade pectoral is like the one on the stele Ruston found. I told them what I knew about the stele, the meaning of the glyphs, the pectoral. They really became animated then."

Polop paused, remembering.

"They believe the painting proves the Petén was theirs from the beginning, before the Spanish invaders arrived, before foreigners claimed their world. According to them, Tikal, the Lacandon Reserve, and all the other parks have to be reclaimed, ranchers have to be driven out, the cartels eradicated. Even though they are working with Los Zetas for the moment, they don't care. Every non-Mayan trace has to be destroyed." He drummed his fingers nervously on the arm of his chair. "They're on the warpath and they want to find that pectoral. It's the symbol of kingship, according to them. Oh, and something else, they have an early Spanish document that completes the story, but they need someone to piece it all together. They said they found it with some old papers in Kan's grandfather's trunk."

Great. Kan again, and the pectoral, too. I could feel my stomach tighten.

~ * ~

It wasn't until the final day of the month that anything new happened, not that Polop's return counted as nothing. The weather had been well below zero most nights during the previous two weeks. Ice like granite made many sidewalks impassible. Side streets were reduced to one-lane roads, two hard ruts through frozen slush. The wind was vicious.

I'd been reading, curled in my old recliner with Rosie warm and kneading in my lap, during what I hoped was the last big blizzard of the winter, but I was having trouble concentrating. I set my mystery aside. Some of the things Polop had said had been nagging at me. First of all, how did the Nuevo know about Ruston, unless they were part of what had happened, and second, how did they know about the stele? They weren't researchers, after all, nor were they privy to the latest archaeological gossip or bulletins. Additionally, how had they come to consider the jade pectoral as a link between Ruston's find and their discovery without additional information? On top of it, Kan was their leader. There couldn't be that many Kans in that part of Guatemala, could there? Yet, even the Riverview businessman's bride was named Kan. Odd.

Maybe Luis and Zoila would have an idea. I'd give them a call, blizzard or no blizzard. I could hardly hear Zoila over the static once she answered. It must have been the wind disrupting the signal.

I told her what I'd been thinking, Kan, pectoral, and all.

"I don't know if this has anything to do with the Nuevo, but we got an email from Luis's brother this morning. You know, the one we stayed with near Xela," Zoila said. "According to him, there are rumors an indigenous group in retro garb is helping Los Zetas establish themselves in the Petén…Yukatek speakers from southern Yucatán, he said. It reminded us of those kids in Flores you told us about, but they wouldn't speak Yukatek. Other people must have joined in."

I could hear Luis talking in the background over the rattling of my storm windows and the static on the phone, but I couldn't make out what he was saying. Zoila repeated it for me. "Luis says the danger isn't over. Snow or no snow, he wants to throw seeds tonight, and he wants everyone involved in the Ruston stele business to be here, too. He said attacks against Mayan scholars have to stop and all the related problems, too. Something isn't right. I'll make supper— tortillas and soup. At least we won't starve. How about six?"

I groaned. The ancestors were up to something, I could tell.

~ * ~

Bill, Pat, and I bought flowers and a pint of vodka on the way to Luis and Zoila's. Bill threw in a pack of cigarillos, just in case. I'd slid the vulture pendent, smelling faintly of parsley from its hiding place in the jar of dried herbs, into my purse before we left Burr Oaks. Maybe it was time for it to put in an appearance.

As we were finishing our meal, unsure of how to proceed, I carefully placed the pectoral in the middle of the table.

"Oh, my God!" Polop said.

Zoila gasped.

Luis gently picked the treasure up with his good hand, cradling it in his palm. He closed his eyes, perhaps feeling the thousands of years of stories running through the tiny object like water, perhaps sensing its connection to another world.

We took our coffee to the living room after dinner and arranged ourselves in chairs facing the balcony. I'd put the pectoral in my shirt pocket in case it was needed. Luis sat in his recliner facing us, tucked under his red and purple blanket.

"I pulled our altar closer to the doors, so it would be sheltered from the wind," Zoila said as she slipped outside to feed more pieces of incense into the potsherd of smoldering copal on the low flat stone just beyond the windows. She placed the flowers and tobacco next to the shard and poured the alcohol over the altar. The wind sucked the curtains through the open door, as if someone leaving the room.

"I'll get Luis set up," Zoila said as she came back in, pushing her hair out of her eyes with the back of her hand, "then we can start." She placed the small table with its bright striped cloth over Luis's lap and positioned the sack of crystals and beans where he could reach it easily.

"Put the pendant here, too," Luis said. "Right where we can see it." He indicated a spot near the front of the table. I slipped it into place. As the sweet smell of copal filled the room, Luis poured out the seeds and crystals, placing ten of the largest stones in a row behind the pectoral. He began to chant, his voice barely audible over the sound of sleet against the windows and the rattling doors; he swayed with the rhythm of his words.

Hypnotized by the chant, the sound of Luis's hand brushing against rough fabric, and the quiet questions he asked the ancestors, I closed my eyes as well. It was as if time itself had unfurled in the room, called forth from the seeds and crystals, the pale green pectoral, and the sighing wind.

When I went home that night, I left the pendent with Luis and Zoila. It was theirs, after all: they're Maya. With the experiences of Ruston and Polop, they needed as much help from the ancients as possible, but they'd have to be careful. Who knew when some weirdo would come after them?

As I went out the door, Luis told me not to worry.

~ * ~

The same night that Luis cast seeds, a popular campus stand-up comic, known for his dirty mouth, outrageous patter, and bottomless need for attention, overdosed on heroin at a fraternity party where he was performing. He was found dead early on the morning following the festivities, covered with snow, half hidden in the leafless hedge that surrounded the colonial style house, and his face in a small pool of frozen vomit.

The police investigations were fruitful. Substantial quantities of marijuana were found in several students' pockets and in a baggy stuffed behind the cushions of the couch in the living room; an enormous supply of Molly was discovered in a cookie jar in the pantry. Several bongs ringed the coffee table in the TV room, and two mirrors streaked with white powder formed its centerpiece. There was no evidence of larger amounts of heroin or cocaine except for the mirrors, a few empty glassine bags in the kitchen trash, and the dead man in the shrubs.

Two days later, the medical examiner confirmed that the comic had died of an overdose of heroin and cocaine—a speedball—an often lethal combination. The minute quantity of powder in the bottom of a small glassine bag in his pocket tested positive at the state lab for unusually pure heroin. His drug paraphernalia contained traces of heroin and cocaine. The young comic joined the innumerable other entertainers who died injecting the deadly mixture.

In the investigation that followed, a spreading area of rot, like the decay in the center of an otherwise unblemished apple, was uncovered, for the fraternity was found to be one source of the increasing supply of drugs that had spread across campus since the previous summer. Thanks to an anonymous tip to Crime Stoppers, four fraternity members were found to be dealing drugs in substantial quantities—heroin, cocaine, Molly, marijuana—from their off-campus apartment a few blocks from the fraternity house.

Twenty thousand dollars in cash was found in the oldest student's room; drug paraphernalia, scales, measuring equipment of a variety of sorts, and a vast supply of small bags were discovered in the kitchen. The drugs themselves were stored in four closets on floor to ceiling shelves installed behind clothes. In all, the entire haul— drugs and cash—was worth hundreds of thousands of dollars, and the students, though they denied knowing anything at the start, soon indicated they'd set up shop the year before with the help of a contact known only as Jorge, whom they'd chanced to meet in the parking lot of a local restaurant.

All of this information came out in fits and starts over the next week and served as a main topic at our Friday cocktail evening. Bill had the most to say, since he and his friends on the police force discussed the situation at the gym every time some new detail emerged—off the record, of course.

"One of the students claims that Jorge had heard them talking about buying drugs while they were eating in Cinco Gallos on a Thursday night," Bill said. "He approached them in the parking lot. The police checked. No one of his description or with his name works at Cinco Gallos, or anywhere nearby. The story seems suspicious. What the hell? Was the guy hiding under the table or, does he just hang around in the parking lot? It doesn't make sense."

"When do drugs ever make sense?" Pat asked.

Bill conceded the point with a shrug. "The authorities' main interest right now is that part of town is beginning to seem to be part of a drug trail. First the Cintas truck crashes right behind Cinco Gallos. Then someone skulking in the restaurant's parking lot is trying to drum up business."

"I find it interesting the priest from the church right near I-74 is the one that was murdered," I added. "Might that be part of a larger picture, or is it just another coincidence?"

No one replied.

The priest's death and the source of the drugs remained a mystery.

Twenty-two

Yucatán, Mexico, April

The house was quiet when Eduardo Guzmán and his bodyguards left his brother's ranch and headed southwest toward Tikal. Eduardo told everyone at dinner two nights ago he'd like to visit an old school friend on his ranch near Tikal. He'd be back three days later, he said. His brother offered to loan him the Land Rover, thank God, since the driving wasn't over paved roads, but Eduardo turned down a chauffeur. He couldn't afford to have anyone knowing where he was going; or what he was doing once he got there. Arturo, one of the guards, could drive.

When they finally bumped along a dirt road into the airfield and construction area after hours, Eduardo was hot and irritable. Arturo, usually phlegmatic, had cursed under his breath most of the way, as he tried to avoid the biggest ruts and gaping holes. Juan, beside him in the passenger's seat, had remained silent most of the way except for sudden intakes of breath, his knuckles white on the dashboard as he braced himself against the worst of the jolts. Arturo pulled up next to the brush shelter and cut the engine. The sudden end to the shaking and noise was like dropping into a hole. The men sat in silence, rattled. Finally, Eduardo eased out of the car.

The first thing he wanted was a cold drink, with ice, if possible. Then he needed to pull himself together. After that he'd be ready to tour the site, to see if they could start making full-sized shipments to Ciudad Juarez. Though he wasn't looking forward to it, he'd have to address the airfield's manager's current concerns—tagged buildings, vandalism, theft.

"Theft, for God's sake, in the middle of a jungle! Who the hell is out there to steal anything? What's wrong with the guy? Why can't he handle it himself?" Guzmán asked no one in particular, as he headed toward the office.

~ * ~

From the start, the situation was as Eduardo expected-—no ice, no comfortable place to sit, and no possibility of a really good lunch—but the work was finished. Streams of trucks poured in from the countryside, loaded with bags labeled cacao, or large boxes, and then backed into the loading docks of the sheds with the Maya Gold logo. Men darted along the dock with trollies loaded with gunnysacks and unmarked cartons. Hangers, planes, bunkhouse, mess hall, office, all carrying the Maya Gold logo, were bustling with activity. It was as he'd hoped, but he soon saw that the manager's worries about vandalism were valid. The NM, whoever the hell they were, had tagged the hangers and even a plane near the gas pumps. If that weren't enough, according to the manager, tools, building materials, and gas had been stolen, and someone had broken a window in the office.

"Worse yet, the runway lights quit a few weeks ago when a plane was landing. Someone pulled a breaker, but there was no sign of who did it," the manager said. "We can't have this screwing around as shipments increase. There won't be room for errors or darkened airfields with a growing number of flights."

"If the tagging means anything, the NM must have something to do with it," Eduardo said as they turned toward the mess hall. "Maybe one of the guys at lunch will know something more."

Over the meal of beans and rice, the men filled Eduardo in on what they knew about the Nuevo. It wasn't much. One of the mechanics overheard talk in a bar near Flores of a stele found deep in Tikal's jungle, a fragment, which seemed to enflame the nationalistic desires of a small group of Maya.

"Strangers from northern Mexico are showing up all over, too," a warehouseman from Lacandon added. "Ogling women in the streets, getting drunk, starting fights in the bars. My family is worried. Something is going on."

"There's talk Los Zetas are making a grab for territory by supporting the indigenous people, using them to take over territory Los Zetas will control from behind," another man from an *aldea* near Lacandon added.

Nothing was definite, but none of it sounded good. Maya going back to the old ways was as unappealing as Los Zetas on the move, and if that weren't enough, the increasing drug activity in Big Grove was calling attention to his business in Illinois.

Eduardo would have to get in touch with the boss. Tell him what was happening before the airport development went sour, or the police found something incriminating in Big Grove after the recent flood of heroin ODs in the area. The trouble all started with that asshole priest. Somehow it was his fault. For the first time since he started this job, Eduardo was uneasy as well as angry.

Twenty-three

It was the prodding of Luis's ancestors, concern over disappearing Mayan scholars, Bill and Pat's desire to see Tikal, and my inquisitive nature that pushed me into flying to Guatemala the first week in April with everyone else, even though I had been offered an archiving job by St. Patrick's parish on the northwest side of town. Since Father Diego had been murdered the previous autumn, they needed help sorting and disbursing his papers. I called the office and let the secretary know I would be available when I returned. "That's fine. Just so we can have things done by July," she said.

Happily, with two more people, the logistical problems of Luis, the chair, the walker, and the bags was easier than before, even though my hand was still giving me trouble. Bill managed Luis with a minimum of fuss and kept his eyes out for problems at the same time. This last part Luis was sure wasn't necessary. Who would grab an old guy in a wheelchair who'd had a stroke? he had asked.

I'd booked rooms for the first night in the city at the Posada Belen Museo Inn, where I'd stayed before, and I made arrangements for rooms in the Tikal Inn after that. They'd been able to accommodate Luis before, and the reservation clerk was eager to have a party of five, since things were slow—the summer tourist season hadn't started yet.

Polop, no surprise, refused to come. He was adamant. He didn't care what the ancestors had in mind, he said; he wasn't going anywhere near Guatemala. Besides, if the ancestors had been paying attention, he wouldn't have spent weeks with a group of thugs trekking the length of Mesoamerica and then end up getting shot.

"No. Not again. Not so soon. My leg still hurts, I can't sleep, and I have panic attacks. Forget it," he said when Luis asked him if he wanted to join us.

I emailed Ochoa the day before we left to let him know when we were arriving and to fill him in on the latest events. I described the increase in drug activity that radiated from Big Grove: the growing amount of unusually pure heroin flooding our community and its surroundings, the comedian's death in the hedge, and the investigations and arrests that had followed. And I shared my concerns for Luis. It was clear someone was stalking Mayan academics. Luis would be a sitting duck in Guatemala, since he'd be in the open at archaeological sites, museums, libraries, hotels, restaurants.

Ochoa's reply came back later that afternoon. "I'm on it with Luis. I have something to tell you when you arrive. Things are moving. Tell Bill to be ready for anything. He'll know what I mean."

Guatemala City, Guatemala, April

We ate supper in the hotel dining room, next to the courtyard filled with jungle plants, palm trees, and shrieking green parrots. Earlier, while the rest of us unpacked, Bill had made arrangements to visit a friend that evening.

"I'm going to see a guy I haven't seen for years. Lives here in the city," Bill said, finishing his meal. "He's a former SEAL, married a Guatemalan woman, owns a trekking adventure business. He sends groups all over Mesoamerica, the Andes, the Amazon. I'll be late, so don't worry."

~ * ~

Even though his room was next to mine, I didn't hear Bill come in. He was quiet when he arrived for breakfast next morning; he wasn't smiling, either. While the rest of us devoured fruit, granola, sweet breads, and café con leche, Bill toyed with his enormous pile of pancakes covered with fresh fruit, butter, and syrup. Something was wrong. Bill never fools around with pancakes.

~ * ~

The flight later that morning to Flores was easy: the plane was half full, and there wasn't a hassle with luggage with three of us to carry bags. Bill was quiet the entire time. Even Pat couldn't get anything out of him. I'd have to get Bill alone if I was going to find out what was happening.

We checked in at the Tikal Inn at two o'clock, plenty of time to get settled before we met Ochoa at four in the lounge.

~ * ~

We'd just settled into our chairs near the front desk when Ochoa appeared dressed in his usual park service outfit, but unlike before, he was wearing a sidearm. He and Bill gave one another one of those looks. Something was up.

"It's good to see you all again," Ochoa began. "I wish this could be something simple like an archaeological/anthropological visit with friends, but since you were here last, things have become difficult in the park. It seems as if the cartels and the nativist group, Maya Nuevo, have begun to get into one another's hair in a serious way.

"The Sinaloas built an enormous drug transfer point just over the Guatemalan border in Mexico. Los Zetas are working on something in the Lacandon Reserve, also just over the border to the north."

"The Sinaloas and Los Zetas are rivals?" Pat asked.

"Yes, and now add in the NM—we call them the Nuevo. They began using the park as a corridor and a place to hide after harassing the Sinaloas, at least part of the time. Tikal is caught in the middle.

"This morning we were informed by headquarters in Guatemala City that the Nuevo attacked the Sinaloas last night. At least we think it was the Nuevo. Really caused damage. They were masked and dressed like commandos; they snuck out of the jungles of Guatemala and into the airport armed to the teeth with automatic weapons, small arms, ammunition. There must have been a dozen of them according to one source. They were trained, too."

Ochoa paused and took a breath. "The airport personnel fought back, but they were caught off guard. The commandos burned down a drug shed and tried to burn another; they vandalized a couple of planes. Three employees were killed. The depot is going to need some repair before it's back in business. The attackers faded back into the jungle with no casualties, as far as we know."

He finished his update and asked, "Questions?" He looked at Bill.

"How do we know?" Bill said.

"The Forest Service has been keeping their eye on the situation since the beginning and so has the border patrol. Local folks who aren't eager to have a drug depot on their doorstep are willing to report what they see, too."

"And the Nuevo? Who could tell if they were masked? I asked.

"The local folks probably know them personally, and one or two folks reported seeing tattoos of the outline of a temple on a couple of the guys' hands. Now how they got that close or saw their hands without gloves, I don't know. They wouldn't say."

Many anecdotes equal data, or at the least some information is better than none, I thought. This gossip was something, but I could understand why people weren't talking much. They were caught with no place to go. Everyone else could leave. For them it was home.

"Where the hell did those guys get arms, uniforms, training?" Bill asked, "And who's the leader?"

"This is just rumor, but folks are saying that Los Zetas are funding a private army to destroy competition from other cartels, take over new territory. There are plenty of trainers available in this part of the world—former Special Forces, mercenaries from years of conflicts in several countries, rebels, disgruntled army personnel. If Los Zetas were willing to pay for their services, well—"

"And the leader?" I asked.

"Esperanza's been poking around in Flores. It isn't the center of the action, but it is the capitol of the Petén, and there are flocks of tourists to provide cover for all kinds of activity, plus it has easy access to the main road and the airport. She's talked with everyone— business owners, fishermen, housewives, kids. This is more speculation, but she heard it's a guy named Kan, K'in Kan."

I nearly jumped out of my chair. Kan again. K'in Kan, the mural model; Kan the family name of the pudgy Riverview banker's indigenous wife. How did this tie together? Or did it?

"We're going to have to be careful," Bill said. "I heard something similar from a friend of mine in Guatemala City last night—murmurings of open warfare, automatic weapons, real training. It seems that the Nuevo are not just a bunch of wannabes; they're serious. They may be responsible for Ruston's and Polop's kidnappings, too."

"There are a couple of reasons that might be the case," I said. "First, the Nuevo want to legitimize their role as First People and rightful lords of the Petén using archaeological material—the steles, the mural—to substantiate their claims—and second, they are eager to remove the blight of drug dealers from their territory. I'm not sure how they feel about the rest of us, but it probably isn't good."

Bill and Ochoa both nodded. Luis looked grim. Pat and Zoila shifted nervously in their seats. Now I could understand why Bill was so withdrawn at breakfast. His friend had told him we were walking into an armed conflict, and now, talking with Ochoa, we'd learned it was as dangerous as Bill feared.

Twenty-four

Tikal National Park, Guatemala, the Following Day

The mist was still rising the next morning as we set off for the Central Plaza. Pat and Bill, despite the mounting tension outside the park, hurried behind Ochoa, eager for their first glimpse of the ancient city. Luis was mounted on Poncho as before. Zoila and I trailed behind. The sound of the pony's hooves knocking against occasional stones provided counterpoint to the thin high cries of jungle birds and the chattering of several families of spider monkeys in the nearby canopy. A howler called in the distance, his hoots muffled by the moisture, the trees, and the thick jungle air. By the time we reached the plaza, my shoes were wet with dew. Temples I and II, soaring in the morning fog, fierce, otherworldly, seemed to lean over the plaza, overwhelming the steles, the altars, our little group. Pat and Bill were stunned by their first view of the temples' enormity and their vast brooding timelessness.

Pat spoke first. "No wonder people are fighting over this place. It feels like the center of the cosmos."

Ochoa nodded. "It always seems like that to me, too," he said, as he led us into the center of the plaza. "This is where my world began."

~ * ~

Hours later, as we settled in a thatched shelter near Temple IV over plates of cold chicken, fruit, and tortillas, we planned our afternoons. Luis and Zoila were eager to get to the library. I was, too. They had scholarly agendas. I hoped to dig up something on Kan's antecedents. Pat and Bill wanted to see parts of Tikal further from the Central Plaza, to develop a sense of the city's complexity and its place in a difficult environment of jungle and limestone.

We separated into two groups after we repacked the lunch basket. I untied Poncho from the nearby railing, where he had spent his break drowsing in the shade. He was as happy to follow me as he was to obey Ochoa, especially since we were heading in the direction of his stable outside the park.

"Be careful," Bill called as we started out. "Keep your eyes open."

"Don't worry," I said and waved as we turned toward the complex of buildings that housed Tikal's offices and museum.

Jaime's nephew, sitting in the shade of the museum, was waiting to pick up Poncho as soon as we rounded the corner of Temple I. He'd placed Luis's wheelchair and walker on the porch before we arrived. So far, everything was going according to plan, though the sky was beginning to darken with an advancing storm.

Later that afternoon, drowsy and stiff from bending over books in the stuffy archives of the museum, Luis wanted a break. I needed one, too. Maybe a short walk would help. I strapped Luis in his chair; the path to the central site was fairly rough, and I didn't want him sliding out. Zoila remained behind, absorbed in her work.

We'd gotten as far as the path leading toward the Central Plaza when it became clear that something wasn't right. For one thing, the world was silent: no birds, no monkeys, no insects, nothing. The only sounds came from the early rainy season storm moving in; thunder grumbling in the distance. A branch snapped behind us, to the left of the path, then snuffling, and what sounded like a muffled cough. It sure as hell wasn't a jaguar, too small, too noisy.

I hurried forward. Maybe it was just an animal creeping through the bushes, sniffing, but I wanted distance between us before whatever it was revealed itself. When the path became rutted, I steered Luis onto the grass and headed toward the Central Acropolis. Pushing him over vegetation turned out to be little short of murder. There's nothing worse than propelling a wheelchair over rough ground, especially with a bum hand. It's like shoving a push plow through unbroken sod, and Luis's chair threatened to overturn every few feet in hidden ruts, forcing me to wrestle it back onto its wheels like a wrangler roping a steer. Luis was a trooper, though: he didn't let out a peep. He just gripped the armrest with his good hand, knuckles white, jaw set.

The storm was over Tikal now, moving fast. The thunder intensified. Rain began to fall: fat drops increased to sheets in a matter of seconds. My glasses streamed like a glass shower door as I turned back toward the shelter of the museum. I peered through the lashing trees and water to see if we had company, hoping we weren't running straight into trouble.

A few feet further, the chair jerked to the left on the rough ground and into the tangle of low jungle growth that edged our route. My still bum hand couldn't hold it straight. The bottom dropped out. By the time we came to a stop, Luis was upside down, his face in the mud, and I was sprawled beside him on my back.

"Must be a reservoir," Luis said when he could finally talk. "You okay?"

"Yeah. You?" I whispered back.

"Yes, though it feels like I ripped off half my face, but so what? Everything else seems fine as far as I can tell," Luis said wiggling those bits that still worked after his stroke.

"I figure we'll feel like hell tomorrow, but maybe we lucked out, nothing broken," I said, shifting my legs and arms.

We froze in place, listening. The overhang of sod and undergrowth shielded our location from anyone above, but in between the sounds of thunder and pounding rain, intermittent scuffling could be heard from various spots on the edge of the reservoir.

"Where'd they go?" a man shouted in Spanish through the storm.

"Don't know. Maybe they fell into the reservoir," another man called as he pawed the bushes that formed our cover. "I don't see anything in it though, not even skid marks, but its dark, and this rain—"

No surprise about the missing marks since we'd dropped straight down. But now we're trapped like mice in a larder with a prowling cat. No way can I get Luis upright and out of the reservoir without being seen.

Luis slowly turned his head sideways so he could breathe more easily; otherwise neither of us changed position. They wouldn't be able to see us unless they looked under the overhang from the other side of the cistern, but if they came down into the reservoir, they'd see us immediately.

"They're from the Yucatán," Luis said quietly.

"How do you know?" I asked in a whisper.

"Some of what they're saying is in Yukatek." He squirmed slightly to get more of his face out of the dirt.

A third voice called in Spanish from further along the path. "I don't think we're going to find them in this rain. They could be anywhere by now. We need to try again when we have the old man alone."

"I'll check over here just to be certain," the man on the far side of the pit shouted over the storm.

There was crashing in the undergrowth on the rim across from us, as if someone forcing his way to the edge, rain or no rain, just as the storm redoubled its efforts.

"Nothing. I can't see a thing," the man on the far side yelled through the downpour.

Finally, the sound of searching stopped. The calling faded. Maybe we were safe, but I wasn't going to chance trying to see over the rim. They could be biding their time under a nearby ledge. Who knew?

~ * ~

There was nothing to do but huddle, silent, wet, and chilled under the dripping overhang of sod, hoping someone would find us. I unfastened Luis's safety belt and lifted the chair to the side. I pulled him further under the overhang...at least he would be more comfortable. There was no way I could get him out of the cistern; the rain made the muddy sides slick as glass. And I wasn't going to leave him to go for help. We crouched together, trying to stay warm under his sodden red and purple blanket, trying not to call attention to ourselves in case the men were still somewhere overhead.

It must have been another half an hour before the rain began to taper off. I could hear sounds from the direction of the museum and library, faint at first then, then growing louder as Bill, Ochoa, Jaime, and a couple of men whose voices I didn't recognize drew closer, tracking us, reading the few signs of our flight, the broken bushes, and the blundering path made by our circling pursuers.

"Look, the grass is chewed up here," I heard Ochoa call from somewhere near the rim of the cistern, "looks like the chair slipped on the edge of a rut."

We were safe. No one would grab Luis now. "We're down here!" I shouted. "In the reservoir."

Getting out of the pit was harder than getting in. It took two hours, if you count the time it took for the rescue crew to arrive and the interval needed to raise Luis and his chair to the surface. Getting me out was nothing—a safety harness, ropes, and two men pulling—in a matter of minutes I popped over the rim like a rodent out of a hole.

We weren't in great shape. My teeth were chattering, and my hand was killing me; Luis was blue, drowsy, and confused. The rescue crew had blankets and coffee in the emergency vehicle. They swaddled us for the ride to the hotel, where Zoila and a doctor were waiting. I sipped a mug of hot coffee on the way, but Luis was too far gone to swallow.

~ * ~

Everyone, including the hotel staff, crowded into Luis's room, tracking mud, grass, and water across the clean tile floor as the EMTs slid him onto his bed and pulled off his wet clothes. "What's this around his neck?" one of them asked as he removed the last of Luis's shirts. He held up a soft green jade pectoral. It was the vulture.

"He needs that," I said quickly. "It's holy. I'll keep it for him till he's better." Zoila nodded in assent, and the tech handed it to me without a word as the other EMTs piled Luis with blankets.

Doctor Gomez tried to shoo us out as soon as she arrived, but no one moved. "Hypothermia," she said as she examined Luis and dressed his cheek. "He's old and frail, and that makes it worse. Keep him warm. Keep him quiet. Call me if he doesn't begin to improve in a couple of hours. I'll check on him again later tonight."

One of the hotel staff took Luis's chair to clean it.

Then Dr. Gomez turned to me. "Nothing much wrong here, at least nothing that couldn't be cured by getting warm and dry. The only other damage, aside from being cold, is a skinned left shin and a couple of bruises where the wheelchair hit you on the way down."

After the doctor gave me the go ahead, Pat took me to my room for a warm shower and a change of clothes.

An hour later Bill, Pat, Ochoa, and I settled down in the dining room, so I could have something hot and tell my story at the same time. The soup was good. Between it and my several sweaters, the shaking faded as I told them everything I could remember, including Luis's remark about the attackers' language.

"We've learned a couple of things from this adventure," Ochoa said. "Someone *is* watching Luis, but we'd guessed that before, and clearly some of them are Yucatekan," Ochoa continued. "The attempt on Luis was feeble, but if we add that to the attack on the drug depot, it looks like things are hotting up."

"Feeble? It depends on your perspective, I'll bet. Just ask Ann," Pat said, biting into a piece of bread she'd been worrying since we sat down.

Ochoa nodded. "It seems there are two groups—clumsy kidnappers and not too bad insurgents—stupid as that description sounds. Of course, there's word Los Zetas are behind the insurgency part, and a guy named Kan is the leader of indigenous Yucatekans, but are they running the kidnapping operations? And there's the Sinaloas as well."

"There's nothing solid about how everything fits together?" Bill asked. "Is it one group? Two? Three?"

~ * ~

An afternoon in the bottom of a wet pit had finished me off. I'd been fading throughout the conversation and missed half of what was said.

"Bed?" Pat asked as she rose from her chair.

I nodded as she took my arm and steered me out of the dining room.

I was gone as soon as my head hit the pillow.

~ * ~

I woke late the following morning, feeling like dirt. Everything hurt, as if someone had beaten me with chains. The fall must have done more damage than I thought, or maybe I was getting old. I eased out of bed and crept to the bathroom. Maybe a hot shower would help. I turned the water on full. It wasn't much, but today it was more than the usual drizzle. I stayed in as long as I could, then reached for a towel. More bruises had appeared since last night. I looked like one of those awful contemporary fabric prints that resemble random paint splashes on a garage floor.

I am getting tired of the ancestors, the relentless search for who knows what, I thought as I toweled myself off. *Is this probing going to get us anywhere? Ruston was dead, Polop half nuts, Luis recovering from an afternoon in the bottom of a reservoir, my hand hurt, and I looked like hell. What next?*

Just as I was pulling on my pants, something clicked. The answer hit me that had been under my nose the entire time. It was like the fabrics I hate so much. If you laid pieces of the material side by side, sooner or later its pattern would repeat itself. Maybe the Maya/Tikal problems were like that, bits and pieces that eventually form a discernable arrangement.

The Mayan scholars, for example, could fit in this way: an epigrapher to explain the boundary markers, an art historian to interpret an ancient mural, and an anthropologist/literary expert fit it all together. Not so silly after all. It was a carefully crafted attempted to make meaning, to describe a world.

Then there was the water thing that seemed to create a matrix. No water, no hope of inhabiting Tikal and environs again. What was done in the past could suggest solutions in the present, and the ancient symbols, the vulture for example, pulled it all together—the past and present—and verified the power of the Mayan leader, a new Vulture Lord.

The vulture pectoral was the key, and the Nuevo were after it. The cartels, well, they formed a subplot, as they manipulated the Nuevo to their advantage.

An idea, that had flitted into and out of my mind ever since our rescue, solidified. The pendant had to be put somewhere safe, somewhere the Nuevo, or the cartels wouldn't be able to touch it, somewhere casual violence couldn't reach it. Where that might be, I wasn't sure. I needed to think.

~ * ~

Pat and Bill were drinking coffee when I arrived in the dining room.

"You look terrible," Pat said.

"As my mother used to say, like something the cat dragged in," Bill added.

"Thanks. And I was just beginning to feel I might live." I sat down. "Any news on Luis?"

"When I checked this morning, Zoila said he's doing better," Pat replied. "He spent a quiet night, and the doctor has checked on him a couple of times. Said he is on the road to recovery."

"Thank God for that," I said. "Now if we could only unravel the situation here, life might return to normal." Then I told them what I'd been thinking.

Bill nodded. "Sounds reasonable. It explains everything that is going on, even the fascination with the pectoral.

"I found out something from Ochoa yesterday, after you went to bed. They may have a line on the indigenous base. There's talk of an encampment on the southeast edge of Tikal, toward the border with Belize on the edge of Bajo de Santa Fe. There's water in the Bajo during the rainy season, then it slowly dries up over the rest of the year. Not a bad place to hide, since it's forested around the edges and there's water. He said they're going to check it out."

The toucan, my buddy from my last visit, fluttered across the dining room to see what he could glean. Pat let out a squeak as he flapped over her shoulder and pushed his way between the breadbasket and her coffee. He looked at each of us in turn, shuffling his big feet in greeting, then bowed toward me. I swear he knew who

I was. He didn't waste any more time on pleasantries, though. He headed for the remains of the fruit plate in the center of the table, clacking his beak with excitement.

"You have to admire his spirit," I said, handing him a piece of banana.

"Huh, if you say so. Just so long as he keeps out of my food," Pat said as she moved her coffee from behind the bird's heaving tail.

Twenty-five

Tikal National Park, Guatemala

A week following the incident in the reservoir, Ochoa pulled out of the Forest Service parking lot before the sun came up, and headed for Bajo de Santa Fe. Jaime sat in the seat beside him, sipping coffee from a thermos. Ochoa was groggy; it was too early to talk, even to Jaime.

The night before, Ríos had them into his office for a strategy session. "We're in trouble. We've got to act before things get worse. Look at it this way," he had said. "The Sinaloas have a drug depot just over the border in Mexico; a world-famous scholar was killed, in an ugly way, right behind one of the main temples; men in weird garb or combat gear have been spotted sneaking through the jungle after hours, and another scholar turned up at the Flores airport half nuts and shot in the leg.

Now, someone has tried to kidnap Luis. It's got to stop. All of it." Ríos had pounded his desk with his fist. "We've have to find out what's going on, who the hell is behind it, and then we've got to call in the military if necessary and put an end to this crap once and for all."

"What have you got in mind?" Jaime had asked.

"We know about the Mexican depot, so let's scout the Bajo area next. People who have traveled through the area have smelled smoke and there's water in one or two small ponds that would make it a good campsite. Then we'll have to tackle connections outside the park. The Nuevo seem to have a foothold there—Flores, Santa Elena, even the Lacandon Reserve."

Ochoa had nodded. He could just see the National Army pouring into the park, Special Forces swarming the priceless buildings, armed conflict in the plaza. Ancient buildings and monuments shot to pieces. Armored vehicles grinding over causeways. Pure hell.

Two days after Ochoa and Jaime returned to headquarters from the Bajo, the situation in the Petén went toxic. No surprise. They'd counted at least two dozen men at what was clearly a military base—headquarters, barracks, mess tent, jeeps, ammo and arms storage; noted their uniforms, their leaders, their drills, their long hair carefully knotted in buns over their foreheads like Mayan warriors; watched the preparations for some sort of maneuver. So, when armed men assaulted the Sinaloa depot across the border for a second time, no one in the Tikal Park Rangers' office was particularly startled.

~ * ~

Eduardo Guzmán was basking with his wife on the beach in Cancun, even though a hurricane was creeping toward the coast. He'd just smeared María's back with suntan lotion when a waiter from the hotel trotted toward them over the blinding white sand. "I have a note for you, sir," he said, handing Eduardo a folded slip of paper. "It's an emergency, the man said. He wants you to call him. Now, he said. Now, or forget it."

Even with his newly acquired tan, Eduardo blanched.

"I gotta use the phone. It's the boss. Emergency. You stay here," he told María as she sat up on the towel beside him. He left his flip-flops behind as he sprinted for their room. *If I don't get this straight,*

I'll lose my ass and maybe worse, he said to himself as he ran, ignoring the hot sand burning his feet. *That fucking priest. It all started with him. It's like the tide turned against me when that priest died.*

"A group of men, the Nuevo my sources tell me—they all wore their hair in goddamn buns—attacked Maya Gold last night," the boss snarled as soon as Eduardo picked up the phone. "Burned the place to the ground. All that is left is the mess hall, bunkhouse, one shed, and a couple of planes. Ten of our guys were killed, including the manager. Everyone else disappeared into the jungle while you're rolling around in the sand without a care in the world. Just what the hell?"

~ * ~

News spread fast. Ochoa walked into headquarters the morning following the attack to discover everyone there in turmoil. Ríos was shouting on the phone. Jaime was checking his duty belt to make sure everything was in order. Half a dozen other rangers and five or six guides were milling about in the break room. Even Luisa Cabrillo, the new blonde curator from the museum, was there asking questions in a shaky voice.

"We need to know what's happening," she said. "We have to find out what's going on, so we can secure the collection."

"I'd act as if the park was under attack, if I were you," Jaime said looking up from his belt. "By the time we get it straight, it may be too late."

"*Jesús y María.*" Ochoa asked, "What's happening now?"

"The Nuevo attacked the Maya Gold depot last night," Jaime said. "Several people killed—mainly Mexicans, but a couple of guys from Flores, too. Nobody we know, but still—and the depot was burned, except for a couple of buildings. Ríos is trying to get the details."

"Are we sure it was the Nuevo? We just checked them out a couple of days ago. Not that that told us much, but they didn't look like they were going to move just yet," Ochoa said. "No obvious preparations to pull out; everyone looked more or less relaxed."

"People seem to think it was them. Had their hair in foreheads buns. Who else?"

Ochoa grunted in agreement. His worst nightmares were coming true.

~ * ~

The rainy season came early that year, with lashing winds and pounding rains, as a hurricane battered the coast. Hurakan, Heart of Sky, was on the prowl, as ancient forces stalked the land. Clouds boiled over the jungle canopy, and the sky, a low gray cover of clouds, churned over the tips of the roof combs of the main temples. Thunder and lightning punctuated the thick air, agitating monkeys and driving macaws into noisy flight deep in the trees. Cancun, further to the north, was deserted.

The wind rattled the windows in the Tikal Inn dining room as Pat, Zoila, Bill, Luis, and I finished breakfast. No one wanted to go out, not till the storm cleared. Besides, Luis had just begun to feel like himself after his week of convalescence, and he wasn't up to a trek in driving rain. We'd begun to discuss what to do while we waited out the storm, when the manager beckoned Bill to the front desk.

He returned a few minutes later looking grim. "It was Ochoa. Things are heating up," he said, "or maybe the change in air pressure is making everyone nuts. The park is in lockdown. You need to stay put. Ochoa's orders and mine, too," he said giving me the beady eye as he pulled on his slicker. "When the Nuevo attacked that depot a couple of nights ago, it really threw the fat in the fire." He crossed the lobby and headed into the rain toward the Tikal Park Rangers' office.

~ * ~

It wasn't until that night things really got started at the inn. Zoila and Luis had gone to bed, and Pat and I were using my room as base camp, trying to read and work out what the hell was going on. We couldn't hear or see anything through the storm; the inky blackness was absolute. We couldn't get any information from the hotel staff, either. All we could do was theorize.

It was ten o'clock when Bill tapped on the door; then he stuck his head into the room to make sure we were okay.

"It's like something out of *Ben-Hur* out there," Bill said, as he shed his slicker and settled into the chair next to the bed. "People attacking one another from every direction. Chaos, confusion. According to sources, the Maya Gold group has regrouped. Reinforcements arrived from Mexico. Some guy with family over the border said they saw an unmarked convoy coming this way. The Nuevo are pulling themselves together in the Bajo getting ready for another go, I'd guess."

At last, something was going to happen to break the sense of impending disaster, I thought. Between the storm and the tension, I was ready to scream. I figured Pat was, too.

"A cadre of Mexican cartel types has been spotted moving into the park from across the Usumacinta River. They mean business. They're dressed in battle gear, armed to the teeth, and heading toward Tikal," Bill continued.

"Captain Ríos has the park rangers patrolling and protecting the center of the site, and the army has a detachment guarding the perimeter. Ann, you've got to stay here. No snooping around. It's dark, pouring rain, and we're heading for serious trouble. Everybody is on the move. I'm going with Ochoa and Jaime. When it's safe to leave the hotel, I'll let you know."

I tried to look harmless. I'd made some stupid mistakes lately, notably taking Luis out for air and nearly getting him killed.

"Don't get smart, Ann. This is serious."

I nodded. Even I could see he made sense. I'd just be in the way.

~ * ~

Pat left around midnight. We hadn't solved anything by talking, but that night I went to sleep in my clothes on top of the sheets—wearing a nightgown in the middle of a battle would be stupid.

It must have been two o'clock when the door of my room eased open, sending a slice of light from the hall across my bed.

"Bill, is that you?" I asked, half asleep. It wasn't Bill, and the men with forehead buns or hoods that pushed their way into my room weren't talking either, nor was Luis, who was tied and gagged in his chair in the hall. I sat up and tried to scream, just in time to have someone slap a hand over my mouth and push me back into the pillows. I thrashed and twisted, trying to escape the suffocating grasp.

"Where is it?" the tall man, the apparent leader, hissed from the far side of the bed.

"What?" I asked into the smelly leather palm that covered my face.

"The vulture pectoral, *señora*. Give it to me and we'll leave you and Luis alone."

I don't know if the ancestors pay attention to gringas, *but if they want the pectoral safe, they better get on it,* I thought as I struggled. Someone on the hotel staff must have ratted us out. How else did these guys know Luis gave it to me and where to find us?

"I don't have it!" I managed to snuffle. "It isn't here."

"Then where the hell is it?" The man made another hissing noise.

"It's safe. The ancestors are watching over it." Maybe that would work. Talk of ancestors should put them off; they were Maya after all.

It didn't do a thing.

~ * ~

The rest of the night was a blur—a jolting ride in the back of a noisy van through the rain, as the jungle pressed in from every side, Luis mute beside me in his chair, the silent men in front. Even though it was hard to see through the windscreen of the enclosed vehicle, I glimpsed the dark figures of several Tikal Park Rangers and a small group of Guatemalan forces near the edge of the park, watching roads and jungle paths. They didn't see us through the dark and rain.

The driver steered down dirt tracks and worse, circled, dodged roadblocks, pulled off into the jungle every time a patrol or official jeep appeared, desperate to avoid leading anyone to our destination. The roadways and paths were miserable, a nearly endless succession of small lakes and mud flats; the jungle trails were invisible, and the storm intensifying at intervals made things worse.

Sometime near dawn, we pulled into a small farmstead at the edge of a spreading wetland.

Two men lifted Luis's chair out of the van, carried it to the house through the sucking mud, and shoved him inside; the remaining man hauled me behind him like a sack of grain, dumping me in a chair near a table. *It could be worse,* I thought as I squirmed to make myself comfortable. There was a fire in the hearth that helped take the edge off the damp that followed us into the room, and I smelled coffee. A granite *mano y matate,* a grinding stone with traces of tomato on its work surfaces, sat on the top of the shelves near the hearth, along with some other kitchen implements. Clearly someone lived here. Odd.

Not so odd, though, as when the inhabitants appeared.

~ * ~

K'in Kan, Flores fisherman, model for the Mayan lord in the Ixchel Museum mural and presumed leader of the Nuevo, entered the room with Luisa Cabrillo, the museum curator. Jesus! I never would have guessed. Lucky I hadn't asked her instead of the director for help when I hid the pectoral under a pot in a case near the museum entrance.

If that shock weren't enough, there was something creepy about the whole setup. Luisa seemed giddy. The way she flirted with Kan gave me the willies: she was a cross between a teenage girl and Mata Hari, all touches, slinky postures, and significant looks. And he was interested, too, though he pretended not to be. It was like a bad *telenovela*, a charged interaction meaning nothing but sex.

"Where is Zoila," I asked Kan, when he shifted his attention away from Luisa for a moment. "Is she okay?"

"She's fine. She's tied to the headboard in their room," a tall Nuevo answered for Kan.

What was he? The mouthpiece? At least Zoila's safe, I thought, as I shifted in my chair. Now, all I had to do was save our bacon, since the ancestors hadn't shown up. The ropes around my wrists had loosened on the journey from the hotel; as the Nuevo talked among themselves, I set about working my fingers and scraping the ropes against my chair to loosen them further. *If only I could grab a kitchen knife from the nearby shelves*, I thought. But there was no way I could move fast enough, tied to a chair.

A half dozen other Nuevo, all with buns or ponytails on their foreheads and inlaid teeth, arrived, filling the little space, leaning against the walls, or sitting on the floor, drinking coffee. Something was up; otherwise why the gathering?

Luis and I were pushed toward the shelves out of the way.

At a nod from Kan, the tall man took the floor, his inlays catching light from the kerosene lamp on the table. "The Sinaloas and Los Zetas are moving in—Los Zetas from the southwest, Sinaloas from the north. The park service and the army have thrown a net around the park; the site itself is guarded. We have a couple of goals. First, drive the Sinaloas north and push Los Zetas back over the river. Second, locate the vulture pectoral. That's where our guests come in," he said, looking at Luis and me. "So, where is it?" He advanced toward Luis, who was huddled in his chair.

"May we have some water?" Luis asked, as if he hadn't heard the question, as if he did this every day.

Though he grumbled, one man filled a mug from the large thermos near the sink and held it to our lips in turn, so we could drink.

The water was balm in the desert—lifesaving, sweet, cooling my cracked lips and parched throat.

"Well?" Kan asked. "Where is it?"

Neither of us said anything.

Even though he knew I had the pectoral, the tall man grabbed Luis's shoulders, shook him, slapped his face. Was he picking on Luis because he imagined he would give in more easily, or did he think I'd leap to Luis's defense and tell him? Rage began to tighten my throat.

The curator shrieked.

"Answer, you little dick," the tall guy said. "What do you care about hanging onto it? You're not Maya anymore; you're an American professor. You speak English. You eat with a knife and fork instead of just a spoon—I've seen you in the dining room when I clear tables. The vulture is ours. It belongs to the Maya. The *real* Maya."

That's where I'd seen the guy. The inn, I thought, hazy with adrenaline. At least that explains how they found our rooms; how they had gotten in, and how they knew we had the pectoral.

"I don't know where it is," Luis said through clenched teeth.

What was this? Revenge for Luis's use of a fork? Time slowed as my focus sharpened. It was as if I'd been taken over by powers beyond my control, forces that obliterated thought and tightened my body like a spring.

The table lantern went out as the guy hit Luis again.

Shivering, overwhelmed by the unstable mix of murderous fury and my competing inhibitions, lifted out of my chair by invisible strings, I lurched forward toward the shelves, the chair dragging behind me as I wrenched my right hand free. I grabbed the *mano* and, swinging the grinder with every bit of strength I could muster, hit the tall guy shaking Luis. The guy didn't see the *mano* coming in the dark. He squalled, fell. I watched myself swing again, slamming him over the head as he buckled. If I could have clearly seen what I was doing, I would have killed him.

The Nuevo closed in from every direction. Using the *mano* like a club, I struck out at the grabbing hands and arms, the jostling bodies, trying to connect with something important. The noise was deafening—I howled like a witch; the Nuevo shouted or cursed in pain; the curator screamed; it sounded as if someone was breaking up the furniture as they struggled to escape, or seize my arms in the dark.

"Grab her."

"Get another lantern."

"What the hell…

The sound of the door splintering was nearly blotted out by the din.

"Hold it. Don't move. Don't touch your weapons or you're all dead."

A group of park rangers pushed their way into the room, flicking the flashlights on their sidearms around the surging space. More park rangers shoved in the small back door, which lead to the shed out back. All that could be heard in the sudden quiet was the snuffling and mumbling of the man on the floor.

Even in the feeble flickering light I could see the damage I'd done with the *mano*. His face was a bloody ruin.

~ * ~

The rest of the night was a blur. Luis and I ended up in a ranger's Land Cruiser, parked near the edge of the Nuevo's compound, while the rangers sorted out the situation inside. As the adrenaline and the rage that lifted me from my chair began to fade, nausea moved in to take their place. I was shaking and disoriented. Luis motioned me closer to him on the seat, pulled me to him, took my hand.

"You have been waiting for the ancestors," he said gently. "Now you have met them, *mi hermana.*" He held my hand, stroking it as if it were an injured bird. "*Pobrecita.*"

I slumped against his shoulder, eyes closed. I could feel my terror drain away as he held me close with his good arm. I slept, safe with Luis... and his ancestors standing guard.

~ * ~

The sun was just coming up when the assault on the ranch was over. The sudden silence and Luis stirring, woke me in time to see the rangers carrying several stretchers to the waiting ambulances and two dozen handcuffed Nuevo led to police vans. I spotted the curator's bright gold hair as she was shoved into the back of a Land Cruiser. I didn't catch sight of K'in Kan.

Two rangers, both of whom I recognized from the park, approached the SUV.

"*Buenos días, señora y señor,*" the driver said as he slipped under the wheel. "*Yo soy* Francisco. *Este es* Esteban. We're taking you back to the inn." The driver turned onto the muddy road heading in the direction from which we'd come.

The roads had not improved overnight. If anything, they were worse. The surface had been churned into endless mire by the rangers' vehicles. The traffic, especially for a jungle road, was heavy. Periodically, clots of Guatemalan military trucks and smaller groups of rangers forced us to swerve into the undergrowth that lined the track, so they could pass.

"If you're wondering why we are heading this way, we're avoiding the Central Plaza," Francisco said as he pulled the SUV onto the road after avoiding a group of military jeeps heading the direction from which we'd come.

"It's too open for one thing, and there were skirmishes near the main plaza last night," he said as he addressed the uneven trail, tacking south then west as he angled toward the hotel.

Luis gripped my hand to steady himself as he peered through the windshield. "Any idea where those groups are now?" he asked, shouting to be heard over the roar of the Land Cruiser's first gear as the SUV gnawed its way along the path.

"The Sinaloas and Los Zetas were the ones that tangled in the middle of the plaza last night, but who knows where they are this morning," Francisco yelled over the grinding engine. "The Nuevo, you know."

Luis snorted.

Just as Ochoa feared, fighting in the plaza, I thought, as I tightened my grip on Luis and the back of the seat in front of me. All I could hope was that nothing major had been damaged by gunfire.

Now that it was light, the sound of the guns became sporadic, just occasional bursts from the plaza and southwest toward Flores, and intermittent single shots to the north. It was impossible to know who was firing at whom.

A sudden volley crackled close to our right, fracturing the morning air, followed by a short burst of return fire. The driver swore as he swerved into the understory near the road to avoid driving into the middle of a firefight. The SUV lurched as it dropped off the path into the gully that lined the roadway. The sound of tearing, thrashing metal brought us to a full stop in the undergrowth, even though the engine was still running.

"*¿Qué es?*" the driver said as he stepped on the gas, but nothing happened. The engine whined but that was it. "*Jesús!* Esteban, get out and take a look."

His partner dropped to his knees just outside the Land Cruiser's door, peered underneath, shook his head, stood, stuck his head back in. "Might as well shut it down. Axle's broken."

~ * ~

Oh, great, I thought a half hour later as we slogged toward the rear of the acropolis, *another day of fear and misery.*

144

Since the gunfire seemed to be moving closer to our path, Francisco and Esteban looked for shelter where we wouldn't be seen. Carrying a backpack, Esteban led our little party, scouting the understory for signs of trouble; Francisco pushed Luis in his chair behind him, and I brought up the rear, hoping to hell I wasn't as exposed as I felt.

It took another hour of shoving through grass, mud, and gravel, skirting reservoirs, and circling ancient Mayan temples before we reached the edge of the palace reservoir and a pathway to the Central Acropolis. On the far side, stretching east to west, the acropolis loomed, its gray bulk spread like bat wings over its platform.

We paused to take in the massive silent form and catch our breath. Esteban wiped his forehead on his sleeve, but Francisco was eager to move.

"We can't stand here," Francisco said, "sounds like the firing is coming closer. We gotta pick up the pace."

We rounded the end of the acropolis at a trot, stopping at the bottom of its massive stairway. Careful not to jostle Luis more than necessary, the men grabbed his chair and started up the worn steps; I followed close behind to steady Luis.

It was rough going at the top as well—the acropolis was a broken field of ancient crumbling buildings, treacherous stairways, empty courtyards, patches of grass, piles of rubble. Francisco struggled to avoid the worst spots, but he had to fight to keep the chair from overturning as we headed across the open ground. Luis's knuckles were white as he gripped his bucking, kicking chair.

"We're heading for Mahler's Palace," Francisco said, guiding skills coming to the fore, even as he wrenched the chair away from a hole. "It's named after the early explorer that lived there when he was working in Tikal back in the nineteenth century." He grunted with the effort as he plowed across a patch of grass.

Luis, afraid to open his mouth, raised a hand to show he understood.

The palace was a long, low rangy building. Three squat doorways divided the facade into equal sections. We headed for the one in the middle, the one where Mahler had carved his name in the lintel, according to Francisco.

"No hope of getting back to the hotel in broad daylight," Esteban said once we were inside. "We'll have to sit tight. I've got water in the backpack, some chocolate, cereal bars. We might as well make ourselves at home," he added as he handed out the still cool bottles. "I'll try the radio again, but the reception here is poor."

It was a long day, trying to keep warm in the clammy dark space, listening to the fighting as it flared and faded across the landscape, watching the curtains of a sudden afternoon rain, waiting for the light to fade.

As the shadows lengthened outside our hiding place, the storm became low rumbles and the sound of trees in the wind. Francisco, who'd been quietly talking on and off with Esteban while Luis and I drowsed, began to stir. He pushed himself off the floor with a low groan.

"I'm stiff as hell," he said as he stretched, then checked his duty belt. "I'm going to head out, see if I can learn anything." He raked his fingers through his hair. "I've got my radio, but reception is spotty. Maybe if I'm away from the Acropolis it will improve. Don't move till I say so or it looks like I'm not coming back. Esteban will keep an eye on things here."

Esteban grunted, nodded, checking his gear as he moved toward the door to take up a place just inside the opening where he could watch the courtyard beyond.

The last we saw of Francisco, he was running low, crouched in the shadows of the courtyard wall near the acropolis stairs; then he disappeared.

~ * ~

By the time the sun began to slip toward the horizon and the wind picked up again, Francisco still hadn't returned. I was getting edgy—Luis looked like hell, and I felt almost as bad. Every bone in my body ached, and Luis was in no state to be playing commando day after day and then sitting in a cold cell fasting like a monk while a battle raged outside. We'd covered him with his blanket, and the men had put their jackets over him, too, but he looked droopy.

"How are you doing?" I asked when his eyes flickered open.

"Been better, been worse. The food and blankets have helped," he said, shifting in his chair.

I nodded. When his eyes closed again, I slipped over to Esteban, who had been squatting inside the door since Francisco left.

"Luis can't go on like this much longer," I whispered as I crouched next to him. *Nor can I*, I thought. *If we'd known we'd be taking part in survival training, we'd never left Big Grove.*

Esteban nodded. "We'll wait till it's dark. If we haven't heard anything by then, we're out of here, even if Francisco isn't back. Who knows what's happened?"

The plan made sense to me. We couldn't sit here forever.

I could smell wet jungle as I squatted next to Esteban, but there was a trace of something else in the moist air, too. Something smoky, smoldering, spicy. Copal? Burning wood? "Do you smell that?"

"Fires for sure, copal maybe," Esteban said, as what sounded like the growing noise of a celebration gusted in the door with the smoke.

"Drums, trumpets, rattles, cheering," I said. "What on earth?"

Esteban shook his head. "I'll scout it out." He slid out the door, heading toward what seemed to be a *fiesta* developing in the Great Plaza.

The faint noise grew louder as it approached the base of the acropolis, swelling in volume and complexity—cheering crowds, wild music, fierce shouts, the racket of excitement and anticipation. Nearly blotted out by the yelling and drums, I could hear a faint chant that grew increasingly insistent as it drew nearer. Thank God there was no gunfire now, just drums and shouting, and the surging roar of a crowd pouring into the Great Plaza from the north.

I didn't hear Esteban return, but he was agitated when he slipped back into our hiding spot. "*Jesús y María.* You won't believe it! It's the Nuevo; they're holding some sort of ritual, a ceremony and parade, and it looks like there are sacrificial victims being taken to Temple One. One guy is yelling in English. Something about being an American, a restaurant owner; all he knows is tacos."

"God! Tacos!"

The noise grew louder, the shouts and catcalls more excited, the screams of the victims more hysterical.

"I've gotta see what's happening," he said. "Coming?"

"Let me check on Luis, tell him what's going on. I'll be right behind you." After I straightened Luis's blankets, I took off behind Esteban. Whatever was occurring was important, a piece of the puzzle of the Nuevo, cartels, and nativist fervor, and I wanted to witness it.

By the time I settled into a hiding spot behind a crumbling wall at the front of the acropolis next to Esteban, the crowd had reached the bottom of the nearly vertical stairs of Temple 1. They parted, allowing a group of a dozen Mayan warriors in classic regalia to reach the stairs with the captives. It could have been 250 CE. Their traditional regalia was stunning: quetzal-feather and white cotton turban crowns, backracks and bustles trailing long green, blue, and red feathers of jungle birds, high jaguar hide sandals, white loincloths with wide bright waist wraps, jade earspools, necklaces, and armbands, and huge carved pectorals. The group's leader wore a mask of an unfamiliar god—red-faced, curly nosed, with a shrunken head attached to the forehead. He was too far away to see if it was Kan or to tell if the head was real.

The music and shouting grew as the ritual party mounted the steep steps, hauling the three barefoot captives in loincloths with them. At the top of the stairs, in front of the temple entrance, fires burned at either end of the platform. A small circular, flat-topped, limestone altar had been placed in the center between braziers of smoldering copal. A gray granite bowl sat to one side of the altar near the stairs.

The captives, herded into the small space inside the temple, were out of sight.

"I wonder if they know what comes next?" I asked Esteban. I was starting to feel queasy just thinking about it.

Esteban shook his head, never taking his eyes off the temple.

~ * ~

The chanting and music continued as the red and gold banners and streaks of lemon of the setting sun faded to luminous turquoise as the planet Venus, the Mayan god of war and marker of sacrifice, soared into the heavens over the temple's ruined roof comb, silhouetted by the fading light. As the planet reached its highest position, one of the captives was dragged from the temple, head hanging, legs trailing behind him.

"Looks like he's been drugged," Esteban whispered.

I nodded in agreement. *Or maybe he's given up*, I thought, *the way a mouse goes limp in the teeth of a cat.*

In the flickering torch light, the guards pulled the man backward spread-eagled over the altar's flat surface, arms and legs held firmly to stretch his chest over the center of the stone. The masked priest, still chanting, raised a flat black obsidian blade over his head then plunged it into the man's chest and pulled downward, opening a wound the size of an open hand.

"He's done that before," Esteban said, his knuckles white as he gripped the stone wall in front of him.

I gasped. This was more hideous than I'd imagined, and there was nothing we could do to stop it.

With one sure motion, the priest reached into the cavity, pulled out the man's pulsing heart, raised it high for the crowds to see, and then he threw it dripping into the nearby bowl. The crowd howled as

the assistant priests hurled the lifeless body down the temple stairs—
it cartwheeled, slid, bounced, a pale ragdoll splattering the steps with
blood. The second man, also seemingly drugged, was brought
forward, and the ritual was repeated—his heart ripped out, raised on
high, thrown into the bowl. His body, too, was hurled down the
stairs, leaving a dark trail on the steep gray stones.

I was feeling worse than sick, but I couldn't look away. It was
like a horrible accident; I had to see it through to the end.

The third man, the apparent leader, the man who claimed to
make tacos, was last. He was dragged to the altar as the chanting
grew and the crowds' frenzied shouts increased. "Despoiler! Sinaloa
demon. Kill him!"

This guy didn't seem as incapacitated as the first two. He
struggled, screaming, trying to wrench away from the men holding
him.

Just as the priest raised his blade over the final victim, Francisco
slipped into our hiding place. "*Jesús*," he said as the blade descended
and the last captive's heart was torn out. "We've got to get out of
here now, while everyone is revved up over the ritual. If we wait,
we're screwed."

We bolted for Mahler's Palace to retrieve Luis, the noise of the
crowd obscuring the sounds of our scrambling departure.

~ * ~

Even though it was nearly completely dark once we got off the
acropolis, the trip back to headquarters was easier than our flight to
reach it in the first place. For one thing, we hit a pathway maintained
by the Forest Service as soon as we left the building, and for another,
we knew where the Nuevo were and what they were doing. Their
sacrifices and ceremonies would keep them tied up for hours. That
didn't mean we could dawdle; it just meant we weren't jumpy as hell
every time a howler called from the nearby trees.

Once we were out of sight from the Great Plaza, Francisco
dropped back to try his radio again. The reception, which he reported

had been difficult earlier, must have cleared; I could hear him muttering into it. He caught up, looking relieved.

"Here's the plan. Captain Ríos is sending men to meet us, and he wants you two where we can keep an eye on you after we arrive. You're going to headquarters till he finds a place for you to stay. The inn is impossible. It's like a sieve." Francisco said.

"Just a little longer," I said to Luis as I tucked his blanket into place. "We're almost there." *I hope.*

Luis nodded.

~ * ~

By the time we reached the park headquarters, a group had assembled on the veranda. Zoila darted across the grass and launched herself at Luis; Pat and Bill rushed toward me. For the first time in days, I felt safe as they swept me into their arms. Captain Ríos, Dr. Gomez, Jaime, and Ochoa watched from the porch steps, and after we pulled ourselves together, they hauled us into the building in a flurry of greetings.

Dr. Gomez herded Luis and Zoila into an office across the hall from the briefing room as soon as we were inside. "Time for a checkup," she said as she closed the door.

Who knows what state he's in, I thought, feeling guilty. *He's been through something close to hell, and it all started with a walk to clear our heads. What was I thinking?*

Twenty minutes later, Luis reappeared with a bandage on his cheek, looking tired but giving a thumbs up as Zoila maneuvered his wheelchair toward a table near the front of the briefing room. Then it was my turn.

"You and Luis," Dr. Gomez greeted me. "Two of the oldest people here, and you act like you're in the Special Forces. Gun battles. Hand-to-hand combat. Hiding in the jungle for hours on end." She shook her head in disbelief.

I didn't know what to say. It wasn't like we'd done it on purpose.

"Anything particular bothering you?" Dr. Gomez asked as she closed the door.

"No," I said, though flickering images of me beating the guy with a *mano* had been appearing at odd moments. I didn't tell her that, and I didn't tell her about turning homicidal in the first place. It wasn't like me at all. And then there were the sacrifices. I could still see the flashing blade as it descended to slice open the men's chests.

By the time she had disinfected the scrape on my forehead and checked my vitals, Dr. Gomez was satisfied that I was just stiff, tired, and hungry; she let me join the group in the briefing room.

~ * ~

"Ríos wants us out of here as soon as possible," Bill said as soon as I joined the table where he was having coffee with Luis, Zoila, and Pat. "The park's a battleground, and as we've learned, the hotel isn't safe. The Nuevo've got people everywhere, including the inn's staff.

"Ochoa's mother-in-law has a farm just outside Santa Elena. She lives with her youngest daughter and son-in-law, so she has plenty of room except on the holidays when the other kids come home. Pat, Ann, you and Zoila and Luis will stay with her. I'll be live-in security. Jaime and Ochoa will arrange for additional guards. Once we're through with coffee, we are getting you out while it's still dark."

"Wasn't Santa Elena where Los Zetas held Enrique?" I asked, envisioning a leap from the frying pan into the fire.

"Yeah, but Ochoa thinks it'll be okay. His mother-in-law doesn't have close neighbors. Besides, nobody is going to think a little old indigenous lady and her family, people who have lived there forever, would be harboring fugitives."

"If Miguel thinks it will work, it probably will," I said. "But I want to know what the hell is going on."

"It's complicated. Captain Ríos is planning an all-out assault on the cartels with the help of the military. And, since the Nuevo have blossomed into a full-fledged armed insurrectionist group with the help of Los Zetas, they'll have to be eradicated as well, or at least driven out of the Petén. The military is sending the *Kaibiles*—specialty forces who are trained in jungle warfare—to clear the perimeter of the park, as well as mop up inside. Then they'll move into the rest of the Petén."

"This has gotten too big for the Tikal Park Rangers to handle, and the *Kaibiles* are the only force small and nimble enough to do the job," Ochoa said as he took the seat across from Bill. "The military would be like using a tank battalion to kill ants."

"*Jesús y María!* The *Kaibiles*," Luis said. "They like to call themselves a killing machine. *Jesús.*"

"I know it sounds like letting jaguars into the spider monkey enclosure, but let me explain Ríos's thinking," Ochoa said. "*Kaibiles* aren't going to tear the park apart like the army: They work in squads of nine. They don't use heavy weapons. The buildings and the site itself won't suffer the same damage as if the army moved through. Think of what has happened in the Middle East...all those priceless World Heritage sites damaged or destroyed. Ríos wants to avoid that, even if that means he has to bring in Special Forces. Besides, who else is there?" Ochoa paused for a moment and then answered his own question. "Nobody."

"What about the Nuevo?" I asked.

"The Nuevo are a whole other story," Ochoa said. "During the action at the Bajo, four were eliminated and a dozen captured; we got the museum curator and two lieutenants, including the one Ann took out. They're in custody in Guatemala City."

"How's the guy I clubbed?"

"Unconscious, under guard in the hospital. He isn't going to be out any time soon."

At least he isn't dead. I couldn't have stood that.

"Kan's disappeared, though," Ochoa continued, stirring more sugar into his coffee. "Vanished. No surprise after the sacrifices you witnessed. He probably feels he needs to lie low till the excitement dies down. Human sacrifices! If we catch up with him—

"The rest of the picture is fluid as well." Ochoa stopped to sip his coffee. "As far as we know, Los Zetas were originally based in the Lacandon Reserve. We knew they had a foothold there, but it turns out it's more than that: it's a military base. Once they started talking, according to the Nuevo, their former allies Los Zetas or Nortes, as they call themselves now, planned to destroy the Sinaloas, then take over—rebuild the shipping complex in the Maya Gold factory, over the border in Mexico; turn the Lacandon into a drug processing center; and control the Petén drug traffic to the States."

"Where does that leave the Nuevo?" Bill asked.

"They have other ideas. Now the Sinaloas are out of the picture, they want to drive out Los Zetas, too, since they aren't Maya, and they're defiling the Mayan heartland with drugs."

"But where's Kan?" Luis asked.

"No idea. It's not likely anyone is going to rat him out, either. He's got fanatical people around him, determined to create a new kingdom.

"There's talk he's moving further into the jungle till things blow over. Find a place to regroup, plan another campaign, this time against Los Zetas."

"And, don't forget, he isn't done with us either," Bill added. "He needs the vulture pectoral to cement his position as lord. That means Luis and Ann are still on the hot seat."

Ochoa nodded in agreement. "Kan's taking this lord business seriously; people are saying that he *was* the one who sacrificed those men."

"Oh, God," Pat said. "Time's doubled back on itself. Heart excisions on Temple One. Drug wars. *Kaibiles*. The Vulture Lord. It seems to have started with Ruston and his stele—" She shook her head.

I'd been watching Luis. Tired or not, he was up to something. He was looking elsewhere, his eyes distant, as if he were peering over the far edge of time, and he was talking softly to someone, someone I couldn't see.

Santa Elena, Guatemala

Two hours later, as we settled into Esperanza's mother's kitchen, a small building at the back of the farm compound, the storm, which had been threatening since sundown, finally broke. Thunder shook the scattered farm buildings, driving the chickens squawking into their coop, or under building overhangs and the dog under the porch. Raindrops as big as pullet eggs hammered the tin roofs at the same time the wind tried to tear the corrugated metal off. Through the open kitchen door, lightning strobed as it cut the sky into jagged fragments, silhouetting the farmstead with fierce light. The air smelled of ozone, mud, rain. The farmyard ran with water.

"It's *Hurakan*," Zoila said with satisfaction. "Nobody is going to be sneaking around tonight with that Ancient on the prowl. We can sleep without worry."

~ * ~

The next morning, by the time the great red disk of the sun pushed over the horizon, dissipating the thick morning mist and throwing distant neighbors' roosters into increasing frenzies of competition, *Hurakan* was gone.

I'd been beyond tired when I lay down; this morning I felt worse, if that was possible. Everything hurt. My back. My head. The scrapes and bruises that seemingly appeared in the night. Between the sizzling storm and fragmentary nightmares of sacrifice and dismemberment and near homicide, I'd only snatched a few minutes of rest at a time.

Then there was the yet unexamined sense of who I am nibbling at the edges my consciousness. Mild-mannered archivist? Retired professor? Killer? I groaned as I sat up.

"What time is it?" Pat asked, her voice muzzy with sleep.

"I don't know. My watch stopped sometime in the Bajo, but whatever time it is, *señora* has been up for hours, and Bill's long gone," I said, inspecting the haphazard pile of garments next to my bed.

Pat sighed as she wrapped herself in her blanket and lowered her legs over the edge of her mattress. "I'm afraid the real trick this morning is going to be getting back in my filthy clothes. I don't think I've had anything clean in days."

I gave her the beady eye. "Put yourself in *my* place," I said as I pulled on my muddy cotton pants. "At least you didn't spend days hiking in the jungle, on top of everything else."

"Still," Pat said, slipping into her slacks, "I smell like something in the zoo."

"A mandrill, maybe," I said, smelling myself as I dragged on my crusty shirt.

"Thanks a lot. Female, I hope."

"Of course," I said, as I stabbed my feet into my sandals, thinking of the brightly colored, notably smelly males. "What else?"

Pat stuck out her tongue.

~ * ~

The mud between the several farm's structures was inlayed with silver pools and braided with still trickling runnels from last night's pounding rain. Small rocks formed islands in the twisting patterns left by the water; tiny rivulets sparkled in the sun.

Half a dozen slightly disheveled brown chickens, their feathers not yet smoothed after a night in the rafters, pecked at corn scattered near the kitchen porch. The scent of wood smoke and coffee mingled in the still cool damp morning air.

Once we left the comfort of our room in a small building near the front gate, the swampy expanse to the kitchen made conversation difficult.

I picked my way through the mire. "We're going to have to get everyone together. Talk about what comes next, what we're going to do about the pectoral, find out when the airport reopens and flights resume." I said as I tried to balance on a small flat rock surrounded by water.

"Logistics, you mean," Pat said, pulling her sandaled foot out of the mud.

"Yes, but first, coffee."

We left our shoes on the kitchen porch near the dog who was basking contentedly in the thin morning sun after his night under the porch. Inside the dim space, breakfast had been laid on the table near the hearth. A fire hissed and popped, as the youngest of Esperanza's sisters plied us with coffee and rolls. Outside the building, the chickens fretted over the remaining corn, but otherwise the meal was quiet. I sipped my coffee, too tired to chat. Pat wasn't doing much better.

Suddenly, the drowsing dog lunged to his feet, barking wildly; the chickens squawked as they fled across the yard.

"It's all right. Good boy. Remember me? I'm a friend," Bill said as he stepped onto the porch. The dog, after he assured himself that he'd met Bill before, settled again in his patch of sun with a soft snort.

"I've got some news," Bill called through the door. He dropped his clotted boots near a bench piled with rusty farm implements and entered the room. "I took off before sunrise to patrol the perimeter of the farm and check in at headquarters." He slid into a chair next to me.

"Coffee? Rolls?" Esperanza's sister asked.

"Both, please," Bill said, as he accepted a steaming mug.

"What's happening?" I asked, too impatient to wait for him to eat.

"Your bags have been moved from the inn to headquarters," Bill said, taking a sip of coffee. "They'll be shipped home when the airport opens. If we bring them here, it will lead anyone who is interested in your whereabouts right to your door.

"According to the night officer, Ríos feels if things go according to plan, the Flores airport should open on Monday. If it's quiet we probably can get out Tuesday." Bill took a roll from the *servietta*-lined basket.

"But between now and then, things are going to be intense. The *Kaibiles* arrived last night and are deploying inside and outside the park. Los Zetas seem to have pulled back into the Lacandon, and there's no sign of the Nuevo. It's early days, though. Someone is bound to spot them. They aren't invisible.

"There's another tricky part, though. The pectoral. We either go for it now before something else happens, or we leave it where it is and hope no one discovers it. Oh, and something else, one side of the reservoir collapsed from all this rain. Looks like there might be an opening behind the rubble."

"Huh," Luis said as Zoila pushed his chair through the doorway. "We go for the pendant."

Twenty-six

Tikal National Park, Guatemala

The morning following the storm, the sun turned the mist to floating tissues of gold as it rose slowly above the miles of jungle that stretched in all directions. In the woodsman's shack hidden deep below the jungle canopy, Kan woke slowly, stiff, unfocused.

The night had been broken with difficult dreams—his grandfather's stories of long ago: how Great-grandmother had been taken as a bride to a flat land where corn grew in searing summers and winter's cold locked the dried brown stubble in ice as the sun grew feeble and pale; how Great-grandmother's husband ignored her loneliness; how she escaped with her children and return to Flores. She died a short time later, grandfather would say, but at least we children were here.

There was another story his grandfather told, too, an older one from a more distant cycle of time, of a young man named K'in Kan, a Tikal lord's son, and his journey to the distant coast to a city where he found a bride and brought her home.

Like Great-grandmother, Grandfather said, the woman grew sad in the young lord's city. She, too, pined for a place where she could raise her children away from the foreign town where people laughed at her accent and made fun of her unfamiliar ways.

One night, the lord, moved by his wife's endless misery, led his young family away from the city of stone temples, endless ceremonies, strict rules, stucco plazas, and sprawling buildings to begin life deep in the jungle with a small group of companions similarly eager to build a world free from the restrictions of Tikal.

Now, time had replayed itself again. Kan, too, had found a partner from another world, but she had been taken by the enemy, and he would never see her again—her hair like golden sparks, her eyes the color of birds' eggs, her skin as pale as moonlight.

Kan shifted on his pallet in the small building in the Nuevo compound, considering time's fierce repetitions. He wanted the vulture pectoral with all his being, but tonight as Hurakan raged, he wanted the woman with bright hair more, and he swore he would kill the little Mayan man who was responsible for his loss.

As he lay, eyes closed, listening to Hurakan recede to the north, he replayed his frantic escape from the farm house, his flight through the jungle night, and the hasty bivouac here, wherever the hell here was, till he could figure out what next. He had to take stock, call in more fighters, find a camp where it would be safe to regroup, and most of all, finally snatch the jade vulture from the hands of that stringy *gringa* and the smug little Mayan prick in a wheelchair. Only then would he be the lord of the Petén with no questions asked, only then could he reign over Tikal as he was destined to do both by blood and by right.

Kan pushed himself to his feet, knotting his tangled hair in a bun on top of his head as he shoved aside the ragged curtain into the next room. The dozen men sprawled on the floor were only beginning to stir, their guns still stacked out of the way against the water-stained walls. Other Nuevo could be seen through the door, standing guard outside the opening, or watching the jungle from the edges of the clearing.

"Get up," Kan said, savagely kicking the closest man's foot. "We have work, much work, to do. And we don't have time."

The men groaned.

"Skip the coffee," Kan ordered as he stepped into the mass of sleepy Nuevos. "I want people down at the park office watching Ochoa *now*. He's been in the middle of this thing since the beginning. He's friendly with the Americans; he was their guide, and he's pulled his wife into it, too. She was dragging that nosy *gringa* around Flores not that long ago. I even talked with them down by the boats—"

He kicked a man in the posterior who was too slow to rise.

Twenty-seven

Santa Elena, Guatemala

Luis started talking as soon as he got inside the kitchen. "During the last twenty-four hours, I've had lightning under my skin—my back, my front, my sides—and during the rainstorm last night, Hurakan sent me a sign in the lightning as well.

"It's clear. We've got to wrest Tikal from all these lunatics—cartels, nativist groups, whomever. And we got to keep the Vulture Lord jade out of the hands of idiots, otherwise there will be no end to killings like Ruston's, no end to kidnappings like Polop's, no end to public sacrifices, no end to stupid plans to reestablish a world gone for a thousand years.

"The *Kaibiles* will take care of Los Zetas, but the jade is our problem and ours alone."

Despite the effort to talk, Luis continued. "It seems to me we have three things to accomplish: We've got to retrieve the pectoral. We've got to deposit it where it belongs. Then we've got to get the hell out of here."

The talk of returning the pectoral made me wonder. "So," I said, "all we know about the pectoral is that it was likely connected to the original K'in Kan during the period when Tikal was just a village. Who does it belong to now? We can't go back in time—"

Luis gave me one of those looks, as if he could see through me into a place I couldn't comprehend. It gave me the willies.

"All these storms so early in the year, the battles, the murders, are signs that something is wrong. There's a tear in the fabric of time, and nothing, *nothing*, will go back to normal until its pattern is reestablished. One cycle has bled into another; unfinished business from long ago has erupted into our lives.

"Ann, you know where the pectoral is, and I can guess where the portal into that earlier world might be. You have to get the pectoral. Then we return to the reservoir behind Temple One.

"We have to be like *las hormigas*, the ants, when their nest is kicked. We have to scatter, scatter in daylight when people don't expect us to move, and each of us do something to achieve our goals. If we just sit here—"

Luis's speech gave me a boost. He was right. The only hope was to return this place to the state it was in before Ruston fell over that damned stele. Then we could go home.

"Makes sense," Bill said, "Your story about the *hormigas* got me thinking—"

By the time we finished breakfast, we had a plan.

~ * ~

As soon as we finished our coffee, Pat and I went back to our room to prepare for Operation *Hormigas*, as we called it. We had to change for our parts in the action—Pat into a touristy outfit that Esperanza provided to avoid being recognized as she bought tickets, and me into something sturdy for caving that Ochoa had dug up— boots, jeans, long sleeved shirt. I packed the Forest Service backpack with caving essentials—flashlight, cereal bars, plastic bags, and the spare batteries Bill had handed out at breakfast.

"I don't know about this caving business," I said as I stuffed a handful of Ziploc bags into my pack. "I'm so claustrophobic I can hardly stand a crowded elevator, never mind a cave with who knows what inside."

Pat nodded in sympathy. "You'll do all right. With everything on your mind—transporting Luis, delivering the pectoral where it needs to go—"

"And that's another thing. All my life I've tried to preserve the past—save documents, conserve photos, protect historical objects—and now I'm supposed to help Luis toss a priceless piece of ancient Mayan heritage into a presumably bottomless hole somewhere under Tikal. If the Guatemalan government knew, they'd go nuts; the archaeologists would kill us."

Pat grunted as she pulled on elastic waist white pants under a bright flowered shirt.

"How do I look? Do you think the bad guys will recognize me?" she asked, clipping on a large pair of gold hoop earrings and slipping a white plastic bracelet over her wrist. "Do I look like an ordinary tourist buying tickets to the States?" She struck a pose.

"Perfect. If I didn't know better, I would think you were the real thing."

"Thanks, I guess," Pat said. "At least it's a compliment for Esperanza's costuming abilities."

~ * ~

Later that morning, when the sun had become hot iron on bare skin, inside the open gate of her mother's yard, Esperanza and her older brother helped Pat into the brother's pickup. Heading for the airport, the truck turned toward Santa Elena when they reached the main road. Half an hour later Zoila, dressed in *traje*, traditional dress, and Luis, wearing a baseball cap pulled over his eyes and a poncho that reached his ankles, left the farmyard in a truck driven by Esperanza's youngest brother.

An hour after the second truck's departure, Ochoa pulled into the farmyard. He carried a box labeled *sopa* to the kitchen and deposited it on the shelves to the right of the hearth. When he left a few minutes later, Bill and I, dressed as backpackers, had crawled under a tarp in the back of his Land Cruiser on top of the heaps of gear that Ochoa had loaded from the ranger supply closet earlier that morning—coiled ropes, climbing harnesses, helmets with head lamps, flashlights, coveralls, underwear, knee pads, gloves, water bottles, a carefully packed plastic sled, the kind EMTs use to extract the injured from rough places, and a collapsible barebones wheelchair, just in case. I squirmed into the heap, trying to make myself comfortable.

We turned toward Tikal on the main road, following the route Zoila and Luis had taken earlier.

~ * ~

When Ochoa drove into the parking lot behind park headquarters, Jaime, talking with a guard at the rear of the museum next door, waved him over. Ochoa parked as close as possible to the men, leaving the door open as he slid out of SUV.

"*Buenos días*," Ochoa said as he rounded the rear of the Toyota.

"*Buenos*," Jaime said as Ochoa reached him. "Listen to this—"

The men talked for several minutes, Jaime waving his arms for emphasis, the guard adding comments at intervals, Ochoa listening quietly.

Thunder growled in the distance, startling parrots in the nearby trees into squawking flight, and spider monkeys into flurries of complaints as Ochoa and Jaime finally turned toward headquarters, stopping first to straighten the tarp in the back of the Land Cruiser, talking as they did so. Satisfied, the two men turned toward the park office.

Ten minutes later, Bill and I slipped from under the tarp, exited the SUV, and headed for the museum, our baseball caps pulled low. The waiting museum guard opened the rear door as soon as we reached it, locking it behind us.

The museum's air was musty, smelling of ancient objects and long dead dreams, as if the spirits of Tikal rose with the motes drifting from the display cases. Its tomb-like atmosphere was increased by its darkness; the shadows dispelled only under two small skylights.

Bill was behind me scanning the blackness for movement, for anything out of place, as I headed for the case where I'd hidden the pectoral. The display shelves where I'd put the vulture seemed especially murky, the orange and cream pots with delicate painted images of Mayan royalty mere dim shapes in the gloom.

I switched on my Maglite, sweeping its thin beam across the vessels on the bottom shelf to make certain nothing had changed, and then I aimed it under a cylindrical tripod vessel near the middle of the case. The vulture pectoral glowed bright green in the slender shaft of light, like a slice of avocado between the pot's flat rectangular legs.

By the time we left the museum a few minutes later, as an afternoon storm blew in over Tikal, the pectoral was safely tucked in a woven purse pinned inside my bra.

Twenty-eight

Tikal National Park, Guatemala

Late afternoon, as the storm raced over the tops of the ancient temples, Kan's luck changed. One of the men watching park headquarters returned with news.

"It was like a *fiesta*. First, two older Maya and a little boy and a pony showed up behind the museum and stopped under that big ceiba tree. The couple sat down on that beat up old bench that's been there forever like they were waiting for a bus; the boy and pony left.

"Then Ochoa pulled into the lot. He parked next to the museum's back door where Jaime and the guard were smoking. The three of them talked for five minutes or so; then Jaime and Ochoa headed toward the Tikal Park Rangers' office, and the guard finished his cigarette."

Kan waved a hand as if to hurry him along. "Skip the details, get to the good part."

"This *is* the good part, as soon as Ochoa and Jaime went into headquarters, two *gringos* got out of the Land Cruiser. I didn't see them when Ochoa pulled in; they must have been hiding in the cargo area. They headed straight for the rear of the museum; the guard knew they were coming...he had the door open before they reached it.

"Ten, maybe fifteen, minutes later the *gringos* came out, joined the folks under the tree. Then Ochoa and Jaime showed up again."

"Did they have the jade?"

"I didn't see it, but it is small, isn't it? Ochoa helped the old couple into his SUV; Jaime took charge of the rest of the party. It looks like they're all going toward the Central Plaza. Ochoa's in the lead. A second Land Cruiser followed right behind them."

"*Jesús*! What the hell is happening and where are they headed with a storm coming? And what's the story with the pony?" Kan paced for a moment, making a decision. "Take some guys; follow them. I'll be behind you."

Twenty-nine

Tikal National Park, Guatemala

It was *Hurakan* again, no doubt of it. The ground shook with each bolt of lightning and the peal of thunder that followed, chasing the last parrots out of the trees near the Central Plaza and deep into the jungle for shelter. It was as if *Hurakan* was declaring his displeasure with what was going on in Tikal.

There were ponchos in the back of the SUV, and as the storm drew closer, we put them on. No sense in being drenched before we even began our descent into the reservoir behind Temple I.

When we reached the basin—the same one Luis and I had fallen into a few days earlier—it had begun to sprinkle. It became clear that not only had the previous rains left additional water in the bottom, but the torrent had also caused the bank to fall away in several places, turning the depression's sides into viscous mud that slumped toward the water. On the far side of the reservoir, under a collapsed portion of rim, a recently exposed heap of large boulders had tumbled into the water below.

"One of the rangers checked that pile yesterday," Ochoa said clipping on his headlamp and slipping a lanyard with an extra flashlight around his neck. "There is an opening behind it. He didn't go very far, just flashed a light around, but it looks like there might be a passage that leads toward the Central Plaza. According to Luis, that's where we are headed."

Luis nodded.

"I'll go first," Ochoa said as he tucked his sidearm and holster in his pack and headed for the basin's edge. "I'll check for a path to the cave. We need something that Luis can use and that doesn't involve landing on the pile of boulders."

He rappelled down the west side of the reservoir, landing on a shelf of limestone protruding from the wall twenty feet below; then he inched his way toward the cave just as it began to pour.

~ * ~

By the time Ochoa returned to the outcrop below, the deluge had lessened, and Bill and Jaime had outfitted and harnessed the rest of us in preparation for our descent.

"It looks like this ledge will work," Ochoa called up. "It's wide enough for Luis's walker if we're careful."

Transporting Luis had required planning. His walker made sense on the outcrop, but inside the cave, who knew? He couldn't get far with his paralyzed leg, walker or no walker. Ochoa had a rescue sled from the emergency supply closet at headquarters. The two rangers in the second vehicle would be able to carry Luis without trouble once we entered the cave.

It had been weird getting into the caving gear in a jungle in the rain. It was hard to squirm into a jumpsuit under a poncho, and for another thing, it fit like diving gear. The garment was clearly meant for a smaller person; the arms and legs were six inches too short, and I could barely pull up the front zipper. My only consolation was Bill, who'd ditched his poncho, looked as funny as I felt, bulging out of his too tight garment as if it were something he'd borrowed from a child.

Dressing Luis in his outfit had taken two of us: me to hold the clothes as his limbs were slipped in and Zoila to work his paralyzed leg and arm first into long underwear—Luis was always cold—then coveralls. We added a polypropylene poncho as the final layer for added warmth. *"At least your outfit is the right size,"* I said as I settled the poncho around his legs. "It could be worse; it could fit like mine."

"Bill, you come next, then Ann, then Luis. The three of us can grab Luis when he lands," Ochoa shouted from below.

Bill began to lower himself.

"Another day in Special Forces training," I muttered under my breath as I slipped my flashlight's cord around my neck. "I can hardly wait."

I clipped onto the rope and followed Bill over the edge. I could feel the vulture pectoral pressing against my chest as I began my descent. *I still ache from our escape from the Nuevo,* I thought as I was lowered down. *When I get home, nothing is going to lure me into anything more strenuous then my daily walk. Nothing.*

I dropped down the wall to the rim of limestone, trying not to think of Ruston, or Kan, or the water and snakes below as I swung out from the reservoir's face and pawed at the narrow ledge to gain footing.

Jaime lowered Luis next. We grabbed him when he landed and pushed him into his walker to keep him upright. I gripped Luis's belt from behind; Bill stood in front of him keeping the aluminum frame steady. Then Bill walked backward as Luis inched along the ledge's rough surface toward the rocks while Ochoa led the way. Zoila and Jaime followed Luis down the side, and the other two rangers brought up the rear: Esteban with the sled in its yellow carrier bag, and Francisco with a backpack of extra supplies.

The cave opening was big enough for us to stand; it breathed out that cold cave smell of mold, water, guano, and air trapped underground for years.

"This is it," Ochoa said as he flashed his light around so we could get our bearings. "Not much room here, but it may open up further along. Let's get Luis onto the sled. Esteban and Francisco follow me with Luis. Then Ann and Zoila. Bill, you follow the women. Jaime, come with me."

We loaded Luis into his rescue sled, strapped him in under a blanket, and settled him into the foam lining of the hard yellow shell. Esteban and Francisco took the straps at either end.

Then Ochoa stepped off. "If you need anything or see something of interest, let the rest of us know."

The inky darkness and the crushing weight of the tons of earth above my head made it hard to breathe, as if the ceiling were pressing down, flattening me with its awful weight. The only thing that kept me from bolting was Bill blocking the tunnel behind me.

We switched on our headlamps as we followed Ochoa, our lights thin sabers of illumination in the thick dark.

~ * ~

Half an hour into our hike, the downward slanting passage suddenly opened into a gallery that must have been seventy meters in diameter; its soaring ceiling disappeared into the damp gloom. Curtains of brown stained minerals undulated down the cave walls and across the floor on the far side of the chamber; crystals twinkled like tiny stars on the stalagmites and stalactites that covered the floor and ceiling. On the far side of the space, a dark opening was barely visible between sheets of ocher drapery flowstone.

Ochoa's sweeping flashlight stopped at the gap. A man-made partition partially blocked its lower half from view.

"A wall! And this chamber probably hasn't been visited by people for a thousand years," Ochoa whispered in awe. He fumbled in his pack for his camera. "That means the partition has been here for a millennium at least! Amazing!" He shook his head in disbelief and moved toward the construction for a closer view.

I gasped. Suddenly Luis's ancestors felt close, as if they were waiting for us somewhere further into the cave just as they had waited for worshipers since Tikal had begun.

"This has to be it," Luis said. He squirmed on the sled for a better view. "The portal has to be somewhere beyond. I mean, look at it! The wall was clearly meant to limit access to what lay beyond, to indicate a boundary, or maybe to serve as an entrance to an inner sanctum where water and fertility can enter our world, where men and gods can mingle."

For the first time since we'd begun the Ruston–vulture pectoral adventure, Luis looked happy.

~ * ~

The pause in the gallery was a welcome break from creeping like a beetle in the entry tunnel. I could stand upright without worrying about hitting my head, and the level floor made it easier to keep my balance. The chance to be in an open space and the sense we were on the right track also lightened my mood.

"How are you doing?" I asked Luis as I stretched my tired muscles.

"Okay," he said. "But I hate being carried."

I nodded in sympathy. "It must be rough. Have some water. No way are you going to be able to drink when we start up again."

"Good idea," Ochoa said. He put his camera into its waterproof bag and pulled out a water bottle. "Everyone, have water or snacks. We're going to push on for another hour or until we see what Luis's ancestors have in mind."

We began moving again a few minutes later and headed around what proved to be a half wall that partially covered the opening on the far side of the gallery. Luis swayed like a baby camel in a sling between the rangers; Zoila and I followed behind them.

By the time Ochoa called the next halt, I'd begun to feel like time was repeating itself, or maybe it was just unspooling like thread as we crept through the tunnel behind the first chamber's opening. The passage was clear except for a few breakdowns or heaps of fallen ceilings, but it was smaller than the first one, forcing me to remain partially crouched most of the time and to duck repeatedly to avoid low protruding rocks.

Not only was my back killing me, but forty-five minutes in the narrow walkway had just about made me nuts. I'd had an MRI years ago that had left me crazy with nerves by the time I was through; it was nothing compared to the claustrophobia that had gripped me by the throat ever since we left the first gallery.

You are all right, I repeated over and over as I trudged behind Esteban's muscular back. *Breathe slowly through your mouth and unclench your hands.* If relaxation techniques work in the dentist's office, they should work here.

"I hear water dripping up ahead," Ochoa called from the front of our party. "Let's break a minute. Get ready for the final push. I think we're almost there."

A small scrabbling noise somewhere in the dark tunnel caught my attention, raising the hairs on the back of my neck.

"Bill, do you hear that?" I whispered before we began moving again. "Someone's fooling around behind us. It can't be rats this far underground. Bats? And I swear I heard someone sneeze."

Bill turned his head the way we had come. Another sneeze. This time muffled.

"Jesus! Someone *is* there—someone with mold allergies, I'll bet. I gotta tell Ochoa," Bill said as he began working his way toward the front of the group.

Bill was back in a few minutes. "Ochoa said just keep going. Nothing we can do about being followed now. The passage is too narrow. Once we leave the tunnel, we can figure something out. Jaime and I will ride shotgun, though," he added just as Jaime passed us on the way to the rear. "You and Zoila stay behind Luis and the guys."

~ * ~

The next gallery appeared as if conjured. Our headlamps' slender beams probed the darkness, illuminating minerals that glittered on the walls; stalagmites and stalactites, luminous as alabaster, glowing as if lit from within.

We clustered together a few feet beyond the passage, stunned; the sacred space opened before us like a vast stone flower.

"My God!" I took a shuddering breath and stood in awe.

A circular raised platform with six-foot high walls of fitted blocks stood in the middle of the splendor. Its stairway faced the passageway from which we'd come. A spillway ran down an incline next to the steps, directing a stream of water toward a small lined course that rounded the base of the structure and then turned toward the back of the gallery, where it disappeared into a carefully constructed opening in the wall.

"The heart of the holy place! The portal! The spot where ancestors and humans meet and fertility enters the world. I'm sure of it. I can feel it in my blood." Luis struggled to get a better view from the litter.

"I hate to break in," Ochoa finally said after we had a few moments to try to take in the spectacular gallery, "but we can't enjoy this now. We've got to figure out what to do about the company behind us, find out if they're still there. I haven't heard anything for a while. Has anyone else?"

I hadn't heard anything either but with our scuffing boots, heavy breathing, and scraping, who would?

We paused, holding our breaths, straining to listen; we heard nothing but water splashing somewhere ahead.

"I've been thinking," Bill whispered after a few silent minutes. "Let me know if this makes sense. We have to have guards watching people's backs while some of us try to locate the portal. Then we've got to get Luis where he can offer the pectoral to the ancestors. And finally, we've all got to get the hell out. What if Jaime and I take over door duty? That means the rest of you can look around without worrying."

"Sounds reasonable. Let's get Luis settled somewhere before we split up," Ochoa said. "Back there looks good." He waved toward a breakdown in the rear corner of the gallery that was barely visible in the narrow beam from his headlamp.

"He'll be safe if something goes wrong, and we can explore without dragging him around for no purpose. We'll get him once we think we've found what we are looking for."

"We're on it," Esteban said as he and Francisco grabbed the sled handles and hustled toward the rock pile.

"I'm going with Luis," Zoila said, following the men into the inky darkness.

"Now, the door guards. Someone needs to be behind that big stalagmite near the opening; Jaime, can you tackle it? Maybe Bill behind that breakdown on the other side of the pathway further in?" Ochoa asked as he began to sort things out.

Bill nodded as he pulled his Sig Sauer out of his backpack and slipped in a magazine. "We have to be cautious. We don't know who is back there. It may not be Kan and his buddies, after all. Whoever it is may not be a problem."

Jaime grunted. "If we can find out who they are and stop any action at the door—" Jaime trailed off as he pulled his Glock from its holster and began to check it over. "There can't be that many of them. There wasn't that much noise, and the tunnel is so narrow, there couldn't be more than a handful. Besides, the Nuevo can't have that much caving equipment."

"We've got to be careful we don't form a two-sided firing squad."

Jaime grunted again.

Ochoa nodded. "Esteban, Francisco, and I will look for the portal. Ann, do you want to join us or go with Zoila and Luis?"

I hesitated for a minute. Explore the cave, or look out for my friends? Friends won over my usual insatiable curiosity. I turned to follow Zoila into the cold dark.

"Wait a minute, Ann. Ever used a gun?" Ochoa asked before I had taken a step.

"I've done some target practice with Bill," I said. "I'm okay, but not great."

"Here," Ochoa, handing me a holstered Glock from his pack. "It's loaded and ready to go. If worse comes to worse, don't be afraid to use it."

"She's not bad," Bill's voice came from somewhere in the dark to the left of the entry. "She'll do all right."

I headed after Zoila, the holster tucked in my pack.

My trip across the cave took more time than I had imagined. The floor's several heaps of breakdowns caused me to scramble and swerve, and artifacts from countless ceremonies made the going rougher than if the Maya hadn't been here first. By the time I slid down into Luis and Zoila's hiding place, I'd stubbed my toe a couple of times and turned my ankle.

"I don't know what's going on by the entry, but you and Luis should stay hunkered down till we figure things out. If something happens to me, Zoila, you'll have to take the sled by yourself. You'll do okay. I'm going to stand guard up behind the breakdown." I gestured toward the pile of rocks that sheltered us from the rest of the cave. "I'll let you know what's happening."

I scrabbled my way up the incline to the heap of collapsed ceiling. Just before I flicked off my headlamp, I took a quick look around to orient myself. On the back of the platform was another stairway, not as wide as the one facing the tunnel, but wide enough for two or three people to use at once.

Maybe the stairway leads to the ritual area and the portal. It could be a way to get the pectoral back where it belongs without being spotted. I slid down the incline to tell Luis and Zoila.

Luis got excited the minute I told him about my discovery.

"We've got to get up there. See what's on top," Luis said. "If nothing else there has to be a source for the stream, maybe just a small spring, a tiny opening of some sort, but maybe there's something bigger, a pool maybe. If it is, it has to be the portal we've been looking for. We can't wait forever for things to go crazy or resolve themselves, sit here doing nothing until someone nails us. We've got to move now."

"The sled is built for varied terrains," I said. "There are diagrams on its storage bag, one even shows one woman hauling it up a ladder on its little bottom wheels.

"Zoila, if you push and I pull, we should be able to handle the steps." I grasped the strap at my end. "Once we're up there, I can poke my head over the rim and we can go from there."

"Ready," Zoila said, grasping the handle at the rear of the sled. "Let's do it."

The sled worked perfectly at the start—up the incline, around the rocks, along the back of the platform, but then it turned into an implement of torture. Dragging the sled up the sharp-edged steep stairs was nearly impossible. The narrow stone steps seemed to catch against the soft plastic wheels, keeping them from turning and in between them the knife sharp treads scraped the sled's plastic shell like razors, causing it to slew from side to side.

I could hear Luis sucking in his breath, but he didn't say anything. Zoila was silent too, but I could hear her breathing heavily as she pushed.

I wasn't much better off. The strap I was using to pull the sled was slicing into my shoulder like steel cable and causing the pectoral to dig into my chest. I felt like I was having a heart attack. My hands, skinned by the rough woven tape, were beginning to cramp, making it hard to grip.

Just before my head rose over the lip of the platform, I stopped. "Let's hold it here. Let me check it out before we go over the edge," I said. "We have some cover this way."

"Zoila, can you hold the sled by yourself?" I whispered.

"I'll be okay," Zoila said. "Just don't take too long."

I took a quick peek over the edge of the platform. Turning my Maglite on low with my free hand, I used it in tiny bursts to avoid calling attention to our position.

The structure was enormous, a round flat stage built to provide the priests and lords a podium on which to perform. In the center, a circular pool, probably the origin of the spillway, shown like black glass in my dim light, its rim lined with broken pots and bits of charcoal. To one side of the pool, a stained flat stone altar and a deep ceramic bowl suggested that other rituals might have taken place— maybe bloodletting and sacrifice, too.

I murmured a description over my shoulders.

"I have to see it myself," Luis said. "Shove the sled up to the edge."

Luis's head and the front end of the sled slowly rose over the lip as Zoila and I strained at the strap and handle. From the other side of the platform, he must have looked like a giant insect rising out of its hole or a creature from another a world. Once we had him positioned, I handed him the Maglite.

"This is it." Luis's low voice came back as he clicked off the light. "Get me to the pool's edge."

Then the world exploded in a shower of shouts, muzzle flashes, and gunfire.

Amplified and echoed by the stone walls of the cave, the sudden barrage was deafening. It sounded like a major battle, each shot repeated over and over by the cave's rocky interior.

"We've got to get off these steps. Zoila and I can't hang on forever," I shouted over the din.

"Head toward the pool," Luis said between volleys. "It looked like it has a bank before you reach the water's surface. If we get down below the edge we won't be so exposed."

Zoila and I grabbed the sled, heaved it over the lip of the platform, and crawled for the pond like war dogs, dragging the sled between us, hoping that no one would notice our activity in the confusion and the explosive bursts from the firefight.

The trip to the edge of the water was miserable. Broken pottery used to burn incense a thousand years ago cut my hands and knees as I dragged myself along. Zoila couldn't have been in better shape than I was, but we kept going, stirring up a thousand years of dust and rattling potsherds. Luis picked out our path with the Maglite's low beam.

"Give me back the light and hang on, Luis," I said as we reached the pool. "We're going to push you over the rim. The sled floats, so you will be okay if you slide into the water."

We dropped our handles and shoved the sled sideways over the edge down a three-foot drop to the narrow shore that lined the water, black as obsidian, smooth as a sheet of glass.

The gunfire and shouts died; the silence was broken only by the sound of voices and an occasional groan. *Who knew what the hell has happened,* I thought as I slipped down the embankment and squirmed in next to Zoila on the ceramic strewn ground. Luis bobbed nearby, Moses in his basket, safe for now. I couldn't bear thinking about Bill, Ochoa, Jaime, and the other rangers. Had Kan and his mob blasted their way into the cave, leaving everyone dead or injured? If they had, what then? What chance did we have to get out alive?

Shuffling sounds broke the silence at the top of the small back stairway.

"They've gotta be up here," someone said. "Let's try the pool; it's the only place we can't see from here."

It sounded like Kan. There was no escaping the SOB—first he kills Ruston; then he chases us into the reservoir behind Temple I, and Luis nearly dies of hypothermia; then his thugs kidnap us and hold us hostage in a remote farm somewhere in Tikal and now this, caught like rats in a granary by the bastard. He was persistent as hell.

I slipped my Glock out of its holster and squirmed into a comfortable firing position. And what did he mean the pool was the only place they couldn't see? I couldn't see anything anywhere in the absolute darkness unless I turned on my headlamp, Maglite, or the light on my gun.

I quickly swept the low beam of my Maglite over the edge of the pond's bank. My question was answered. Two men stuck their heads over the lip of the drop off into the pond wearing infrared night vision goggles. No wonder they'd gotten this far into the gallery without trouble. They were next to invisible if they remained hidden from our group's headlamps, and they could see all of us plain as day.

I had no way of tracking them. All I had was my flashlight and gun to pick out their dark shape. I would only make our situation worse if I turned the flash full on, it would be like a solar flare on the black backdrop of space. The headlamp wouldn't be better. It would light me up for an easy shot.

"There's that little prick floating on the pond like a rubber ducky."

"Give me the pectoral, Luis," Kan said. "Now, or I'll kill you." He fired into the water to underline his point.

They must have been so concentrated on Luis that they didn't see Zoila or me, or if they did, they didn't think we mattered. Was he going to kill Luis outright, shoot him while he was helpless in the pond strapped to the sled?

Kan fired again. Luis yelped.

I looked at the gun in my hand, my last resort, and began to shiver with nerves. Luis was helpless. Luis would die, then Zoila, then me. Kan was going to kill us all unless I did something.

The detached feeling from the farmhouse swept over me again. I was being dragged out of myself, lifted out of my skin by an alien force. My body tensed, humming with rage and fierce, focused energy, aware only of the gun in my hand and the two men looming over the rim.

Using the light on my gun to aim, I shot Kan and then shifted to the man next to him, practicing everything I remembered from the range—aim for the center of the mass, slowly squeeze the trigger, take three shots.

The men dropped from view one at a time.

I scrambled up the bank, illuminating my path with the light on my gun, just as a third man appeared at the top of the stairs. I rolled into a firing position, raising my gun, but before I could pull the trigger, the man disappeared with a jerk, clattering down the stairs, shouting as he fell. The sounds of a scuffle below the platform were followed by silence.

"Ann, it's me," Bill yelled from the stairs. "It's okay. The guy is done. Put down your gun. I'm coming up."

Bill appeared over the rim, his headlamp searching.

I closed my eyes. Bill was there. Then Zoila. I couldn't understand what they were saying though: I was numb.

Through my fog, I spotted Ochoa and Jaime pulling Luis over the embankment to safety at the edge of the pool.

~ * ~

I don't know how much time passed. I was shivering, exhausted. Ochoa wrapped me in a blanket. Bill gave me a bottle of water. Zoila held my hand when she wasn't fussing with Luis, next to me on his sled.

"Luis, what happened?" I asked when I finally was able to talk.

"I got hit when Kan fired the second time," Luis said.

"It's a flesh wound," Jaime said. He finished bandaging Luis's arm. "It's gonna ache, but that's probably all. The doctor will do a better job when we get back to headquarters."

"It could have been worse," Luis said. "It's my paralyzed arm. I've been trying to ignore it since my stroke, so what's a little more inconvenience on that side? The main thing is we've got to return the pectoral before something else happens.

"Can someone get me to the edge of the water so I won't miss my throw? Ann, come with me; can you hand me the pectoral when I ask for it?"

I followed Bill and Jaime as they dragged the sled to the edge of the pool and oriented Luis so he could toss the pendant without trouble. I tried not to watch Esteban and Francisco as they hauled two bodies toward the stairs.

When we reached the pool's bank, I unpinned the purse from my bra and removed the jade vulture I'd found in Ruston's study...years ago it seemed.

In the light of my headlamp, the pectoral glowed green in my hand, the color of a sunlit sea or young corn. The vulture stared up, alien, inscrutable.

"Here," I said, tucking it into Luis's good hand. "It's time to send it where it belongs, back to the ancestors."

Cradling the pectoral in his good hand, Luis began to chant, quietly at first, then louder, as if he were communicating with someone on the far side of the pool, or another time and place; he tossed the vulture toward the center of the water.

~ * ~

The slog back out of the cave must have been like the way in, though this time I had something else on my mind besides caving— the fact that I was responsible for two of the five bodies that had been brought to the front of the gallery while we were regrouping for the hike out.

Unlike the journey in, there were two Nuevos with us, too, both with wounds—one shot in the shoulder, the other in the hand, if their bandages meant anything. Their functional arms were cuffed to their belts, and they were tied between Esteban and Francisco with caving rope. They were quiet for the most part in the narrow tunnel, with only an occasional groan or intake of breath when they tripped on something in the half-light of their captors' headlamps.

There was another difference as well. It was most obvious when we reached the first gallery. Water was pouring in: rivulets down the walls, showers from the ceiling, pools in most of the hollows, and a small stream that wound toward the tunnel leading to the outside.

"Has it been raining the whole time we've been in here?" Ochoa asked as we paused to catch our breath and stretch before we began the push through the final tunnel. "Let's get going. We don't want to get caught if the tunnel floods."

Luis looked pensive, chewing on his lower lip, his brow furrowed.

"What is it?" I whispered. "Why the water? Why now?"

I had to lean over the sled to hear him.

"This whole thing has been about water from the very beginning—water for Tikal and the city on the coast—for crops, for drinking, for everything else. The vulture was the symbol of water and fertility, it still is—farmers burn their fields, the vultures come to feast on the remains of the animals caught by the fire, the rains come, the corn grows—and the vulture pectoral was the symbol of K'utz Chman, who controlled both rain and fertility. It was an image of his power. Now the pectoral has been returned to the ancestors, but not without pain, bloodshed, and battles with men with murder in their hearts. And you, *hermanita*, have been made to suffer as well, though you will heal with time.

"The water is a sign, a warning. Tikal must be cleansed. The Nuevo who have perverted Mayan ways must be eradicated. This world is not meant for them or the cartels either."

We moved off into the tunnel, Ochoa in the lead, Bill bringing up the rear. The water grew deeper as we walked. It was over the tops of my boots, and we splashed, not scuffed, through dirt and stones.

There seemed to be a growing cold wind at our backs, too. It had begun as a whisper, but then it had increased to a serious steady draught, as if a glacier were exhaling in the depth of the cave behind us.

Something wasn't right. I dropped back to tell Bill what Luis had said about cleansing. With the water and the gusts of air, it felt as if the ancestors had already started in on it.

I'd just returned to my place in line when I heard a roar from deep in the cave. The wind became a gale.

It sounded like a jet engine—something huge, howling, grinding, pitiless—tearing its way through the cave toward us.

"Run!" Bill yelled. "Run like hell!"

Thirty

Tikal National Park, Guatemala, the Collapse

Terror washed over me in a wave as the world unmade itself. Water smelling of something ancient and long-buried churned and rose around my legs as the cave roof collapsed, crumbling its way toward the tunnel opening. By the time the full flood hit me, it was up to my shoulders, a solid wall of bone-chilling icy water swirling with rocks and nameless debris. Bill slammed into me, grabbing my arm to keep us both from being knocked down; then we smashed into Zoila.

I lost my footing in the roiling flood, flailing my arms as I sank under the surging water. Bill dragged me to the surface by my collar. *If chaos has a smell this is it: water and rock and icy air*, I thought, choking and coughing as he steadied me in the buffeting river.

Zoila was screaming for Luis somewhere in the dark and I could hear Ochoa yelling further toward the entrance. Esteban and Francisco shouted to one another as they struggled to maintain their footing and keep the Nuevos' heads above water at the same time.

At least Luis's sled floats, I thought as another wave from deep in the cavern roared into the tunnel. I was sucked down this time and carried toward the entrance, rolled like a stone along with the rubble that poured toward the opening, heading for the rock pile, the reservoir, the open air.

It was impossible to orient myself in the churning water. Unable to avoid the boulders at the cave's mouth, I slammed into them like a runner taking a fall on cement, then was scraped up and over their rough surfaces as the racing current swept me out into the reservoir. Lungs exploding, ears ringing, choking, I finally broke the surface on the far side of the pool; an elastic band had kept my glasses on, but trying to see through the film of water on the lenses was difficult. It was raining too, making it hard to recognize details in the half-light of approaching evening, but I thought I spotted several dark shapes bobbing on the surface nearby.

Once my glasses cleared, I could see Zoila hanging on the end of Luis's sled as it floated on one side of the reservoir. In the middle of the pool, two men were dragging two others out of the full force of the flood, and I could make out three heads below the outcrop pathway we had used to reach the cave. Relief swept over me. We were all going to get out.

I had relaxed too soon. A deep groaning noise came from the direction of the cave opening, and the earth itself seemed to tremble and rock. The reservoir water rose and fell, climbing almost to the rim as it sloshed from side to side, gaining speed and height with each undulation, as the wall containing the cave entrance collapsed forward into the water with a roar. The force of a growing sinkhole sent a churning geyser far into the darkening sky and ten-foot waves across the reservoir.

I could hear Ochoa shouting over the tumult as I swam toward the trail that led upward to the rim. Getting to the pathway from the surging water proved to be excruciating. There were no convenient protruding rocks large enough on which to stand. I was forced to claw my way up the slippery surface, like a cat up a curtain, by using the smallest protrusions as means to steady myself as I inched toward the ledge, water thundering below, hurling spray into the air as the chaotic subsidence gnawed its way around the rim.

Exhausted from caving, my struggles in the surging water, the climb, I could barely haul myself over the edge of the outcrop. I rolled away from its rough edge and lay against the reservoir's steep side, panting, resting for a moment till I could begin the climb upward. I had to get out of there. Who knew how much longer the earth's sinking would continue? Maybe the entire area would fall in on itself. The only safe place was somewhere as far as possible from the reservoir and its collapsing geology.

It was pitch black and the rain had settled into a steady downpour by the time I climbed over the rim. I'd kicked off my boots escaping the pool; I'd lost my hardhat and my headlamp then, too, and as far as I could tell, I was alone. I staggered toward the service road that led to ranger headquarters. I had to find help for anyone still trapped in the reservoir.

~ * ~

By the time Ochoa, Bill, and Jaime hauled themselves up the path to the rim of the reservoir, Zoila had grounded Luis's sled on a small limestone outcrop near the bottom of the ledge. Esteban and Francisco had dragged the Nuevos onto a rocky protrusion across the pool from what remained of the cave opening.

"I can see everyone but Ann." Ochoa scanned the still heaving water.

"I saw her swimming toward the ledge after we left the cave, but then I lost sight of her as the rim started to collapse," Bill said.

"I didn't see her after that, either."

"Jesus," Bill said. "I hope she made it out."

"We've got to get everyone out and keep an eye out for Ann at the same time," Ochoa said between coughs. "I've got extra rope in the Range Rover, blankets, coffee, our clothes, the radio. Let me call headquarters first, tell them what's happened, that we need folks out here, let them know about Ann; then let's get Zoila and Luis out of the water. We're going to need help and more equipment for the guys and our captives."

~ * ~

As I stumbled through the sucking mud, the feeling I'd had off and on since we first entered the cave—that we were an essential part of the story of the reservoir and the cavern—returned, along with the idea that we were living out something that began long ago. It was eerie.

First the Vulture Lord and K'in Kan, then the classic Maya and their cave, and now us, beginning with Ruston's murder.

It were as if—

Several sets of headlights suddenly caught my eye as they dipped and rose, heading toward me on the saturated trail through the dark needling rain. *I hope to hell it's the rangers*, I thought, slipping into the thick understory at the side of the road, *not the Nuevo, not Los Zetas*.

When I spotted the ranger's insignia on the door of the lead Land Cruiser, I plunged out of the undergrowth waving my arms.

"Stop! Help! We've got to go to the reservoir. Now! The walls are falling in. Everyone's trapped," I yelled as I lunged into the road.

The car jerked to a stop. The ranger in the passenger's seat rolled down his window. "Ann?"

I nodded.

"Get in. The others are okay, but they're having trouble getting everyone out of the reservoir. We're headed there now. Here," he said, opening his door, "get in front with the heat. I'll sit in back."

I crawled into the seat directly in the blast of the Land Cruiser's roaring heater. The ranger whose seat I'd taken dropped his jacket around my shoulders and handed me a cup of coffee from his thermos. Between sips I tried to explain what had happened—the roaring water, the grinding, spreading collapse of the cave, the sinking walls of the reservoir near the cavern's opening, my separation from everyone in the chaos of the expanding sinkhole and rising water.

"*Horrible*," the driver said, shifting into second gear. "At least everyone's alive. It sounds as if they're just cold and wet. Ochoa radioed headquarters to let us know what happened." He swerved to avoid a washed-out spot in the road. "They're worried about you."

Thirty-one

By the time the entire caving party and the captives arrived at the Tikal Park Rangers' headquarters a couple of hours later, *Hurakan* had moved off muttering, probably disappointed we'd gotten out. We could hear him complaining in the distance as we sipped mugs of steaming coffee in the break room.

After Dr. Gomez gave Luis a proper bandage, as well as a sling, and inspected the rest of us, we were given dry clothes. We were tired, but nothing a night's sleep wouldn't mend. Even the Nuevos in the holding cell at the back of the building had made it through the sinkhole collapse with nothing more than a few contusions and raw spots.

"Do you think there will be any way to get back into the cave?" Zoila asked Luis stirring sugar into his coffee. "I mean all the structures, the artifacts." She paused. "They're priceless."

"We'll have to see what is left of the cave itself, once we can get somebody out there to check," Ochoa said, "a caving expert, someone who is familiar with karst typography. We have to make certain the entire area is stable before we start a dig. All this rain, the water's weight on the cave system, the underground erosion eating away the rock over the years—the entire cave may have turned into a giant sinkhole or may be about to become one."

I shuddered and wondered if not being able to go back into the cave was such a bad thing after all.

"At least we'll have some images of the platforms and galleries. My camera didn't get wet and it's in one piece, *gracias a Dios*," Ochoa said.

Santa Elena, Guatemala

Later that night, back in our room at Esperanza's mother's place, I was less concerned about the cave and artifacts than I was about having killed two people. I could hear Pat turning restlessly on her narrow bed, apparently mirroring my own miserable attempts at sleep.

"Pat? You awake?"

"I can't turn my mind off. I'm still trying to digest everything. What hell. And your awful experience taking care of Luis—"

It was kind to put it that way. Taking care of Luis, not killing.

I sniffled, blew my nose. "It's as if something broke—or a shift occurred deep inside. Who am I now? I don't know."

"Try not to worry about it tonight," Pat said. "You can think about it later." She switched on her flashlight and got out of bed. "Benadryl might help." She found a bottle of water, dug a container from her travel bag, and shook out two bright pink tablets.

I obediently swallowed the pills she handed me. I felt like I did when I was a kid sick at home from school and my mother was giving me medicine.

"Thanks."

"That should do something," Pat said, switching off her light and getting back in bed.

She was right, after a few minutes the Benadryl took effect.

I slept, dreamless, until sunrise.

~ * ~

Bill, as usual, was the first one up; we passed his room's half-open door on the way to the kitchen. Esperanza's mother was busy adding wood to the hearth and making coffee when we settled at the table. Esperanza's sister was mixing dough in a bowl on the worktable nearby.

On the far side of the little room, the old dog slept under a bench curled in a ball, feet twitching in a doggy dream. The chickens fussed and clucked near the porch, scratching at the corn that littered the ground.

"*Buenos días señoras.* How are you this morning?" Pat asked.

"*Buenos días.* We are fine and you?" our hostess answered, smoothing her apron over her *corte* with one hand as she deposited a basket of rolls on the table with the other. She returned with two cups of steaming coffee.

The warmth from the fire felt good. *Maybe breakfast will help my fragile state*, I thought, taking a roll, though food had all the appeal of a piece of wallboard.

Pat and I were drinking a second cup of coffee, and I'd managed to eat a piece of roll when Bill joined us, bringing the scent of early morning into the kitchen with him... moisture, jungle, farmstead. Esperanza's mother handed him a cup of coffee as he sat down across the table.

Bill peered over the rim of his cup at the fragments of bread piled in front of me.

"It isn't easy," he said. "But the important thing is you saved Luis's life. Without you, the story would have a different ending; you and Zoila probably wouldn't be alive, either."

I shredded the remains of my breakfast while he was talking, then looked up.

"I feel horrible. I can hardly stand to dispatch an insect, but I shot two men and one was Kan himself. It's a nightmare."

Bill placed his hand over mine.

Suddenly I was crying, silently, painfully. Pat and Bill drew closer and did their best to comfort me.

Thirty-two

Several days after our arrival at Esperanza's mother's farm, as the sun began to slip behind the fringe of communities that ringed Lake Itza's far shore, four of us gathered in the kitchen. In the jungle to the north, a howler called, another answered from farther east just as Bill stepped into the kitchen after his latest trip to headquarters.

"According to Ríos, the situation has finally turned a corner. The park is cleared of Nuevos, and the *Kaibiles* have returned to their base," Bill said.

"It didn't take long once the *Kaibiles* got here. Kan's followers had a camp, almost a little pueblo, in the middle of Tikal Reserve. It wasn't hard to find once we started looking. There were thirty men plus wives and girlfriends." Bill poured himself a fresh cup of coffee. "The few that remained have been taken to prison in Guatemala City. The women are in jail too, till someone can figure out what to do with them."

"How about the cartels?" Luis asked.

"The Mexican army completely demolished the Maya Gold transfer point to the north. Now they're mopping up Los Zetas in the Lacandon Reserve. From now on, the cartels will be Mexico's problem, and they aren't going to fool around."

Pat, who had been nibbling on a salted tortilla, had more personal news. "I got tickets for us to fly out on Saturday," she said. "The airline personnel assured me now the Nuevos have been rounded up and the cartels contained, the airfield is safe."

We all cheered.

The sound of an approaching truck broke into our excitement.

"Looks like company has arrived," Bill said as Esperanza's brother-in-law parked in front of the porch.

Company? What didn't I know?

The dog barked wildly; the chickens fled as another vehicle entered the farmyard, then another.

Bill stepped outside. "It's Esperanza and Ochoa and Jaime and his wife."

A fourth pickup could be heard working its way past the gate and into the crowded yard.

"Esperanza's oldest brother and his wife just showed up," Bill called over his shoulder.

"Will someone tell me what is going on?" I asked no one in particular.

The women, carrying platters covered with dishtowels, began to file into the kitchen.

"What's that?" Bill asked, indicating the platter Esperanza carried as she slipped through the door.

"Tamales, for afterward," Esperanza said. "Where do you want them, Mom?"

"Over here," her mother said, waving her hand at the shelf running along the back wall of the kitchen. "They'll be fine until we need them."

Captain Ríos, Francisco, and Esteban exited Ríos's Land Cruiser at the gate and joined the group in the farmyard.

"Will someone tell me what is happening?" I said as I joined the growing crowd outside the kitchen.

"'Listen up," Bill shouted over the din.

Luis, dressed in a Guatemalan shirt and hand-woven shawl with images of spread-winged vulture-like birds draped around his neck, waved his good arm for silence. Once he had everyone's attention, he began.

"We've been attacked, injured, and forced to do things we would never have considered possible in order to thwart the Nuevos and to return the vulture pendant to the ancestors. Since we've all been affected by recent terrible events, we must have a ritual to restore balance and order to our lives and the world.

"Ann, Bill, and Jaime had the most difficult roles and are in special need of healing.

"I didn't say anything about this earlier because the ceremony didn't come together until the last minute. I didn't want to let you down if it didn't work out."

I guess that makes sense, I thought. I was so prone to weeping at odd moments, who knew how I'd respond to disappointment? I wasn't certain myself.

"There is a holy spot, a spring with an altar, at the edge of the jungle near the site of an ancient pueblo. We'll hold the ceremony there," he said, as Zoila began pushing his chair toward the nearest vehicle.

Luis was tucked between Esperanza's mother and her son in the lead pickup. Zoila, Esperanza, and I rode behind them in the bed of the truck; the walker, travel chair, two bags of fertilizer, and a large box of copal took up the rest of the space.

Everyone else fanned out into the remaining pickups, crowding into the cabs or taking seats in the beds, trying to make themselves comfortable on bags of seeds or farm chemicals. It felt like a hayride, except no one was giggling or tossing straw.

The muddy track toward the jungle was miserable—rough clumps of weeds and portions of crumbling bank filled the old ruts that were barely visible from the pitching vehicle; only the high walls of the ancient roadway clearly marked the path's location. We were thrown from side to side, along with the other cargo, as the pickup lurched its way toward the jungle's edge. No one talked; we'd bite our tongues.

An hour from the farm, as the rose-gold light faded and streaks of lemon and pale blue edged the western sky, we stopped at the edge of a still empty cornfield near the tree line. With the trucks silenced, the metallic songs of insects deep in the nearby jungle closed around us.

"This is it," Esperanza's mother said as she eased her way from the cab.

I crawled over the tailgate with my two companions.

We had parked as close as possible to a tumbled pile of rocks that backed up to an upturned ledge of limestone protruding from the weedy margin of the field.

My legs felt like rubber as I wobbled closer to the outcrop. I wasn't the only one that felt shaky from jostling down a dirt track in the back of a pickup. Everyone else looked unsteady, too.

A thin thread of water flowed from under the rock pile and formed a small pool at the base. It drained into a slender rivulet, disappearing in the direction from which we'd come. A flat stone altar, the size of a kitchen table, lay near the spring surrounded by piles of broken pottery.

I headed back to the truck. There wasn't a lot I could do for the ceremony, but I could help Bill with Luis.

Bill gently lifted Luis out of the cab while I hauled his wheelchair out of the bed and held it steady as Bill placed him in the chair. I fastened his seat belt and covered his knees with his purple and red blanket. He'd need it; the evening would be cool.

"Ready?" Bill asked. "If the road was any indication, it's going to be rough getting to the altar."

Luis nodded and grasped an armrest with his good hand.

Slowly Bill wheeled Luis across the uneven ground to the gray stone altar, picking his way carefully to avoid the worst of the rugged spots.

Everyone had been busy while we had been getting Luis settled. Esperanza and Zoila had arranged armloads of white canna lilies around the site and lit copal in the largest pottery fragments. Someone had placed clusters of tiny white candles, flickering in the evening breeze, between the cigarettes and small bottles of *aguardiente* on the altar; a fire had been lit in a nearby ring of stones.

~ * ~

Luis sat in silence in front of the altar, his eyes closed.

Slowly he began to chant, swaying slightly in his chair. "I ask for curing for those who protected the rest of us from harm and recovery for those who suffered during the chaos. Dispel the evil that has enveloped us all—"

His voice dropped, blending into the sounds of the jungle as he continued to sway, his words part of the night and the place itself.

Thick blue clouds of copal rose from the shards, coiling like the Vision Serpent into the evening air, enveloping us in thick, sweet fog. I breathed deeply, my eyes closed, abandoning myself to Luis's voice, the incense, and the warmth of the fire.

He must have prayed for another hour. A breeze came up, ruffling my hair, brushing my face like tiny wings. The smoke from the fire and the copal, the soft chanting, and the jungle sounds merged into an enveloping darkness, thick, soothing, curative, as if I were tucked under the soft breast of an enormous bird, or held dreaming in the cool arms of Ixchel, the moon goddess, deity of healing.

By the time the ritual ended and the fire was reduced to embers, the goddess and her rabbit familiar sailed high in the sky; Venus trailed behind her, watching us with cool distant eyes as we headed home. I drifted with the copal between this world and the next.

As we jolted along the dirt track to the farm, I reflected on the ancestors. First, they got me into this, and now they seem to have pulled me out. I was too tired to be amazed, too spent to do more than accept things as they were.

The farm kitchen and the main building across the farmyard were brightly lit when we pulled in an hour later. The dog barked once or twice from the kitchen doorway, then went inside. Smoke meandered in wisps across the sky from the back of the kitchen.

Esperanza's mother and the other women had been busy while we were gone. The cool night air smelled of tortillas, tamales, and coffee. A cousin who had been helping in the kitchen directed us toward the scene of the meal as she carried a platter of tamales for the festivities across the yard to the main building.

The women had been at work in there, too. Boards on sawhorses had been set up to form a long table between the family altar and the door to a bedroom. A collection of bright table clothes covered its surface; steaming platters of tamales, baskets of tortillas wrapped in *serviettas*, large bright squares of hand-woven cloth, bottles of soft drinks and beer crowded together along its length. A single light bulb in the center of the ceiling illuminated the space...candles on the table and altar added to the glow.

"There's coffee on the hearth in the kitchen," Esperanza's younger sister said. She held open the door for Luis as Zoila pushed his chair into the welcoming space. "I'll bring a tray."

"Like a funeral, wedding, holiday—first the ritual, then the feasting," Luis said as he surveyed the dishes. "Food nourishes us and weaves us together at the same time." He looked tired, but the sight of the feast seemed to perk him up.

After the last several days of deprivation, misery, and terror, the tamales were pure ambrosia: served in their cornhusks, the fresh steamed masa contained shredded pork with red chili sauce...rich and spicy. A bowl of extra sauce stood near each serving platter. Using the wrapping as plates, we ate the tamales straight from the husks, tossing the empty coverings into a basket at the end of the table when we were through.

I licked my fingers as the juice leaked from my fourth tamale. If I could purr, I would have then. I headed back to the table for another tamale and a tortilla to sop up the extra sauce.

The food worked its magic. By the time the tamales and tortillas had disappeared, conversation had turned from the terror of the cave and the ancestors' fierce demands, to what was needed to preserve the site. Ochoa took out his camera.

"You have to see this, and now is as good a time as any," he said, as he turned on the camera. "The cave is even richer than we thought. Look at the painting! Look at the artifacts!"

He held the camera down so Luis could see. The rest of us clustered around Luis's chair.

In the background of the photos Ochoa shot in the second gallery, handprints and images of rain covered the walls, the ancient rain god Chac peered from the center of the panel. Large ceramic jars, also references to water, sat along the floor. Water. It was the focus of much ancient Mayan ritual and a link with the vulture pendant left in the cave under Tikal, the city where the story of K'in A'jaw began thousands of years ago. I could feel the hair on my neck stand on end, as if a cold breeze had suddenly blown through the warm room.

Barely visible in the light of the flash, pathways in the cave floor led toward the platform and to the altar near its base where a jumble of bones lay on the ground behind it.

"Those may be jaguar bones. Everything was so chaotic then I didn't see them, and it's hard to tell in this image," Ochoa said, squinting at his camera. "But I think I can make out a feline skull. Jaguars were special sacrifices during important rituals, as well as indicators of high-ranking officials and lords."

"Why a jaguar?" Pat asked.

"The jaguar was a symbol of power, strength, ferocity; it's the top predator in the rain forest, the ruler of its world," Luis said.

"I don't believe it! Wall paintings. Water images! A jaguar!" I was stunned.

Then everyone began talking at once.

"We've got to get back in," Ríos said. "That cave is a treasure. Nothing like it's ever been found. Who knows what else is in there? I hope the water hasn't scoured the place clean. But first we have to have geologists examine the site. As far as we know, the thing is a death trap. It's going to need to be stabilized."

Ochoa nodded. "No way can we get in until we know we can get back out."

"Once things settle, you will find a way," Luis said. "I hate to break things up, but I've got to go to bed, I'm exhausted."

"Thanks for the wonderful meal. The tamales were perfect," Zoila said to the women seated on the bench along the back wall. She grabbed the handles of Luis's chair and headed for the door. "It's been a long day; we need to call it a night."

Ochoa slipped the camera into its case, and the women, recognizing the party was breaking up, began bustling the empty dishes from the table to the kitchen.

Ríos yawned. "Let's go, guys. It's late and there's a lot to do tomorrow, so we can reopen the park at the end of this week—assess the damage, pick up shells, make sure we have all the bodies. Then we can start thinking about the cave..." He yawned again.

"I'll drive, Captain," Esteban said as the rangers started across the porch.

Pat and I followed the men out and headed for our room.

"I'm done," Pat said. "The last few days have been beyond belief."

I grunted in assent.

"I can hardly stand the thought of wasting time to get out of my clothes," I said as I took off my sneakers.

I was asleep nearly as soon as I pulled up my blanket.

That night I dreamed of jaguars with jeweled eyes stalking through Tikal's main plaza and a black glassy pool rimmed with fist-sized lumps of jade. Around the pool and in between draperies of stalactites dark shadows flitted and dissipated like fog rising from the jungle. A serpent watched me from the cloud of copal mounting into the air from the far side of the pool.

Thirty-three

Big Grove, First Week in May

Bill's brother Bob drove us home from the airport outside of Big Grove, and if he was shocked by our battered appearances, he didn't say anything. Maybe Bill had warned him.

Spring had arrived while we were gone. Leaves had appeared on trees and shrubs, the grass was lush, and flowers bloomed in beds and porch pots.

After settling Zoila and Luis in their apartment, we headed for Burr Oaks. The old brick buildings looked as they had when we left, except for green bushes and the freshly sprouted canopy of the red maple in front of our building. The entry way was the same, too—brass mailboxes in need of polishing, a recycle bin shoved up against the outside wall—and now with the three of us hauling bags, crowded. We hugged before we started up the stairs to our own homes, dragging our luggage behind us.

I could hear Rosie mewing as I fiddled with my locks. As soon as I was in, she twined around my legs, churring, hopping up and down, trying to reach up as far as possible, glad to have me and not the cat sitter come through the door. I dropped my gear as she slammed into me like a tiny brown footballer. I scooped her up, pressed my face against her little whiskery cheeks, headed for my recliner, eyes filled with tears. We settled in together, Rosie kneading my chest, her muzzle in my ear, her purr blotting out everything except her squirming body, stiff whiskers, silky fur.

I could hold her forever, I thought, pressing her close. I can't go through something like Tikal again. It would kill me.

Thirty-four

Big Grove, Third Week in May

A week after we returned, I reread the letter from St. Patrick's parish to remind myself what they needed done. I'd called before I'd left, but I needed to phone again to set up an appointment.

Dear Ms. Cunningham,

The Parish Council of St. Patrick's Catholic Church is tasked with organizing and removing our former priest's private papers from his offices before the arrival of our new priest in July. You have been recommended as an outstanding archivist by the cousin of one of our parishioners and a friend of yours, José Polop.

As you may recall, Father Diego Muldonado, died last autumn. Since no one in our parish has the skills to undertake the task of categorizing and dispensing his papers to appropriate destinations, we are hoping you would be willing to do so. If you are interested, please call the church office to make arrangements.

Sincerely,

Tomás Castillo, president of St. Patrick's Parish Council.

Their needs were clear. I called the church office to arrange to begin work in two weeks. That would give me time to settle into my life again and to cope with my still shaky emotional state. Bill insists it's PTSD. I'm not so sure. Maybe I'm just tired.

Later that evening, as I sat with Rosie warm and heavy on my lap, it occurred to me that I'd just accepted another job where my skills were required after someone had been murdered. Strange. I'd become a compiler of violently shortened lives—sifting through papers of the suddenly deceased—trying to make sense of the jumbled papers and scraps, partial messages, old lists, diaries. It was like being a forensic pathologist reading someone's remains like a catalog.

Maybe I should mention something on my business cards, "Specializing in the papers of murder victims, or the suddenly departed—" Rosie stretched and yawned, turned, settled again. Ruston was the last such job, and look where that went. Tikal. Drug cartels. The Nuevo. Kidnapping. Gun battles. Heart excision. *What incriminating material could possibly turn up in a priest's papers?* I asked myself, sipping the last of my whiskey.

Father Diego's murder hadn't been solved, and some people had even begun to suggest it had merely been a random act of violence, not something more sinister. I wasn't so sure—neatly placed .22 bullets didn't sound like a mugging gone wrong.

~ * ~

That same week Pat, Bill, and I settled back into our regular pattern of BYO Friday night cocktails. We were still kicking around Ruston's murder as the beginning of the problems in Tikal, at least as far as we were concerned.

We didn't have anything specific regarding his demise...like proof of who killed him—but after seeing Kan's performance on the pyramid steps, we could guess. Kan knew how to carry out a ritual sacrifice, and whoever killed Rustin had done everything right—scaffold, arrows, heart excision.

"But how about Polop?" Pat asked. "He got home in one piece, half nuts, but alive."

"I don't know, but maybe being Maya they didn't feel they could kill him right away—or possibly they were saving him for a more propitious moment, you know, Venus rising in the morning sky, or some big social event like a lord taking his seat or throne," I said.

"But both kidnappings were about the Nuevos' solidifying their vision of a new Mayan world with Kan as its lord," I added. "Our turning up with the vulture pendant was a dream come true."

"We walked into their fantasies with our eyes closed." Bill shook his head in disbelief. "Jesus, there we were with their ancient symbol of lordship dangling from our fingers."

Thirty-five

Big Grove, Same Week

I pulled in next to the parish hall at nine o'clock Monday morning next to the only car in St. Patrick's parking lot. The sky was clear, the sun warm, and wisps of cirrus clouds, like strands of spun sugar, drifted over Big Grove on their way east toward Indiana.

The red brick hall could have been mistaken for a small grade school, and even though the hall lights were off, the double doors were unlocked. The office was to the left of the entry. A small woman, her black hair in a ponytail, sat behind the crowded desk.

"Hi. I'm Ann and you must be Irma, the woman I spoke with on the phone," I said as I stepped into the room.

She stood to greet me, smiling. *"Buenos días, señora,* I'm the church secretary, Irma Villa Lobos. We are so happy to have you," she said, extending her hand. "We haven't known what to do with Father's papers. We desperately need your expertise before the new priest arrives. He said he'd like to move his own things in right away.

"Father Diego's offices have just stayed as they were since he died, since things are pretty quiet here except on Sundays, or when we have parish council meetings," she added, pulling a ring of keys from her desk. "Now there's a rush with the priest arriving in a few weeks.

"Is there anything you would like to know before you start?" she asked, slipping on her sweater. "Otherwise, we can go over to the rectory now. I'll show you around."

"Has anything new been uncovered about Father Diego's murder?" I asked, more to make conversation than anything else, as we headed for the rectory's back door.

"Nothing. At least the police haven't said anything. It's as if it never happened." She slid her key into the lock. "I don't know if we'll ever hear anything."

"Since we have supply priests who come on Sundays then leave, there hasn't been any reason to clear Father Diego's things out till now. No one uses the rectory or his office in the parish hall, either. The house has been cleaned, of course, and his clothes given away, but his library and his really personal things—he didn't have any family—are still here. No one has the heart to dispose of them. His laptop is still with the police," she added as we stepped inside.

The small rear entry was tidy—doormats vacuumed, checkered curtain on the door freshly laundered and ironed—and the kitchen beyond was spotless and empty. Irma switched on lights as she guided me toward the short hall that led toward the front of the house.

"The library was his inner sanctum. He spent hours in here reading and writing," Irma said as she unlocked the heavy oak door to the left of the entry.

"We starting locking it after he was murdered; I'm not sure why. It just seemed safer that way." She pushed open the door and switching on the library lights. "Silly. Who'd want a dead priest's papers?" she asked, crossing herself.

"Make yourself comfortable. If you need anything, let me know. Here are the keys to his desk and file." Irma turned to leave. "I'll be in the office till four-thirty."

The library must have been added after the house was built, since it protruded beyond the house's square floor plan, and the two windows at either end were larger than those in the original building. Built-in shelves lined with books covered the walls from floor to ceiling, except for a small wooden file cabinet behind the desk and a tiny bar to the right of the door. A single crystal glass still stood on its glass top. I sniffed it. It had been washed, but the cabinet below was still stocked—an expensive port, a pricey scotch, gin. For a Franciscan, he was living well.

A well-used mahogany desk, bare except for a green banker's lamp, wooden file tray, and an old-fashioned desk blotter, faced the door. Two library chairs shared a lamp and side table with a large ashtray in front of a window to the right of the door. Traces of cigar smoke still hovered in the air. He must have smoked in here often if I could smell it six months later. It reminded me of Ruston's study.

I settled into Father Diego's chair after retrieving my materials from the RAV4. Might as well clear the desk top first, then the drawers, then the file cabinet, then end with the books if they wanted them removed, too. I'd have to clarify that point with Irma.

The desktop file tray held notes for a homily and the rough draft of a letter describing a parish fund drive meant to begin last February.

The blotter-calendar, still displaying the last month of his life, was more interesting, since he seemed to use it as a diary. "Monday, call Wilson's Heating and Plumbing about rectory furnace. Tuesday make appointment with provincial's office. Wednesday, homily."

On his final day, the fourth of December, "Chicago early, back late afternoon," was written in hasty black ballpoint.

He drives to Chicago, comes home, then he's killed. Was there a connection between the trip and his death? It was an interesting coincidence—was it accidental or something else?

The top-right drawer contained office supplies. The bottom drawer was a small hanging file, with at least two dozen dark green folders dangling from its metal structure. I'd go through it after I developed a sense of his other materials. The left side of the desk was similarly business like.

Maybe the file behind his desk will hold something of greater import, I thought, swiveling to face it, jiggling a tiny key into the top drawer's lock.

The drawer was jammed with manila files, bristling with paper that made it hard to pull open—a lifetime's worth of homilies, as far as I could tell after a cursory inspection. The bottom drawer was only half full. It contained letters regarding parish business over the span of Father Diego's tenure at St. Patrick's, articles from periodicals that had caught his eye, and in a file by itself at the front, lists of large donors and the amounts they had contributed over several years.

I looked at that first. Half way down the inventory, I spotted Eduardo Guzmán, former owner of Cinco Gallos, member of the Sinaloa cartel, and one of Kan's temple sacrifices, according to the local news. I could still hear Guzmán shrieking about tacos as they hauled him up the temple stairs. I shuddered.

It was odd to find that man's name here in Father Diego's office as an important church contributor. He didn't seem the type—more a drug lord and cartel boss sort, according to the Mexican police—but maybe Guzmán was trying to make restitution for his sins. Since his restaurant was only two blocks away, it would be easy for him to seek solace at St. Patrick's.

I leaned back in his chair to think. What did I know: first, someone murdered Father Diego—a professional hit from the look of it, though the police weren't saying; second, he and Guzmán were connected, at least through the church; and third, both Father Diego and Ruston frequented Cinco Gallos and smoked expensive cigars on not too generous salaries. Were there other connections between the two, besides both being murdered, that tied them to the rest of the story, or did they both just like Mesoamerican food, fancy smokes, and have lousy luck?

There was something else, too, though—the truck full of drugs that burned behind Cinco Gallo. Not that the accident was connected to Guzmán just because it was in his backyard, but it was interesting, and what the hell was that truck doing cruising off the interstate into the St. Patrick/Cinco Gallos neighborhood?

And there was Father Diego's fast trip to Chicago on the day he was killed. What the devil was that about? The extravagant contributions from Guzmán to the church were curious, too. Still from what I could tell, the priest didn't sound like the type to be in trouble with the cartels or drugs, either, but that didn't mean anything. A priest would be a perfect addition to the ranks.

Get a grip. This isn't an investigation; it's archiving. Pack, don't pry, I thought as I began to arrange the files of homilies from the file cabinet by date in a banker's box. I picked up the partial sermon from the desk tray to add to the collection.

I hadn't noticed it before, but in the wooden receptacle between the homily and the rough draft of the funding campaign letter, was a dog-eared pocket-sized notebook from a local auto dealer titled, "Oil Changes, Mileage, and Maintenance." I flipped it open to check it out before I decided where it belonged. The oil change and service records were blank, but those headed mileage and gas were filled with notations.

According to the entries, beginning last September, Father Diego drove to Chicago and back in a single day once or twice a week. Before that, nothing. What the hell was he doing? The last trip, the day he was killed, hadn't been entered.

I needed time to think. I slipped the notebook into a Ziploc, then into my purse. I'd scan it into my computer and return it when I wrapped up the job.

A couple of hours later, I stopped in the church office to drop off the keys before I left for the day. Irma, hard at work on the church bulletin, was glad to take a break.

"Mind if I ask about Father Diego?" I asked, unable to completely contain my inquisitiveness.

"*No, señora,*" Irma shook her head.

"I found Father Diego's mileage record for several months before he died, and I wondered, had he always gone to Chicago regularly? It's a couple of hours each way, so it must have been something important for him make the trip so often."

Irma thought for a moment. "He started going last autumn, sometimes a couple of times a week...just day trips."

"I know it isn't my business, but I'm curious. That's a lot of driving. Was it for the church?"

"I don't know what Father was doing. I didn't ask. I just imagined it had something to do with the parish, but now, with his death—He'd leave early, but be back in time for Mass." Irma nibbled thoughtfully on the side of her thumb.

I might as well push for details, I thought, as I plunged on. "Did he go by himself? Take anything with him? His briefcase, computer, anything?"

Irma frowned as she considered. "Usually he left his briefcase and computer here. Odd, when you think about it, if it was a church matter. I know once he dropped off a suitcase in Pilsen, the old Mexican neighborhood, for Eduardo Guzmán, the guy who owned Cinco Gallos. I saw Father carry it to his car. Said a relative had accidently left it in Big Grove after a visit."

Well that was something. Guzmán was involved in one visit at least and probably more. Clearly he knew about Father's trips if he asked him to deliver a suitcase in the city.

I placed the mileage record in front of Irma so she could see what it included. "Do you mind if I copy this and bring it back later this week? I'd like to take a closer look at the dates, see it they fit into any sort of pattern. I keep thinking there is a connection between Father's trips and something in Big Grove."

"Go ahead. It isn't like he is here to worry about his privacy." Irma shifted in her chair, gathering her thoughts.

"I know she may have nothing to add, but would his housekeeper know anything?"

"She probably wouldn't know much. They'd communicate through notes on the kitchen table. Luz'd clean, cook, leave. She wouldn't see him for days.

"Luz and I didn't have much time to talk, either, but she did mention that Father began going to Cinco Gallos pretty regularly. Must have been a year and a half or so ago." Irma carefully worked on her thumb as she considered Luz's information.

"How'd she know if they didn't talk?"

"He'd leave a note telling her he didn't need dinner; he was going out. He also mentioned something about Cinco Gallos a couple of times; once, when they ran into one another, he said he liked the food.

"Oh, she said he'd started to smoke cigars then, too. The rectory smelled like a men's club, she said. It was hard to air out."

"Anything else?"

"Nothing really big." Irma paused. "But he'd been really happy, on top if the world, until he started his Chicago trips, then he got moody, distracted, like he had something on his mind. Didn't even joke much with the kids. I thought maybe he was having a hard time with the new bishop in Springfield, but I didn't pry."

I felt like I was near the end of what Irma knew. I took one last stab. "Did he have health concerns? Anything going on the parish— financial difficulties, issues with parishioners?"

"I can't think of anything," Irma said, handing me the notebook, "but if I do, I'll let you know."

Well, that's something, I thought as I headed for the parking lot. *I'll bet anything Guzmán treated him to dinner and cigars at Cinco Gallo. Maybe the Chicago trips had something to do with Guzmán's previous generosity. It would make sense. Maybe the drug business is part of the picture.*

I slid into the RAV4 and wondered what else was part of the situation. After all, Guzmán had ties to Big Grove, Tikal, the cartels, and now the priest. It was odd.

Once I had everything ready to send to the provincial's office on Thursday, I'd talk with Luz. Maybe she could remember something that would help me sort things out.

~ * ~

By the end of the week, I'd gotten both offices cataloged and packed and had something to talk about during our cocktail hour on Friday besides ·Tikal—the apparent link between Guzmán and the priest and the details I'd dug up since I started work at St. Patrick's.

"It's curious," I said. "Guzmán contributed thousands of dollars to St. Patrick's. Had he suddenly returned to the church? Was he expiating his sins?

"When I spoke with Luz, Father Diego's housekeeper, she didn't have too much new to add to what Irma already told me, except she did say he did begin to have dinner regularly at Cinco Gallos last fall and the booze and cigars started then, too. She would know. She had to deal with the stale smoke and empty the recycle bin.

"It's like a jigsaw puzzle with pieces missing—Ruston, cartels, the restaurant, Father Diego, the Nuevo—"

Pat nodded in agreement as she handed me a platter of celery with dip.

"Then the priest's trips to Chicago started a year later. Guzmán's cousin's suitcase appeared on one of those jaunts then, too, so we know for certain there was a connection between Guzmán and Chicago at that point. The whole thing seems unusual to me, as if Guzmán and the priest had an arrangement.

"I xeroxed the list of contributions. Maybe it will suggest something, if I look at it long enough."

"Too bad you don't have his appointment calendar, too," Bill said, spitting crumbs as he talked through a mouthful of cracker and cheese. "It would be interesting to cross check the dates of contributions and dinners, see how the Chicago trips fit into the pattern."

I worried a piece of celery. "I know this isn't part of my work for the parish, but the cast of characters seem to overlap with what went on earlier—here and in Tikal—and violence crops up in both places as well. Maybe there's even a connection to Ruston."

Pat put down her wine. "You know, it sounds as if Guzmán had been grooming Father Diego that first autumn—dinners, cigars, alcohol, contributions, and who knows what else—then this year began using the priest in some way, maybe as a courier. I mean think about it. What else makes sense? A priest would be perfect in that role. Who would suspect him of being a cartel flunky?"

"I'd love to get my hands on his computer—see if his schedule is there—but Irma said the police still have it. Can't they give it back to the parish?" I asked, turning to Bill. "Surely there isn't any reason for them to hang onto it."

"I'll ask the guys at the gym. Find out what's going on. If they haven't learned anything from it by now, they aren't going to discover something in the future, either. I'll tell 'em the church needs it."

The week's other big news was that after much coaxing, Ochoa and Esperanza, according to their most recent email to Pat, had finally set a date for their visit to Big Grove.

"They're packing. They've applied for visas. Once those come through, they'll buy tickets. Right now, they're thinking it will be the second week in June."

"Ha! It will be just like before—Ochoa, cartels, murder," Bill said, grinning happily.

"I wouldn't say that to Esperanza," I said, finishing my scotch. "She'll cancel the trip."

Thirty-six

The morning after Esperanza's and Ochoa's arrival, the sky, pale blue as Persian turquois, was clear, scrubbed clean of clouds by last night's wind. Everything was reassuringly familiar outside my kitchen window. The man in the small brick house across the street from Burr Oaks was watering this spring's basket of pink impatiens hanging from his front porch roof. His elderly neighbor fussed with boxes of red geraniums lining her railings.

Burr Oaks' gardeners had set out the white metal lawn furniture and sun umbrellas behind the buildings. Residents had dragged out their barbeque grills and parked them along the back of the garage facing the condos.

The cardinals nesting in the spirea below my window flew in and out of their hiding place, their bodies carmine in the morning sun. *Maybe the pair that lived in the shrub last year*, I thought pouring a second cup of coffee, *or maybe one of their children is starting a family.*

I took my coffee and the morning newspaper into the living room and settled into the recliner. Rosie was stretched out, asleep on her carpeted window perch, basking in the morning sun that slanted through the corner window behind my chair.

Not much had changed in Big Grove since we'd left, but the lead article in the business section caught my eye. "Cinco Gallos Has New Owner," the headline read. "Oscar Olivera, Chicago businessman, replaces Eduardo Guzmán at the helm of the popular Guatemalan restaurant in northwest Big Grove," the article began.

"The menu is more or less the same with a few additions that will change throughout the year," Olivera said when asked. "We'll try to explore cooking from various parts of Mesoamerica, treat them as specials.

"I bought Cinco Gallos from Eduardo Guzmán's widow, but since I still have businesses in Chicago, I'll only be here part time after we get things rolling."

Huh. I wonder what the cartel has to do with this? What is going to turn up on *its* list of new offerings?

~ * ~

Since I was free to poke around while Zoila and Luis spent the day showing Esperanza and Ochoa Big Grove and the nearby countryside, lunch at Cinco Gallos seemed in order. I might as well check things out. As usual, the parking lot was crowded. People and vehicles struggled to avoid one another in the narrow space between the restaurant and the tall wooden fence that surrounded the property.

On the way to the front entrance, I spotted what I'd bet was Olivera's car, a black Jeep Cherokee with smoked windows, parked near the back door. It gave me the willies, considering what had happened to Polop.

The tiny entry was packed. The crowd milled, waiting for tables: I could barely wiggle my way into the surging mass. There didn't seem to be any alterations in the lobby that I could see, new owner or not—even the posters on the front desk were the ones that had been there for as long as I could remember, but maybe they hadn't had time to redecorate.

I had a better chance to look around once I was seated. Nothing had changed in the dining room, either—same décor and staff, even the menus were the old well-worn editions except a piece of paper had been inserted into the front announcing daily specials. My *sopa*, when it arrived, was familiar, too—hot chicken broth with rice, greens, and fragments of egg and a plate of sliced avocado and lettuce to add to the bowl.

Maybe modifications will come later, I thought, as I spooned up the *sopa, but I hope they leave the food alone.*

Later, on the way home to Burr Oaks, I considered what I'd seen. It wasn't much. There were no real changes at Cinco Gallos...yet, except for a new owner and his creepy car, but that suggested something else—it was probably business as usual and that business likely included drugs.

~ * ~

The following night, Zoila and Luis gave an official welcome dinner for Esperanza and Ochoa. Zoila had gone all out—roast turkey, tamales, a huge fruit plate with slices of papaya, mango, pineapple, and magenta-colored pitajaya.

"My friend Rosa and her family made the tamales," Zoila said later as she refilled the serving dish for the third time. "I'd still be in the kitchen if I'd tried to do it."

It was a night of nourishment of all sorts—friends, food, laughter—a rich mixture of companionship and pleasure. "How has your first day been?" Pat asked our guests once we'd all begun to slow down on our feasting.

"Luis and Zoila took us everywhere...I can't remember it all, but I took plenty of pictures," Ochoa said as he took another tamale. "The countryside is astonishing: huge, flat, like a savanna, and countless squirrels in town. *Never* have I seen so many squirrels. My brother and I would have counted it a miracle if we had seen half as many when we were hunting as boys."

"The thing that amazed me was the size of everything," Esperanza said. "Fields larger than the main plaza in Guatemala City, farms that go on forever. And the university! It's a city!"

Conversation threaded its way from their visit to the clearance sale at Bill's sports shop, and the mob of children and mothers that had descended on the library while Pat was working, and finally the cave. Even Polop, despite his recent kidnapping, was interested.

"Not much new there," Ochoa said, "except we've put a fence around the area and the water in the reservoir has drained back to its former level. The geologists will be arriving next week to see whether it is safe to go in. Who knows what is left of the artifacts after that collapse and flood, but we've got to find out. *Gracias a Dios* we have those pictures."

I didn't have anything, so I told the story of my lunch at Cinco Gallos. "Not a lot to say about the place, except there is a black Jeep Cherokee behind the building. Otherwise, everything looks like it did when Guzmán owned it. I find it hard to believe Father Diego might have got himself killed just frequenting a restaurant full of students and families."

"The murdered priest?" Ochoa asked, clearly interested. "Anything new there?"

Esperanza gave her husband a bleak stare. "This is our vacation, Miguel. You promised not to talk police work, no matter what."

Pat kicked me under the table.

Even though Pat was scowling, after a little prodding from Ochoa, I related the story of Father Diego, his murder outside his church moments before five o'clock Mass, and the fact that his death was still unsolved. What else could I do? Ochoa wasn't going to give up. A murder was all it took to get him asking questions.

Ochoa leaned forward eagerly when I mentioned the priest's apparent recruitment to the cartel's workforce. I had his full attention.

Bill, to elaborate, dug into the drug problems in Big Grove and the death of a local disc jockey at a fraternity party during the winter. "Drugs have become a real issue here," Bill said. "There was even a bust of university kids selling way more than weed a few months ago."

There was nothing like drugs and murder to get the guys back into the groove.

"Sounds like it could be the backstory for our troubles at Tikal," Ochoa said.

Bill nodded.

"That is one way to think about it," Luis, who had been quiet to this point, said joining the conversation.

Polop grunted in assent.

"Let's have our coffee in the living room," Zoila said, breaking the ensuing silence. "It's more comfortable."

~ * ~

The evening air, drifting in the balcony doors, smelled of freshly cut grass and blooming prairie. Conversation slowed as we settled into our chairs. Coyotes yipped in the distance. An owl called nearby.

The thought that Tikal and the cartels might have followed us home made my skin crawl, and the owl, harbinger of death for the Maya, drove home the point. Several worlds intertwined in Big Grove and Tikal—Maya and Euro, criminal and law abiding—and trying to pry them apart seemed to lead to murder.

"Tonight's accounts of Father Diego and Guzmán make it clear there's more to do," Ochoa said.

Luis nodded. "The story *isn't* finished. All these events are part of the same world. Imagine it as an infinite piece of brocade. Time is the background hue, the body; the colors that form images of places, people, events are laid in at each pass of the shuttle."

The owl hooted again, closer this time.

Later, I was still thinking about what Luis and Ochoa had said as I drove home. Maybe they were right about the continuing narrative of Big Grove and Tikal. And maybe the owl meant death here, too. I shuddered.

Thirty-seven

Big Grove, Third Week in June

In the shed at the far end of the row of similar rental spaces in the U-Store-It business nearest the first exit from I-74, the old fer-de-lance slept, satiated by the rat she had eaten earlier. The warmth of the sun on the aluminum building during the day had lulled her and now her nest, a hollow space in the center of the pile of plastic-wrapped bricks of fentanyl-laced heroin, held the heat in, too, making its space even more comfortable.

She didn't know how long she had been there; her journey had been periods of vibrations, jolting, and shouting men, alternating with silence. It felt good to rest with a full stomach in the quiet of the shed.

She would explore her environment later. Maybe she would find another rat in a day or two.

~ * ~

That same night, as the snake drowsed in her nest, Oscar Olivera licked the last of the steak juice from his lips as he sat in his office in Cinco Gallos thinking about business. He had received a text earlier indicating a partial shipment from what was left of the Maya Gold depot in Mexico had safely been delivered to the storage facility on the far edge of the small industrial park that spread along the highway behind the restaurant. Two more deliveries to go and all of Maya Gold's remaining product would finally be out of Mexico.

He'd check on it tonight before he went home, see how much storage space it used, and figure out how much more he would need for the next two. They might have to open another unit for the final load.

He'd seen a real uptick in sales during his short time in Big Grove, particularly to the south and east and even deep into Indiana. Dealers from as far away as Indianapolis and St. Louis were waiting for the shipments, too, though everyone who sold drugs throughout the region was getting interested in fentanyl-laced heroin. He needed the new supply ASAP. Eager to get the drugs on the street, he'd get a few of the bigger dealers over tomorrow night, start the ball rolling.

He'd call it an early night. Tomorrow was going to be busy. The supper crowd was starting to thin; the manager could lock up.

Thirty-eight

Big Grove, Third Week in June

Tuesday morning, I had just finished packing an agriculture professor's office in preparation for his move to the USDA, when my cell phone rang. It was Irma, the secretary at St. Patrick's Church.

"The police just dropped off Father Diego's computer. I don't know if you still want to see it, but I have his password since he never could remember it. I thought some of the material might need to be printed out and sent to join his other papers."

"I should look at it. I'll stop by this afternoon, if that's okay with you. See what we need to do. Will two o'clock work?"

"I'll be here."

"Good. See you then," I said, edging a chart of types of soybeans further into an envelope.

By 1:30 I was on my way to St. Patrick's. The traffic on Sutter was light at that time of the day. Bloomingdale Road was deserted when I turned west except for a black Jeep Cherokee that looked like Olivera's entering the rental storage facility nearest the first Big Grove exit from I-74. The juxtaposition of the type of vehicle that had snatched Polop and a storage facility that could house drugs was intriguing. I drove past the church. I still had ten minutes before I was due to see Irma. Might as well see where the Jeep's going.

I didn't slow down as I past the U-Store-It, since I was trying to be inconspicuous, but out of the corner of my eye I spotted the parked Jeep, an old Hertz truck, and two or three guys letting themselves into the end door in the last row of units. Huh.

When I got to the church at two o'clock, Irma was busy at her desk. Father Diego's computer was on the table behind her.

Father Diego's computer, once she got it running, was not the goldmine I had hoped—emails, of course, but nothing unusual, three dozen homilies, and two folders of letters regarding church business. His schedule, however, was thought provoking: dinners with Guzmán were noted throughout the autumn and increasing numbers of trips to Chicago showed up as well. At least it confirmed my suspicions regarding connections between the two men, and the priest's visits to the city seemed to be linked to his friendship with Guzmán.

Irma emailed me the schedule: it would give me something concrete to think about once I got home. That night, after dinner, I forwarded the priest's schedule to Bill and Pat; maybe they could come up with something I hadn't considered. I mentioned the guys with the Cherokee and the truck at the U-Store-It as well, just to bring them up to date. I even suggested someone should check it out.

Later, settled into my recliner with a small glass of Bowmore 18, Rosie, and a book, it was hard to concentrate. What was going on at the storage place? Excess furniture from Cinco Gallos being stored? Olivera's household goods warehoused till he could find a place to live? Drugs? That end of town seemed to be the center of something odd; U-Store-It and Cinco Gallo were only a few blocks apart, and St. Patrick's Church was in between. And whatever was happening might have to do with all those Chicago trips Father Diego took before he was murdered.

I had trouble going to sleep that night. It was as if shadows were moving just outside my line of vision. Rosie was restless, too. Maybe it was the moon, or what Luis had said about not being done with the story. And then there was the owl. What the hell was with the owl?

~ * ~

Early next morning as a hazy mother-of-pearl sun broke free of the horizon, I staked out the storage units from behind the truck repair shop next door, armed with binoculars, water, and a box of cereal bars. I'd parked behind a dozen fifty-gallon drums and a couple of dumpsters at the rear of the building for cover. The U-Store-It was quiet when I arrived. All that was left was to wait.

The traffic on I-74 was heavy as people headed for work; it drowned out the noise from Bloomingdale Road and silenced a plane angling toward the runway at the airport. Nothing much happened for the next couple of hours, and I was getting restless.

I'd just finished my first cereal bar when a black Jeep Cherokee pulled up in front of the first unit at the far side of the complex. The driver got out and began fiddling with the heavy padlock. I slid out of the RAV4 for a closer look, leaving the door ajar so I could leave with ease; I edged my way behind the closest drum. If I were careful, there was no reason the Jeep's driver should see me, hidden as I was behind the drum and a corner of the repair shop. I propped my elbows on the drum's rusty top to steady my binoculars.

I didn't sense anything until a leather glove clapped over my mouth and an arm hooked around my neck, yanking me backward onto the ground. I squirmed, kicked, thrashed, but it didn't do any good. Jerked over on my stomach with a knee rammed in my back, my arms were lashed together, my ankles and mouth wound with duct tape. I was trussed like a lamb on a spit.

"Gotcha, bitch! We spotted you from I-74 on the way over," the man who had grabbed me first said. "Your RAV4 stuck out like a sore thumb parked with these crappy drums."

The men hauled me like a duffle bag toward unit one, the Jeep, and the man who drove it: a current of terror ran through me as I was dragged and scraped over the gravel between the buildings, writhing, twisting, bleating with terror.

My head hit a cement parking bumper as we rounded the corner of the last bank of units; the world exploded into bursts of colored light. Then there was nothing.

~ * ~

Once my head cleared, I began to slowly twist and wriggle on the uneven surface under me, desperate to assess my situation in the dark enclosure, likely a shed. Turning my head against the tape on my jaw and neck, I felt my hair pull where the adhesive wrapped around the back of my skull. Working my hands under me despite the sticky binding might yield some information about my current position.

I was lying on what felt like large blocks packaged in plastic, similar to vacuum packed cubes of sphagnum moss, or maybe like the drugs that had burned behind Cinco Gallo earlier in the year. If it were the latter, I might as well give up. Though I couldn't pick out the guy I saw fiddling with the storage unit in a lineup, no way was I going to get out alive after being caught spying on him. And now I was wallowing on what likely was his inventory.

Muffled voices came from my right from a nearby unit: then I heard an overhead door being pulled down, a car driving away.

Why the hell hadn't I talked about my snooping with Bill and Pat? Ochoa would have had something to say, too. I was helpless in a claustrophobic space, unable to escape, unable to call for help. The blood roaring in my ears, however, wasn't so loud that I didn't hear something moving further back in the shed, sliding slowly among the packages of drugs in my direction.

Whatever it was, it couldn't be human. I wasn't going to annoy it by thrashing around. I forced myself to stop moving.

~ * ~

Later—maybe an hour, maybe two—my disoriented state was interrupted by the sound of a vehicle in front of the shed. I could hear the two men who had snatched me talking with someone else, likely the guy I thought was Olivera, come to oversee what happened next.

The unit's door rattled open. Light from the orange security lights poured in, blinding me with sudden glare. The men slipped into the shed pulling the door closed behind them. Someone switched on a flashlight.

One of the guys that grabbed me earlier kicked my legs, "You awake?"

I moaned under the tape.

"Good. We're gonna take you outta here to someplace more private," he said, as he and the other thug began to wrestle me upright. "We got business tonight and need you gone." He cut the tape from my ankles so I could walk, and then pushed me toward the door. "Easier than dragging you and less obvious, too."

This was it. The owl's prophecy coming true. I was going to be hauled off, killed, and then dumped in a cornfield. I couldn't even scream. If I was going to do anything, it had to be now. If they got me into the Jeep, I was finished.

I went nuts. I kicked at where legs or crotches would be, slammed my head into the face of the guy holding my arms. He shrieked. I kicked again, this time at the man hovering nearby with the flashlight.

He swore as the light flew out of his hand, smashed on the floor, and went out.

I was hurled back onto the heap of drugs as the men struggled to regain control of the situation.

"What the hell! Open the damned door," the guy who might be Olivera yelled. "I can't see a thing."

I had a front row seat for what came next.

As Olivera scrabbled in the shadows to locate his flashlight, patting the floor with his hands and fumbling with the closest packages of drugs, the snake, bedded down in a depression at the front of the pile, had had enough.

Outraged at the intrusion, the struggle, the noise, the man swearing and groping inches from her new resting spot, the agitated fer-de-lance raised as much of her five-foot body as far as she could on the slippery heap, striking without warning, hitting the pawing intruder on his shoulder. She drove her fangs in as far as possible, hanging on no matter how the man tried to knock her loose. Then, finished, she dropped back into the pile of drugs.

~ * ~

"My shoulder's on fire!" Olivera yelled, staggering from the storage shed holding his upper arm. He fell against his Jeep, pale even in the sickly glow of the yard lights.

"Let me take a look," one of the men said. He pulled down Olivera's jacket, jerked open his shirt. "Your shoulder's bleeding." He tugged aside the shirtsleeve for a better view. "You're bleeding from a couple of holes, like a snakebite, for God's sake. A snake! In the shed? What the hell?"

The second man vigorously wiped his handkerchief over the wounds. "It's starting to swell, and even in this crappy light I can see it leaking under the skin. Why don't we have another flashlight?"

Olivera lurched toward the rear of his car, then fell, sliding into a sitting position in the gravel. "Don't call nine-one-one. I gotta get to a hospital without emergency personnel. If they show up, we're screwed. Help me into the car, let me out near an emergency room. Then leave.

"What was I thinking coming to Big Grove?" he said as he fell flat on his back despite the men's efforts to keep him upright.

~ * ~

I slipped down behind the mountain of drugs. With Olivera on the skids, maybe they would forget me.

It was becoming difficult for Olivera to breathe. I could hear him panting over the sound of traffic. One of the guards tied a tourniquet around his arm, but what good would that do for a bite on the shoulder? It probably would only make things worse.

Then Olivera threw up.

The men struggled to drag Olivera into the back of the Cherokee. "Son of a bitch, he's limp. It's hard to hang on." One of the men grunted.

While he swung Olivera's legs into the vehicle, the other man jumped into the driver's seat, firing up the engine. "Get in," he yelled, "We don't have time. We'll worry about that goddamn woman later. She isn't going to get far covered with tape."

As soon as the second man slammed his door, the Jeep peeled out of the storage lot. They had only pulled the garage door part way down.

The snake, still agitated by the commotion and the screaming men, slid down the plastic pile and out the storage unit's door, staying close to the wall, her dark splotchy pattern clearly visible in the garish light. She rounded the end of the building and headed west, crawling off into the Midwestern night.

I was right behind the snake's vanishing tail as she left the shed. I wasn't going to wait for the guards to come back. I wasn't thinking clearly myself, but I knew I had to get away. No point in trying to reach the industrial buildings to the east, since there wouldn't be anyone there at this hour, or going for the McDonald's several blocks away, since I could hardly totter. No point in following the snake, either: there wasn't anything in that direction, just the exit ramp and scattered warehouses, and who knew how the snake felt about company?

St. Patrick's Church was the closest familiar place. If I could make it there, someone would eventually show up.

It was hard to walk with my arms bound behind me. I stumbled over every clump of grass and depression in the church's athletic field, falling on my face more times than I could count. I couldn't put my hands up to soften my fall, so I slammed my face into the ground a couple of times before I figured out I needed to turn my head to the side as I went over. I was still going to look like dirt, but at least I wouldn't break my nose.

Getting up was an additional agonizing undertaking: roll on side, raise one knee toward chest, plant that foot, rock forward, stand slowly, stabilize, move forward. Without the use of my arms, trying to maintain balance was difficult. I couldn't call for help, either. I couldn't get the tape off my mouth without my hands.

The church was dark except for the porch lights when I finally collapsed at the small side entrance outside the sacristy. Maybe *Olivera's thugs won't look for me here and besides, there is nowhere else to go*, I thought as I slumped onto the cement and leaned against the door. Now that I wasn't floundering across the field, the evening chill began to seep into my body, making me shiver. I closed my eyes. All I had to do is wait, wait and hope someone found me before something else happened...or I died of misery on the same spot where Father Diego had been murdered.

Thirty-nine

Big Grove, Later That Night

It must have been a half hour before I heard an increasing number of sirens coming from the north, on Sutter. *Maybe an accident on the freeway, some multicar pileup outside of town*, I thought as they grew louder. The wailing suddenly cut off somewhere nearby, one siren after another. They seemed to reach their destination west of St. Patrick's, across from the activity field, near the U-Store-It facility.

Then things seemed to heat up: I could hear gunfire over the traffic, and it wasn't just one or two shots. The firing petered off, then more sirens.

What was going on? Even in my wretched state, I wanted answers.

A few minutes later, headlights swung into the St. Patrick's parking lot, passed the office, headed toward the church. No way could I get to my feet and run in time to elude trouble. I was caught like a raccoon in a crawl space.

"There she is," a familiar voice shouted through a half-open door as the car skidded to a stop at the end of the nearby sidewalk. "On the church porch."

"Ann," Bill yelled as he ran toward me. "Is that you?"

By the time Ochoa and Bill pulled the tape off my face and hands, checked me over, and wrapped me in a blanket, I was numb, cold, nauseated. My consciousness flickered like a loose bulb, and I couldn't lift my arms. My legs were worthless, too—I had to be carried to the car.

"We're heading for the hospital," Bill yelled over his revving engine.

Hours later, checked by doctors, detaped, and back at Burr Oaks, Esperanza, Pat, and Zoila took over from the men. Clucking and exclaiming, they got me into a hot shower, dressed me in pajamas, and tucked me into my recliner with a pillow and blanket. Once I was settled, Pat handed me a mug of tomato soup. "Here, drink this. It will help."

I nodded, took the cup carefully, sipped cautiously at the hot liquid. It was heaven. I hadn't had anything since that cereal bar— Lord knows how long ago—and the efforts of my escape made me shaky and lightheaded. After another serving, I felt more like myself and ready to ask questions.

"How did you find me? And how did the police know about Olivera's storage units?"

"That email you sent tipped us off, especially the part that someone should check that storage place," Bill said. "I'd called the cops earlier, just to let them know they should take a look at it, that something seemed to be fishy down at the far end.

"Then, when you weren't home by your usual time, and knowing your nosy nature, we began to worry. Ochoa and I decided to run out there. The police were raiding the storage place at that point. When it was clear you weren't there, the church was a natural place to check. You know the rest."

"Thank God you found me," I said, imagining several more hours encased in tape or worse. I dabbed at my eyes with the edge of my blanket.

Pat broke in before I lost all control. "We should put something cold on your face. It'll help reduce the swelling."

She headed for the kitchen where I could hear Zoila already rummaging in the freezer. Pat returned with a plastic bag of peas and a dish towel. "You'll probably have black eyes from your adventures. They're puffy and bruising now, but you'll feel better once the swelling goes down."

I placed the peas over my eyes and lay back. The throbbing in my face began to ease.

A knock sent Rosie under the bed where she had been hiding on and off since I got home. Bill answered the door. I could hear him conversing with someone in the hall.

"Ann, can you talk with Officer Murphy now?" Bill said from my entry.

"Couldn't this wait? She's barely back to herself," Pat said, scowling from the chair next to my recliner.

"Let him in," I said. "I'm okay."

"I won't take long," Officer Murphy said. "But I want to hear what happened back there. All we have now is four Sinaloa guys in the hospital with gunshot wounds, another dead, and the guy who owns Cinco Gallos in intensive care with snakebite. Snakebite! Here in Big Grove! They say he may not make it since the bite was close to his heart and brain. He'd moved around a lot before they got him in, too, so his body is starting to swell. No one knows what kind of snake it was. The hospital's checking with the zoos in Chicago, see if they can tell them anything.

"The shed you were in is full of drugs that must have just come up from Mexico and Guatemala—a couple of the packages were even labeled Maya Gold, Petén," Murphy added.

"If that's the origin of that shipment, the snake is probably a fer-de-lance," Ochoa said.

"I just got a quick glimpse of it crawling out of the shed," I added, "maybe five feet long, dark brown splotches."

"Sounds right to me," Luis said from the nearby sofa. "A fer-de-lance looks like that. They're especially venomous as well. That would explain the state Olivera is in."

"Might help the guy's doctor to know what it is, but my worry is that snake is somewhere on the west side of Big Grove. We're in trouble if we can't catch it right away, or it finds enough to eat and settles in." Murphy was still muttering as he headed into the dimly lit hall to radio the information. "Poisonous snake loose in summer! Kids running around outside. People in flip-flops mowing the lawn. What hell!"

~ * ~

Two days later, Olivera died of a massive heart attack caused by snakebite, according to the newspaper article that described his death.

"The snake really got him," Dr. Wilson, his doctor said. "Fer-de-lance venom is potent: it causes breakdown of tissues, internal bleeding, thrombosis. Mr. Olivera just couldn't rally after that bite. For one thing, he moved around too much after he was struck; he even staggered into the ER on his own. We didn't learn what type of snake it was until later, and the antivenin didn't arrive until the next day."

The snake, the article continued, was still on the loose.

Forty

From the night of the raid on, the Feds were all over Big Grove. According to the news, millions of dollars of cocaine, heroin, and fentanyl had been stashed in the U-Store-It units. Other sheds in the six-block industrial area next to I-74 were found to have drugs in them, too.

Big Grove, it turned out, was a transfer point, sitting as it does on the intersection of I-57 and I-74—two well-used north-south, east-west interstates—and just a short drive from I-55 and I-70, also major interstate highways, making it an ideal rerouting point. Several cities, including Indianapolis, Chicago, St. Louis, and even Detroit, were within easy reach. No wonder the drug trade had blossomed in Big Grove; how could it not, considering its location?

"After the Feds were through, the drug traffic in town dried up just like that," Bill said over cocktails one Friday, snapping his fingers to illustrate his point. "At least that's what the guys at the gym said. It's as if the whole cartel thing had never happened, that drugs never flooded Big Grove, at least not in the volume the Sinaloas provided."

Big Grove, First Week in July

Life returned to normal in Big Grove. Ochoa and Esperanza returned to Guatemala laden with gifts for family and friends, hundreds of photographs, endless stories—including the recent installment of the Ruston/Tikal tale that featured the snake.

My bruises faded to green-tinged taupe, but my startle reflex was still hair-trigger. I winced or ducked every time anything suddenly moved, or made noise in my vicinity. My fault, really. Why hadn't I minded my own business? Maybe this time, I'd learned *that* lesson.

Every once in a while, during the rest of that summer, someone thought they'd spotted the snake, but it was always a false alarm—a garter snake, a piece of rope, a section of hose in the back of a garage.

School began as usual in the middle of August: students in shorts and Tee-shirts milled in front of campus bars, and parking places disappeared like ice on warm pavement.

I began to feel more like myself as the familiar academic world reasserted itself, but I still wondered about the snake.

Forty-one

Big Grove, First Week in September

On a rocky slope near the culvert that carried a thin thread of water under Patterson Road, the snake lay coiled, basking on a shelf of limestone. She had come to feel the arroyo next to the roadway was her territory, even though the air was too dry to be completely comfortable. It was a good spot otherwise, with several rocky overhangs and sheltered areas, as well as a variety of rodents.

She had regular success hunting in this new world, but the jungle with its moist dense greenery still called somewhere in her reptilian brain. She shifted lazily. At least there was food.

~ * ~

Above the culvert, a state highway worker inspected the guardrail over the little creek. A motorist had sideswiped it yesterday, and he needed to make sure the rail was still sound. The man had just checked the cement at the base of the final post when he spotted the snake curled in the sun. "Whoa! That sure isn't a garter snake! I thought that fer-de-lance would probably be dead by now." He stood slowly so as not to frighten the creature, easing his way to his truck to call 911, just as the highway workers had been instructed to do, if they spotted the reptile.

238

Half an hour later Big Grove Animal Control and the special Snake Task Force from the University Wildlife Clinic arrived at the bridge.

"Now comes the tricky part," the vet in charge said, unloading several large snake tongs, white cotton snake bags, and a plastic carrier box with air holes and handles.

"It's going to move fast once it knows we're here," he said, peering at the snake over the rim of the arroyo. "The highway will help cover our noise. We're just going to get one shot at it, so we've got to do it right. Let me review the drill. We all move at once, slow as possible, and then station ourselves above and around the ledge.

"Folks with tongs will lead. If you have a clear shot at it, grab the snake in the middle of the body. Baggers stay behind the people with the tongs, but keep the sacks open so the catcher can drop the snake in as soon as it's caught."

He oversaw the distribution of equipment before continuing. "I probably don't have to tell you, but stay away from it as much as possible. It's short tempered, and it won't hesitate to bite. Remember, it can puncture your boots. Those of you without equipment, stay back, but be ready to give us a hand on the incline if we need it. This embankment is steep. It's going to be hard going.

"I'm going in from the left rear. It's a little less steep there, and it'll bring me down outside the snake's field of vision. Let me go first. If I miss, close in."

The vet eased his way down the weedy face of the cut. The others, slightly behind him, moved at the same time.

~ * ~

The snake, made drowsy by the sun and the gopher she had eaten earlier, didn't suspect a thing until the tongs closed around her body. Outraged, and terrified, she fought with every ounce of strength she possessed, twisting, winding in the air, striking at whatever held her, desperate to escape. It was no good; no matter how she struggled, the tongs held her firm until something soft and white closed over her. Still she fought, biting, straining, looping with rage.

The shouting that surrounded her agitated her further.

"Got it!"

"Look at that sack thrash!"

"Don't drop it!"

"We'll get it out of the bag once we're back at the clinic. No reason to struggle on the edge of the highway."

"Where's that transport box?"

The white trap swayed and clung, then she dropped, white substance and all, into a hard, small space. There was a snap above her. Sounds faded.

Later that afternoon, released from the white clinging thing, the snake rested, tired but calm, coiled in her container somewhere dark, quiet, soothing. She couldn't see the people checking on her from the far side of the room through the opaque walls of her current home.

Forty-two

Big Grove, Second Week in September

Wednesday evening after the news, Zoila called with an invitation for cocktails on Friday. "I'm going to call Pat and Bill, Polop, too. They are part of this story. You can have your usual weekly festivities here. We'll have drinks and watch the sunset, but first Luis says he wants to cast seeds. Would six o'clock work for you?"

"Perfect. I'll bring the offerings," I said.

When I arrived at Luis and Zoila's condo Friday with gifts for the ancestors—cigarillos, a pint of bourbon, lilies——and a hunk of Double Gloucester cheese for the rest of us, Luis was already in his recliner, his divining table over his knees. Pat, bearing a basket, and Bill, carrying a large shopping bag, were right behind me. Polop followed them with a *servietta*-covered platter. Copal wafted in the open balcony doors, filling the room with the smell of resin.

"Since this is a special evening, I thought I'd go all out," Pat said, putting freshly made bruschetta and dishes of toppings on the table behind Luis's chair.

"So did I, but don't worry. My brother's wife made the dip." Bill grinned as he placed homemade cheese and frijole appetizer near the tiny tapas Zoila had set out. "This is going to be some feast," he added, plugging in his dipping pot.

"My special guacamole and tortillas," Polop said, wedging his platter onto the crowded table.

"Make yourselves comfortable," Zoila called over her shoulder as she carried my offerings to the flat stone altar outside.

"Ever since the authorities caught the snake, the ancestors have been closer than they've been since Tikal," Luis said. "I've had lightning under my skin almost constantly and most nights I've dreamed of a serpent. It is clear we need to make offerings and cast seeds, and we all have to take part to pull the last threads of this story together, but before we start, you need to see what Esperanza sent." Luis pulled the short ritual shawl from around his neck and handed it to me. "It just arrived this week. She found it in a little village in the Highlands, Santa Catarina Ixtahuacan, on one of her buying trips for her shop."

The shawl was unlike any other ceremonial piece I'd seen. Four feet long with alternating figured panels, it was a stunner. Three white rectangles with vultures, wings raised as if basking, and, toward the top, the ritually important double eagle or *kot*, wings and tail spread, were woven in red thread. Between the birds were sections of red serpent-like zigzag forms, each one enclosing a four-pointed star. The shawl was old, worn, frayed.

"The images are amazing and those tiny stitches!" I said, tracing the raised figures with my finger. "I've never seen anything like it."

"It reminds me of our story. It's an outline of the narrative we've just lived. The vulture, the Vision Serpent bringing the ancestors, the snake as protector, just as she was in the storage shed." I passed the shawl to Pat. "But Santa Catarina?"

"As I said, when this entire business began with Ruston and his discovery of the stele," Luis said. "This story was set in motion thousands of years ago. It isn't a surprise to find traces of it, even there."

"The narrative began with the pectoral from Takalik Abaj and runs like a thread to our own time," Zoila said. "The individual actors changed, but the roles remain similar from one age to the next. K'in A'jaw and Kan both tried to form new communities with the vulture as their symbol of lordship, but Kan was seduced by power. It was through him and the Nuevo the cartels began to expand their grip on the Petén and to pollute the ancient site of Tikal."

"In the end, the fer-de-lance was sent by ancestors as their emissary, their means of confronting evil," Luis added.

"Whoa! The fer-de-lance! The ancestors! How did that work?" Bill asked.

"The snake was the ancestors' proxy. She saved Ann's life, and she killed the cartel boss who connected the Petén to Big Grove. She is Ann's *nahual*, her spirit guide." Luis placed his shawl around his neck again, smoothing it with his good hand.

"I can hardly believe it," Pat said. "Here we are in Big Grove, discussing what began thousands of years ago in the jungles of Guatemala. We know the people's names, we've imagined their lives, we've even seen K'in A'jaw's stele where it was placed to mark his village's boundary."

Polop, who had been quiet, suddenly added, "I wouldn't believe it began so early either if I hadn't seen that little painted cave, the lord, the retainers, the offered chocolate pot," his voice faded as he remembered the scene.

"It began then, if not before, led to Ruston, the vulture pectoral, and us—" Luis said, trailing off.

The curtains moved in the breeze. Copal drifted in with the scent of prairie. The moon rose beyond the trees into the sky thick with stars. This time the owl was silent.

Luis cast seeds, his chanting soft, calling on the ancestors and the lords of the *Cauacs* as he swept the seeds and crystals across the table, laid them out, swept again and again.

"Look outside," Luis said later that night as the moon rose higher. "Venus, a symbol of the serpent's power, is keeping Ixchel and her rabbit company."

Big Grove, Late October

Later that autumn, before the weather became unpredictable, Pat and I drove to Chicago for one of our periodic museum days. We'd added something new to our usual list of art, lunch, and more art—the zoo.

I'd called to check on the fer-de-lance—whether she was on exhibit and if we could see her. She was, and we could, the information woman said. "She is in one of our smaller habitats. They are well lit, but the walkway in front is dark. You'll be able to see her clearly."

A few days after my call, as we drove north on I-57 with the morning mist rising from the empty fields on either side of the road, I told Pat what I knew about the snake's new home.

"She's in the Reptile House, along with amphibians and other reptiles. It sounds as if she has a space to herself, a place that reflects her native environment. I know this seems odd, but I'm eager to see her. I feel as if she's my companion, a spirit guide."

"Considering what the two of you went through together, it's no surprise," Pat said. "You *are* bound together. She's your spirit familiar, your *nahual*. Those thugs would have killed you without her intervention."

~ * ~

The exhibition space was dark. The rectangular glass-fronted habitats glowed jewel-like in a single row that circled the room like a diamond necklace.

The fer-de-lance rested on a limestone ledge under the protective shelter of moist jungle foliage behind the central window. Her buff and brown coils seemed part of the stone itself.

As I leaned my face close to her habitat, the snake raised her head. Her yellow eyes looked into mine. I moved nearer to the warm glass. On the back wall of her terrarium I could see the indistinct image of the vision serpent rearing behind her.

Meet J.A. Kellman

J. A. Kellman lives in central Illinois with her husband and two cats. She is a retired professor and has done research in Guatemala.

Visit Our Website

For The Full Inventory
Of Quality Books:

Wings ePress, Inc

Quality trade paperbacks and downloads
in multiple formats,
in genres ranging from light romantic comedy to general fiction and
horror.
Wings has something for every reader's taste.
Visit the website, then bookmark it.
We add new titles each month!

Wings ePress Inc.
3000 N. Rock Road
Newton, KS 67114

An Ann Cunningham Mystery

Made in the USA
Columbia, SC
25 August 2019